The Woodville Connection

To Alastair and Amy with love and gratitude

The Woodville Connection

K. E. Martin

PEN & SWORD
FICTION

First published in Great Britain in 2013 by
PEN & SWORD FICTION
An imprint of
Pen & Sword Books Ltd
47 Church Street
Barnsley
South Yorkshire
S70 2AS

ISBN 978 1 78303 002 6

Printed and bound in England
By CPI Group (UK) Ltd, Croydon, CRO 4YY

Pen & Sword Books Ltd incorporates the Imprints of Pen & Sword Fiction, Pen & Sword Aviation, Pen & Sword Family History, Pen & Sword Maritime, Pen & Sword Military, Wharncliffe Local History, Pen & Sword Select, Pen & Sword Military Classics, Leo Cooper, Remember When, Seaforth Publishing and Frontline Publishing

For a complete list of Pen & Sword titles please contact
PEN & SWORD BOOKS LIMITED
47 Church Street, Barnsley, South Yorkshire, S70 2AS, England
E-mail: enquiries@pen-and-sword.co.uk
Website: www.pen-and-sword.co.uk

Dramatis Personae

At Middleham Castle

- Richard, Duke of Gloucester, youngest brother of King Edward IV; sometimes referred to as Dickon, Richard, Gloucester and my lord of Gloucester
- Anne, Duchess of Gloucester, wife of Richard, youngest daughter of the late Earl of Warwick and sister of Isabel, wife of George of Clarence
- Francis Cranley, musician and close friend of Richard of Gloucester, acceptable with a lute, excellent in a crisis; sometimes known as Frank
- Smithkin, a Sergeant-at-Arms with a grudge
- Fat Nell, a nursemaid and former beauty
- Will Fielding, an old friend in trouble
- Jack Conyers and Tom Tunstall, retainers of the Duke of Gloucester, both merry fellows
- James Metcalfe, a reliably fast messenger

At York

- Master Pennicott, a wealthy and elderly wool merchant with close ties to the House of York
- Mistress Pennicott, his lovely young wife

At Plaincourt Manor

- Sir Stephen Plaincourt, already master of the small manor of Ringthorpe and now also of Plaincourt Manor following the death of his nephew Geoffrey

- Geoffrey Plaincourt, newly deceased, only child of William Plaincourt and his wife Alice, nee Lambert, both also deceased
- Gervase Root, the manor steward, currently absent from Plaincourt
- Blanche St Honorine du Flers, a waiting woman and skilled healer
- Alan Rolf, an aged servant
- Dulcy Rolf, the manor washerwoman and sister to Alan; a good Christian soul
- Jem Flood, the manor cook
- Letice Flood, the cook's wife
- Matthew, a kitchen boy with a peculiar talent
- Cuckoo, a kitchen skivvy
- Walt and John Tench, Sir Stephen's loyal henchmen
- Assorted servants and villagers including a kennelman, stable lads, grooms and messengers
- Father Gregory, priest

At Court and elsewhere

- King Edward IV, known to his closest associates as Ned
- Queen Elizabeth, his consort, born Elizabeth Woodville
- Jacquetta, Dowager Duchess of Bedford, deceased; Queen Elizabeth's mother
- Anthony Woodville, Earl Rivers, the Queen's brother, a Knight of the Garter and the King's close friend
- George, Duke of Clarence, brother to the King and Richard of Gloucester; fond of a drink
- Cecily, Duchess of York, mother of the King, Clarence and Gloucester
- John Skelton, a loyal friend to the House of York

Prologue
London
February 1460

The sound of heavy footsteps and urgent, low-pitched murmurings roused George from his troubled slumbers. Swords clanked against the dank stone walls outside the chamber and keys jangled and scraped against the door's cumbersome metal lock. Terrified, the boy buried himself beneath the bed's silken coverlet, reaching in the blackness for the comforting warmth of his little brother. As the door was flung open, flickering torchlight filled the chamber.

"Rouse 'em quick, my lady," urged a coarse, unfamiliar voice, "we must hasten if we're to make the tide."

Peeping through the bedclothes, George sagged with relief as he identified his mother standing in the doorway, perplexingly in the company of two disreputable-looking, mud-splattered strangers. Tumbling from the bed he ran to her, clutching her crimson skirts against his face as he sought solace from the horrors that had devilled him. She placed a swift, soft kiss on top of his uncombed curls and then, to George's incredulous dismay, pushed him gently towards one of the ruffians.

"Go with Master Skelton," she instructed, "he and his man Fielding are taking you and Dickon to a place of safety.

"They are good men," she continued, interrupting his anguished cry of protest, "and were loyal to your father, may God rest his soul. Now be brave and take care of Dickon for me. With God's grace we shall be reunited in good time."

Too appalled to open his mouth, George watched as his mother passed a small bundle of clothes and a purse of money to the man called Skelton. Glancing momentarily towards the bed where Dickon slept on undisturbed, she hesitated, raising her fingers to her lips in a gesture midway between a blessing and a farewell. Then, mindful of the need for haste, she murmured a barely audible "Godspeed!" and fled to the lonely comfort of her quarters.

Whilst she remained, George had been frozen to the spot; now he recovered and made a spirited dash for the doorway but Skelton anticipated the move. Catching the boy by the scruff of his neck, he flung him unceremoniously over his shoulder.

"Take charge of the littl'un for me," he ordered. "I'd best get this slippery young eel onto a saddle where I can keep an eye on him. Join us at the horses quick as you can."

Impervious to the feeble fists pounding impotently on his back and deaf to the threats and curses issuing from the purple-faced lad, Skelton made his way to the stables, leaving Dickon alone with his silent companion.

Through noise and disruption the seven year old boy had slept on with the tranquillity of unruffled innocence; now, the new silence of the chamber woke him more suddenly than the pealing of a dozen church bells. Opening his clear grey eyes onto the dimly lit room, he was surprised to see a gaunt-featured man standing by the side of the bed, looking down at him from a towering height. As consciousness returned from the peaceful depths of oblivion, Dickon became aware that George was no longer with him and that for no good reason he could think of, he was quite alone with a gigantic stone-faced stranger. He looked at the man's pale blue eyes, his grim, unsmiling mouth and huge, weather-roughened hands. A large, brutal-looking sword hung at the stranger's side and the stains and tears on his clothing told tales of hardship, battle and recent bloodshed.

Dickon knew he should feel afraid and marvelled at his own composure as he was plucked from the warm quilts and arranged carefully in strong, muscle-bound arms. With instinctive trust, he threw a slender arm around the man's broad shoulder and clutched him tightly as he was carried from the chamber. The gesture seemed to gratify the stranger and he smiled fleetingly, revealing teeth large, yellow and wolfish, and breath redolent of meat and strong ale.

"Where are you taking me?" Dickon murmured, as they

passed through unfamiliar corridors and dripping back-staircases.

"Where none shall harm you," the wolfman replied and Dickon nodded, now quite satisfied that he was dreaming still. Resting his head against the wolfman's chest he closed his eyes and slept once more, confident that soon he would awaken in his own bed, with George at his side and this strange creature no more than a memory from a puzzling yet not unpleasant dream.

***

They had been riding for hours and George was feeling sore and sick when Skelton finally slowed his horse's furious pace. It was still dark but daylight threatened to break, the murky emptiness of night giving way to a greyish pre-dawn. The small party dismounted hurriedly and picked their way with caution down the greasy steps leading to the quayside. Skelton ushered an unprotesting George into a small rowing boat moored by the steps while Will Fielding unpacked the saddle-bags. Dickon lay on the ground wrapped in a fustian blanket, half awake and half asleep, fully aware now that this was no dream but too drowsy to fret.

Gazing dreamily into the shadows, he spied four figures emerge stealthily from the gloom with swords drawn and murderous intent writ plain on their grim features. With lurching stomach, he realised that these men were his enemy, come to kill him and his brother. For the first time in his young life he was truly afraid. Will stood with his back to the oncoming threat, whistling a merry tune. Dickon felt sure the big man was unconscious of the attackers' approach. He opened his mouth to raise the alarm but the words caught in his throat, mingling with the bitter taste of terror. He watched, helpless and aghast as one of the quartet veered off in his direction while the remainder continued their advance on Fielding.

Clenching his fists for courage, Dickon gazed up to meet

his doom and saw the assassin's look of triumph change to one of astonishment and then agony as Skelton's throwing knife caught him cleanly between the shoulder blades. Dropping to his knees, the man raised his arms as if in supplication towards his intended victim, then pitched forward and lay still.

Pinned beneath the bulk of the dead man, Dickon watched in horrified fascination as the other three assailants hurled themselves at Fielding. The speedy resolution of the encounter recalled to him the early nickname he had given Fielding, for there was indeed something wolf-like in the way he despatched his foe. The seasoned soldier had been well aware of the approaching enemy and his whistling had been a pre-arranged alarm for Skelton. When the attackers were within a hair's breadth of reaching him, Fielding had spun around and decapitated the leader with one fluid motion of his sword. Stumbling back in temporary disarray, the two survivors met Skelton advancing toward them. They lunged at him with a savageness born of desperation but Skelton had the advantage and he dodged neatly to their right whilst thrusting his sword deeply into the side of his nearest assailant. Fielding finished the job with nonchalant ease, running the final attacker through on his grisly weapon from back to front so that the blade protruded from the unfortunate's belly.

"Clifford's men," he grunted, slicing the livery badge from his fallen foe's sleeve and wiping his sword on it. "Worthless whoresons, making war on helpless children."

To emphasise his disgust for such unworthy opponents, he cleared his throat and spat magnificently, the foamy spittle describing a triumphant arc before landing neatly between the staring eyes of a bodiless head. Sheathing his weapon, he ventured to comfort the shivering Dickon whilst Skelton ran to investigate a curious sound emanating from the direction of the rowing boat. There he discovered George in a dismal condition. Having witnessed the attack with a certain fatalistic stoicism, he now celebrated his narrow escape from violent death by vomiting over the oars.

Left alone with his own frail charge for a few moments, Fielding abandoned his habitual air of soldierly gruffness, replacing it with a clumsy, fatherly concern. Gathering the white-faced child into his gore-splattered arms, he held him close against his chest and gently wiped a salty tear from the boy's trembling cheek.

"Hush now, little lordling," he whispered softly. "All's well now and ever will be, for none shall harm you so long as Will Fielding's by your side."

***

In London their mother spent long, anguished hours on her knees, praying for the news that would announce the safe arrival of her youngest boys in the Low Countries. Racked with misery over the recent killing of her beloved husband and second son, and riven with anxiety for another son who had boldly assumed the mantle of the family cause, still she trembled with fear for the safety of George and Dickon. At last word arrived from Skelton, advising her that all was well and the boys safely lodged in the town of Utrecht. When she read of the attempt on their lives and their escape thanks to the good offices of Skelton and Fielding, Cecily, Duchess of York fell once more on her knees to give grateful thanks to Almighty God for her sons' deliverance.

Amidst her fervent prayers and rejoicing, the Duchess also found time to make a solemn vow that when the fortunes of the House of York were once more in the ascendancy, Skelton and Fielding would not be forgotten for their services to her precious boys in their flight to safety.

Chapter 1
Arrival of a Weary Traveller

My name is Francis Cranley. I am an old man now, bent and withered so that the fresh-faced doxies of the village sit close to me and peck my crumbling cheeks with no fear for their virtue. Oh, my pretty chicks, it was a different story once.

I am comfortable here in this place where I am tolerated by my stolid farm lads and their buxom wenches. When they wish to humour me, they come to my house to feast on meat and ale while I regale them with tales from the old century. They smile and stifle yawns as I speak of the glory days of my youth, the days when I served my long dead friend and master whose name is now reviled throughout the Christian world. False accusations and foul calumny be-slime the reputation of Richard, one time Duke of Gloucester, Plantagenet lion and last true King of England.

I am an ancient, doddering fool. My sight began fading some years since and I dare say my wits are soon to follow. It is over ten years that I last played my lute and near twice as long since I shared my bed with aught more enticing than a flea-ridden hound. My memory is failing. I cannot remember how I broke my fast yesterday morn but I recall with blinding clarity the events of over fifty years ago. But then, why should I forget a time when I was young and lusty, and in my arrogance thought I would stay that way forever?

There are many stories with which I weary my greedy visitors but there is one I never shall tell. While it pleases me to confide this tale to my good friends quill and parchment, I have instructed the stout, dumpling-cheeked widow who sees to the comfort of my house to feed my scribblings to the flames the moment I breathe my last. I do not doubt she will obey my order since I have bought her loyalty with gold and soft words; in any case, the woman is unlettered and has little interest in my ramblings. Thus I would have it. I am the last survivor of those who took part in the Plaincourt Manor affair and for reasons of my own I have vowed to take that secret to my grave.

How well I remember that cold December morn that brought with it the promise of Christmas, and a succulent mystery ripe and ready for the solving. We were at Middleham Castle then and my lord of Gloucester had just embarked on what was perhaps the happiest period of his brief and turbulent life. His bride of less than a twelve-month, the gentle Duchess Anne, was *enceinte* and the Duke was near beside himself with delight at the prospect of his first legitimate child.

Christmas at Middleham in the year of our lord 1472 promised to be a merry occasion. Returning from Westminster at the close of Parliament that December, the Duke came laden with bolts of sumptuous fabrics and precious jewels for his beloved wife and costly wall hangings to bring comfort and colour to the castle's great hall.

At Middleham he was pleased to discover that the dour northerners were warming to his wise and generous leadership. One by one they were pledging him their allegiance, sealing their fidelity by sending him their sons to serve in his retinue. This meant much to the Duke, for the love and loyalty of honest people was ever more important to him than the esteem of self-seeking courtiers.

In this happy atmosphere of hope and goodwill, and secure in the favour of his brother Edward, fourth king of that name, my lord chose to overlook the storm clouds that threatened his tranquil existence. The bothersome Woodville clan, close to the King by means of his ill-considered marriage to the beautiful but scheming Elizabeth Woodville, were known to detest upright, decent Gloucester and longed to shatter his influence over the King.

Powerful as the Woodvilles were, however, their poisoned tentacles had not yet the length to reach into the north and so, for the time being, they remained content as long as Gloucester was absent from Court. Closer to home and much more disturbing to the Duke was the deepening rift between himself and his brother George, Duke of Clarence.

Married to Isabel, the older sister of my lord's own sweet wife, Clarence was envious of the special favour shown by the King to their youngest brother. His wine-fuddled brain seethed with schemes to forge a schism between the two and though his feeble efforts served only to irritate Edward, this lack of success strengthened his rancour and fed his feelings of injustice and ill-treatment. Concerned though he was by George's machinations, my lord misliked dwelling on such unpleasant matters and strove to disregard the scheming as best he could. In his heart he believed that the deep fraternal love he bore for Clarence was returned in full measure and would never be sundered by petty squabbles.

The Christmas season drew on a pace and I found myself greatly in demand for songs and all manner of mummeries. My position at Middleham was an enviable one, albeit unofficial in all but the broadest sense. Ostensibly, I held tenure as minstrel to the Duke and Duchess, although my lute playing was no more than passable and my repertoire of secular songs scarcely appropriate for entertaining the young and pious Duchess. Still, I was in possession of a fine, tuneful voice and I danced, capered and amused with consummate ease.

Perhaps of more purpose to the Duke was the fact that I was a skilful swordsman whom he had known all his life and trusted without question. A word about my origins is needful here to explain the special bond of friendship between Gloucester and myself that enabled him to trust me to the very end of his days. He had my unswerving allegiance throughout his short life and a part of me perished with him on the battlefield at Bosworth.

To explain, then, I must begin by saying that my father was also a Francis Cranley, a gentleman of limited funds serving in the retinue of Gloucester's late father, Richard, Duke of York, who was contending at the time of my birth for his rightful title as heir to the English crown.

My mother, I was told, was a comely but lowborn woman of regretfully easy virtue who peddled her favours in return for food and lodging. The union between my parents was not blessed by Holy Mother Church and thus it fell to my lot to enter this world a bastard, though my father had the decency to acknowledge me as his brat and bestow on me the Cranley name. A scant few weeks after my birth, this worthy man was careless enough to forfeit his life during a bloody scuffle with a band of Lancastrian followers. Upon hearing the news of his demise, my saintly mother exhibited the depth of her sorrow by absconding with the meagre Cranley fortune. So precipitate was her departure that she unaccountably left behind me, her babe-in-arms.

Thus abandoned, I would most assuredly have died but for the intervention of the Duke of York. When told of my sorry plight, he recalled the steadfast service given him by my dead father and resolved at once to take charge of my welfare. Having found for me a wet-nurse, a healthy, buxom girl known to all as Fair Nell, he despatched me at once to Fotheringhay Castle, there to be reared alongside his own younger children. I was of a similar age to Dickon, the Duke's youngest child and so it was cast that we should become playmates and grow to love one another as brothers.

We played and fought and took lessons together and none saw aught wrong with this arrangement. Of a certainty I was always conscious of my humble origins but felt part of the family nonetheless. When tragedy struck the House of York in 1460, with the bloody murders of the Duke and his second lad, Edmund of Rutland, I was of necessity separated from the young ducal offspring when they fled to safety in the Low Countries. I remained in England since there was no call for a nobody such as I to flee but I was soon reunited with my noble friends when fortune's wheel turned once again, placing Edward, their oldest brother, onto England's throne.

When Dickon returned to England from his Burgundian exile my friendship with him continued as before. I was with him the day before his brother's coronation, lending him my encouragement as he prepared for the gruelling ceremony that would make him a Knight of the Bath. I was there again a few months later when the King created him Duke of Gloucester. It seemed a weighty title for a nine year old lad to carry but the King was bent on honouring all his kin, and so I learned to address my friend with due respect, greatly as this chagrined him. In my private thoughts, however, he remained simply Dickon, the intense and slender child with whom I had frolicked so carelessly in the dirt at Fotheringhay.

In his twentieth year my lord was finally able to fulfil his dearest wish and marry his cousin Anne Neville, a tender lass of sixteen who had won his heart as a child. Clarence had worked strenuously to oppose the match as he had no desire to share any part of the rich Neville estates but my lord pressed his suit with his customary tenacity and won his bride in the end. Neither Dickon nor his new Duchess felt fully at ease in the self-indulgent atmosphere of Edward's Court and so they determined to seek out the fresher air of the north. They made Middleham their principal home as it was here that their love had first blossomed years ago. Back then, Anne had been a golden, gracious child watching with shining eyes as Dickon and I matured from ungainly boyhood into flushing, eager manhood under the tutelage of her father, the once great Earl of Warwick.

In order to keep me close by him at Middleham, my lord made me his personal minstrel, a fine position which carried a generous stipend and left me ample opportunity to flirt with the Duchess's ladies. To add legitimacy to my position I duly joined the Guild of Royal Minstrels but in reality my duties were not onerous and I was rarely required to perform in public. This I found all to the good since I was certain that my musical abilities would be insufficient to please a truly discerning audience. In truth, most at Middleham knew that my minstrel's job was a thin disguise for my true role of private counsellor and confidant to the Duke.

Naturally, there were many nobly born men who flocked to serve Richard of Gloucester and he set great store by their loyalty and devotion, but he had in me a unique tool to employ as he saw fit. With my fine education and fighting skills, I was as useful as any of his nobles and yet the circumstances of my birth prevented me from aspiring to high office. Tainted by bastardy and with no family connections of mine own, my one allegiance was to the Duke of Gloucester. He knew I could be relied upon to perform such errands and duties as it might be incautious for him to entrust to any of his higher born companions. Aside from the genuine love that I felt for him, I knew that my own fortunes marched in parallel with Gloucester's. As he prospered, so did I; were he to fall, I would tumble with him.

And so I return to the Christmas of 1472 and the entertainment I was plotting for the festive season. It was to be an informal Yuletide, with none but the Duke's closest friends and retainers in attendance but still there were many arrangements to be made. Gloucester was a young man but he possessed little of the natural gaiety of spirit commonly associated with youth. He enjoyed the japing and tomfoolery of others but his own humour was gentle and wry and his face always wore the shadow of his early struggles. It came as no surprise to me, therefore, when he asked me to organise Middleham's Yuletide revelries that year.

"Make it a merry time," he instructed me one wet December morn. "I want it as splendid as anything they have at Windsor or Westminster. I must show my northern friends that I am more than the King's tax collector. Let them see that I am a man like them, one who feasts and jests and cherishes his wife, just as they cherish theirs."

"Just as they do, my lord?" I quizzed him, thinking of all the stout, red-faced northern matrons I had met, finding it inconceivable that any one of them inspired overmuch affection in their husbands' hearts.

"Aye, just as they do, scoundrel," he repeated, his eyes alight with the warm intelligence that so delighted his friends and inspired even his enemies to respect him.

"Not all men think as you do, Francis. Some even believe that fidelity and goodness are more desirable in a woman than a comely figure and kissable lips. But we stray from the matter in hand. I want to impress my northerners with our Yuletide celebrations. Arrange it for me, Frank. You have a talent for these flummeries. Spend what you will, only make it a success."

We were drawing close to the Auditor's Chamber as we spoke and I was ready to quit my lord in order to set some plans in motion when our attention was caught by a commotion issuing from the Gatehouse. Looking closely, I saw that a horseman had arrived and was seeking admittance to the Castle. Smithkin, the Sergeant-at-Arms, was having none of it, turning the man away with angry words and gestures.

"Whose badge does he wear?" I enquired of Gloucester, pointing to the newcomer. "I cannot make it out."

"I see no livery," the Duke replied, "but the fellow's clothing has surely seen better days. The poor wight is coated in mud and dust from head to boot, Francis. 'Tis plain he has ridden long and hard in this inclement weather. Old Smithkin serves me ill by refusing him entry. This will not do. Come, let's go to his aid and see what his business at Middleham may be."

I fell in with this plan quite readily. Smithkin and I were old adversaries and I ever relished encountering him in company with the Duke, for then he was obliged to conceal his simmering dislike and address me with a courtesy that undoubtedly stuck in his gullet.

The history of our animosity is simply told. Some months before, when I had first arrived at Middleham, I had lost my heart to Smithkin's daughter Margaret, a painfully lovely creature whose honey-coloured hair and ripe womanly body possessed my mind by day and destroyed my rest at night. I knew that she returned my love, our few snatched kisses left me in no doubt on that score, but Margaret was an irritatingly virtuous girl who believed that the marriage bed was the only proper place to celebrate our love. In short, she made wedlock the price I must pay in order to possess her.

I have had much time to reflect on what happened next

and I swear on every holy relic in Christendom that in due course I would have come to terms with the match and taken her as my wife. At first though, and to my cost, I baulked at the suggestion. She was desirable and sweet and I loved her truly but she was not the bride I had imagined for myself. My close friendship with the Duke and Duchess meant the very world to me and maintaining the warmth of the relationship with them was always my first consideration. In all truthfulness, I feared how it might suffer were I to wed the unlettered daughter of the Duke's own Sergeant, a girl who was content to pass her days discoursing with the common people of the town. Could such a one ever become a fitting companion for the gentle Duchess?

I felt severely troubled on this point and so I dallied, tossing the dilemma about in my head as a hound tosses the rabbit betwixt its teeth in order to break the struggling creature's neck. For the first time in my life I kept my feelings hidden from my lord of Gloucester. I knew full well that had he been aware of my affection for Margaret he would have pressed me to marry her with all speed, brushing aside as of no consequence my objection to the match. So I said nothing and behaved outwardly as if all went well with me, whilst inside I gnawed at the problem until I feared for my reason.

It may be that the little I knew of my own mother also inspired my hesitation for, like Margaret, she had been a beautiful woman of humble birth and she had turned out none too admirably. Whatever the reason, I turned away from Margaret whilst I sought to reconcile myself to the match. This does not speak well of me, I know, but I was tempted to put pride and personal ambition before the call of my heart and I paid the full penalty for my pretensions. While I was pondering on my decision Margaret despaired of me and accepted the hand of a wealthy old merchant who had been courting her unobtrusively for many months. She moved with him to York and what my heart suffered I have not words to say but I do not complain for the pain was well-deserved.

In addition to a broken heart, the sorry episode earned me

the unremitting enmity of old Smithkin who justly blamed me for the removal of his beloved daughter. This enmity troubled me not one whit for, in a curious way, the feuding took my mind from my misery and I almost enjoyed the jibing and insults that we exchanged whenever we met. I bore old Smithkin no genuine ill-will and in truth always spoke well of him to my lord of Gloucester. For Margaret's sake, I even helped secure sound positions for her two brothers although I made certain her foolish old father remained in ignorance of my assistance.

My lord and I arrived at the Gatehouse in time to see the newcomer slide silently from his spent horse and collapse at our feet onto the cold December grass. As Gloucester leapt forward to assist the stranger I kept close to his side, fearing this might be a ploy by a hired assassin to launch an attack on the Duke. Even then there were many who would have given much gold to see Richard of Gloucester in his coffin and I was fully aware of the fact. Praise God, in this case my suspicions proved groundless.

Filthy and torn, the simple clothing of the unconscious man bore testimony to the trials of his journey whilst giving no clue to his identity. Turning him gently as we examined him for injury, my lord and I drew back in horror at the sight of a hideous scar covering the entire left side of his face. The skin was puckered and blistered from brow to mouth, looking for all the world as though that side of his face had been set alight. A viscous yellow liquid oozed lazily from the corner of the damaged eye and trickled into the fissures surrounding the wound.

The toughened scar tissue had grown white round the edges and as I poked it gently I found it was quite smooth to the touch, leading me to the conclusion that this was no new affliction. The weeping eye was clearly a permanent condition, a sticky and unpleasant reminder of what must have been an agonising injury. His face bore further wounds including a livid red lesion, recent by the look of it, lying just above his right eye but all paled into insignificance compared

21

with the horror of the ruined cheek. At once I understood Smithkin's reluctance to give admittance to the fellow. In the good Sergeant's eyes such a dubious-looking character was unfit to speak with the noble Duke and should be sent on his way with all speed.

My lord of Gloucester, however, was possessed of greater compassion than his Sergeant. With a few terse commands he had the unlovely visitor transported to the fireside in the great hall where a veritable army of servants was summoned to minister to his needs. The Duchess herself, roused from her solar by the commotion, stood by his side murmuring instructions and after a few minutes of this tender care he opened his eyes. He remained awake long enough to wolf down a hastily assembled meal of bread, cheese and ale and then fell back wordlessly into his slumbers. We let him be until he woke again several hours later. This time cold water was splashed onto his face to rouse him fully and then he was brought before the Duke to tell his story.

"My lord, I pray you will forgive my rough appearance and uncouth manners," the stranger began, "but I am a simple man and know naught of fancy speech and courtliness."

I confess I found the sight of this lumpen great fellow standing against a background of splendid brocades and tapestries as disquieting as a pulsating boil on the face of an otherwise comely maiden. We were sitting in the Duke's privy chamber, just Gloucester, the newcomer and I, and it was clear from the way he glowered at me that he found me as unwelcome as a bishop in a bawdy house. Less welcome, in truth, for I have heard tell of several bishops who relish a good debauch as much as any man.

"He can hang himself if he is reluctant to tell his tale before me," thought I, whistling softly as my fingers absent-mindedly turned over a small scrap of cloth I happened to have about me. For my part I was only too thankful to be present and able to keep watch over my friend who on occasion had a regrettable tendency to be reckless with his safety. I had been aghast when the importunate wretch had demanded a private audience with Gloucester but something about the wild desperation of his manner had persuaded my lord to accede to this unusual request with just one stipulation.

"You will not mind Cranley's presence, I am certain" the Duke had said, forestalling the objection I was about to make to this private meeting, "for he is my true and trusted servant and will disclose not a word of what he hears here, unless sobeit I give him leave. He makes a fair scribe and I would have him set down your tale for me that I might consider it some more when you are at your rest."

Though my lord spoke gently the iron in his voice was unmistakable. As it was plain these terms were not negotiable the stranger had no recourse but to acquiesce to my presence, though he did so with ill grace. This was not the first time that Gloucester had asked me to act as his scribe on a matter of personal business. His official secretary, John Kendall, was a worthy man devoted to the House of York and my lord had great faith in him but he preferred to use my services when dealing with sensitive or potentially dangerous issues that required unbiased advice.

I believe this was because, for all his loyalty, Kendall was a cautious man whose advice, if sought, could be relied upon to be bland and noncommittal. I, on the other hand, as one who enjoyed the privileged position of trusted boyhood friend, would tell my lord exactly what my thoughts were even when their substance was likely to displease him. There was nothing out of the ordinary, then, about me acting as his secretary on this occasion but I did find it passing strange that my lord should deem it necessary for me to record the details of his meeting with this ruffian.

It occurred to me then that the Duke's manner had been somewhat constrained since the audience began and I was hard put to comprehend why this should be so. I readily admit that at this point I felt little inclined to favour the disfigured petitioner and heartily wished that my lord would conclude the matter with all speed and then dismiss the fellow from the castle. My humour was scarce improved when I glanced down at the cloth entangled between my fingers and discovered it to be the soft, apple-green ribbon I had once traded with Margaret for a kiss and which she had returned to me the night she told me of her plans to wed.

"My lord," the man continued, "I come to you to plead for justice. I am wrongly accused of a crime so foul it sickens my very soul and I cannot bear to have the stench of it upon my good name. 'Tis little enough I have in this world but I have ever been known as an honest man and this has been a comfort to me in my loneliness. Now my name is besmirched and I shall not know rest until my innocence be proven.

"Yet for all this, I would not trouble you on my account alone but do so for the sake of one who has risked her own safety to help me. I am driven nigh beyond reason knowing the woman I cherish more dear than my own life may be in dire peril and is surely even now paying a severe penalty for aiding my escape. I will not be easy until I know that she is safe."

I rolled my eyes at this melodrama but not so Gloucester, who looked hard at the man, as if to gauge the sincerity with which he spoke. As he gazed upon the awful, mutilated features of the stranger, something flickered momentarily behind my lord's grave eyes and then was gone. I knew not what he had seen in the man's face but resolved to put all thoughts of Margaret aside and pay closer heed to the proceedings. Dickon would sign to me when he wished me to start scribing and I had better hold myself in readiness.

"Come, friend, give me your name," the Duke murmured, an unaccustomed note of hesitancy causing his voice to falter.

The fellow nodded his head slowly, as if satisfied with the progress he was making. As he did so I discerned that there was something reminiscent of a wolf in his appearance, not a young and powerful wolf, proud and dominant in his bestial glory but rather a lean and mangy elder of the pack, a battered and canny survivor of many cruel seasons.

"I'm mostly known these days as Pretty Will," he replied

after a short delay, rubbing thoughtfully at his wounded face. "'Tis meant most likely as a jest," he added unnecessarily. "You, my lord Duke, once knew me by a different name and for all that you were naught but a frightened child at the time, yet with God's good grace I believe that you shall remember me now and help me in my hour of need."

I noticed with some alarm that Gloucester's pallid face had become more ashen than usual; he trembled as he rose from his chair and moved uncertainly towards the stranger.

"Can it truly be you? We thought you dead. And yet I see it is you," he continued, delighted astonishment blazing brightly in his eyes. "My dear old friend, Will Fielding!"

Unmindful of his ducal dignity, my lord leapt at Fielding like a boisterous pup and clasped the man in a close embrace. As for me, at last daylight flooded my fuddled brain, chasing away the murky shadows that had thus far kept my wits in darkness.

I now understood that this unprepossessing person could only be the soldier hired by John Skelton many years ago to help spirit Dickon and George out of the country following the tragedy that had befallen their family at the battle of Wakefield. I well recalled the confusion and anxiety that had permeated the York's house in London at that time; naturally, being of no political importance I had been left behind in the care of the Duchess Cecily when they fled. Kind lady, though she feared for the safety of her youngest boys and wept for the husband and son she had but lately lost in battle, yet still she found time to share words of consolation with me whenever I showed signs of loneliness or fright.

Master Skelton, I knew, had been well-rewarded for his services, the King having granted him the lucrative office of Surveyor of the Port of London. Fielding, however, had disappeared without trace. It was said that the Duchess had offered a handsome purse in exchange for news of the tough soldier's whereabouts as she had sworn to reward him for saving her children's lives. Years had passed without any news and still the good Duchess remembered her vow and strove to find him. She had long since abandoned any real hope of discovering his whereabouts when a Burgundian cloth merchant arrived at Court with tidings that saddened her heart.

Fielding, the merchant reported, had perished in a drunken brawl in an Antwerp tavern several years since. The clothier had no further details to offer, having gleaned this information through his young 'prentice who frequented the hostelry in question, but the Duchess accepted the veracity of the story and was particularly impressed when the merchant refused to accept the gold she offered him. Small wonder, then, that my lord of Gloucester had turned white as the rose of York when he finally recognised his old protector. I have heard tell of corpses rising from the grave to return and haunt the living but it was plain enough that Fielding was no ghost. Alas for my delicate nostrils, his pungent odour was very much a reality, one which would have shamed the most demonic, hell-spawned entity. How my noble friend could bring himself to embrace the man I was scarcely able to comprehend.

When the first rapture of the reunion had abated somewhat, my lord regained his composure sufficiently to demand of Fielding an account of his life from the time of their parting to the present day, that he might better comprehend the need in which Fielding now approached him. I recount here the gist of what Fielding told us that day in the Duke of Gloucester's privy chamber. The tale was long in the telling and parts of it strained my credulity, not to mention my poor wrist as I struggled to write it all down. My lord of Gloucester, however, listened most attentively to the testimony of his old protector and appeared to give credence to every word that he heard.

Chapter 2
An Old Friend Tells His Tale

"My lord Duke," Fielding began, "when you and your brother returned in triumph to London, I confess that I missed your young company most grievously. Your oldest brother was become King and you had no further need of my protection. Aye, though I rejoiced for the victory your family had sustained, still I nursed a soreness in my heart that you were no longer under my protection.

"Your brother George was a cheery young lad and I liked him well enough but it was you that I missed the most. 'Til knowing you, my life had been rough and empty; I knew only how to fill my days with drinking and cursing and fornication unless I was engaged in battle. This was the time I liked the best, when I could fill up my chest with bloodlust and charge into the fray with no thought but to slay as many foe as possible. I say without false pride that I was known as a fearsome fighter and many brave men were loath to meet me in battle. Master Skelton chose me for his mission for this very reason. I was not a bad man but in battle I had no conscience.

"And then I met you and your brother. The days I was privileged to spend with you taught me that there could be a place for tenderness in my life. I found a new way; serving you gave my life a better, more honest meaning. I learned 'twas more rewarding to the soul to comfort and care for a frightened child than to make empty sport with a lusty trollop or run a foe through on my sword.

"My lord, you were such a fragile child, ailing and ever in the hands of God and yet you were so brave and trusting. Do you recall the name it pleased you to give me? Wolfman it was, and I swear I guarded you and George as fiercely as any she-wolf guards her cubs. Then you left, and with you gone I took leave of my senses for a while and fell in with dissolute company. I returned to my former ways and stayed intoxicated for nigh on half a year.

"With my corrupt companions I caroused by night and slept by day but there was naught of merriment in our proceedings. I drank to fill the aching void in my soul, to drown the desperate sense of worthlessness that assailed me whenever I was sober. Why my companions behaved as they did I cannot say but I know that all men must wrestle with their demons before they can be saved. I was saved at the last, roused from the sodden pit of despondency into which I had sunk by the accident that gave me this cursed scar.

"It happened like this. My fellows and I were drinking in a tavern in Antwerp, soaking up the roughest brews unfit for even swine to drink. After a flask or two of this liquor had burned its way down our throats, we started to sing a bawdy song that heaped insult on the locals. Of course, offence was taken as had been our intention and a bloody fracas ensued. I entered into the mêlée with gusto, banging heads together so hard that the teeth were knocked out of my victims' mouths.

"It was a good fight and would most likely have ended amicably enough, had not one touchy fellow with a split lip and blackened eye come raging toward me with a burning torch which he thrust hard into my face. I made to dodge the blow and caught the full impact on my left cheek, as you can see. The scorching of my flesh was more pain than I had ever known and mercifully I lost consciousness but not before I had struck wildly at my assailant with my dagger. I cut him deep in the shoulder and he fell flailing to the ground, dropping the torch as he hit the floor. In all the mayhem nobody noticed at first when the flames started to lick the ragged arras hanging from the wall. Then, as the fire took hold and the heat became intense, the assembled company was either too intoxicated or too indifferent to organise a fire party. I was told that the tavern went up like a tinderbox. Several men perished in the flames but I was more fortunate. Some worthy soul, I know not whom, saw me lying senseless and dragged me from the building, thus saving me from a fiery death.

"When I came to I was in the home of a cloth merchant, a man I had encountered several times before when buying broadcloth for you and your brother, my lord. This man had discovered me in a ditch by the roadside and had sent his men to put me on a litter and carry me back to his house. I still wore the livery of the House of York and it was this that had prompted him to help me, for my face he surely did not recognise. My countenance at this time was more than sensitive folk could stomach to gaze upon, so terribly disfigured had I been by the burning brand.

"The merchant's good lady cared for my injury and nursed me back to health, enduring without complaint the filthy imprecations that I hurled at her every time she changed the herbal poultices on the wound. At one time, I became fevered and weak as a hatchling but with good food and kind attention I gradually regained both my strength and my dignity. The incident in the tavern had left me full of remorse for my drunken practices and I took a solemn vow to reform my unruly ways. From that moment onwards, it has been my practice to be abstemious in all my habits and I have remained sober ever since.

"When I had fully recovered from my injury the merchant offered me employment in his service, protecting his wagons and mules from the ruthless outlaws that lie in wait upon the trade routes. The work suited my abilities and was very much to my liking. I travelled throughout the Low Countries and beyond, to Paris, Lyon and Venice. The searing pain in my scorched face gradually lessened to a dull ache to which I became accustomed, and I found that the new savageness of my appearance served to discourage the more faint-hearted bandits from making free with my employer's precious trade goods. I never once forgot the debt I owed this generous fellow and I worked hard to repay his goodness. He and his wife became my family and I knew a certain contentment in their company.

"In time, my lord, a rumour reached us that your good lady mother was seeking for me, in order to bestow upon me some kind of reward for my past services. My kind benefactor was much pleased for me and urged me to set out for London at once but I recoiled in horror at the suggestion. With all my sins upon me, to present myself before the gracious Duchess in order to receive her blessings and bounty was more than I could bear. Even the thought of it made my heart churn up in shame. I cannot explain, except to say that I felt as if the excesses of my drinking and whoring days still clung to my presence like an evil toxin which would befoul the purity of your noble mother.

"And I thought also of seeing you, my lord, the little lord Dickon who had so favoured me with his boyish affection. I knew I had never been a handsome man but neither had I looked a monster, a nightmarish creature like to terrify children. The thought of you looking upon my ruined face and turning your head in revulsion brought tears of self-pity to my eyes. I explained all this to my employer and although he did not fully understand my reasoning, after much argument and with sympathetic encouragement from his lady he finally agreed to journey to London in my stead.

"He presented himself to your noble mother at Court and gave her the story that the man she sought had perished in an inferno at a tavern in Antwerp several years since. In truth, the virtuous man misliked lying on my behalf but saw for himself how tortured I became at the thought of facing you again, so I beseech you not to think ill of him for his deception. Having completed his mission to my satisfaction, my master returned home and I remained happy in his service until his untimely death of the sweating fever some two years since.

"I had been thinking for some time of returning to my homeland and the demise of my erstwhile employer brought my hankerings to a head. His widowed lady retired to the cloisters and the business passed into the hands of their daughter's husband, a surly brute who disliked me and lost no time in dispensing with my services. Much to my surprise and gratitude, I found that my master had willed me a modest legacy, small enough to escape resentful notice from his foremost heir but adequate enough, if used sparingly, to support me for the remainder of my days.

"Possessed now of the means to feed my body, I searched about for ways to feed my soul. I needed a purpose, someone in trouble to protect, as you had once been, my lord, or else someone kind and worthy of my service, as the merchant and his wife had been. Returning to England in 1470, it did not take me long to find such a one.

"I had been staying in Lincoln but a sennight, passing myself off as Will Yorke in order to conceal my true identity, enquiring in kitchen and in tavern for news of any likely employment, when word reached me of a young lordling in need of a new body servant. The story went that this poor lad was naught but a cripple, fortunate in being lord of a rich and fertile manor at the tender age of twelve, cursed in the infirmities that denied him any pleasure in his inheritance.

"My informant told me that the boy was weak and ailing, his limbs as crooked as a Venetian moneylender's reckoning. This unhappy lad, one Geoffrey Plaincourt, was not expected to survive to manhood and on his death his estates would pass to his late father's younger brother, the comely and elegant Sir Stephen Plaincourt. Sir Stephen had inherited from his father the smaller, neighbouring manor of Ringthorpe and was thereby adequately provided for but he was said to spend all his days at Plaincourt, tending to his nephew's grander affairs with a diligence born of greedy anticipation. It was he that sought a new body servant for Geoffrey and so I rode out at once for Plaincourt in order to present myself to Sir Stephen.

"On my arrival at the fair manor of Plaincourt I quickly deduced how the land lay for young Geoffrey and my heart ached with pity for the sorry lad. I discovered that the boy was kept to his chamber all day, denied fresh air and daylight on the grounds that being abroad too much would overtax his feeble strength. No person, excepting the meanest servant, was allowed to visit him without the consent of his uncle, Sir

31

Stephen, who put it about that company over-excited the lad and brought on one of his plaintive fevers. Sir Stephen was a smooth and plausible liar but I have met his type before and I guessed at once his unkind purpose.

"By keeping his nephew a prisoner in his own manor, he thought to drive him to despair and from thence to an earlier death than nature intended, whereupon he would become lord of Plaincourt in title as well as in fact. There was no-one at Plaincourt with the inclination or the means to stand as friend to poor Geoffrey. Sir Stephen was the boy's legal guardian until he came of age and as such was within his rights to impose his own rule over the manor. Although I saw all this for myself in a very short time, I kept my own counsel and worked hard to ingratiate myself with Sir Stephen in the hope that he would hire me to tend to the boy.

"As it turned out, I need not have tried so hard for the black-hearted villain took one look at me and resolved at once to make me his nephew's keeper. Guessing his true character as I did, this was not hard for me to comprehend. My face is the stuff of boyish nightmares and the rest of my appearance so unappealing, so coarsened by dissipation it disgusts even myself. The rude manner of my speaking is the only language I know. Every callus on my hands, every crease upon my brow holds witness to the brutal life I have led up to now. Oh yes, I could see why the treacherous serpent would think me the perfect tormentor for young Geoffrey. I would be wielded by Plaincourt as an odious tool, one that with careful management would topple his nephew over the edge of despair and into a lonely, premature grave.

"It was well for Geoffrey and myself that Sir Stephen was a poor judge of men, yet it cannot be denied that the boy's initial encounter with me was all that Sir Stephen had hoped for. He introduced me to the child as 'Pretty' Will Yorke, telling him with calculated cruelty that I had been selected as his special servant on account of my reputation for dealing with fractious children. Geoffrey shrank from me in terror but I treated him gently and it was not long before I had won for myself his affection and his trust. Indeed, 'twas easily enough accomplished, for the ill-kept child had been so starved of softness that the simplest act of kindness brought him wonder.

"Ah, poor Geoffrey! He was a right pitiful sight to behold with his bony, wasted frame, darkly shadowed eyes and cheeks hollow as caves in his sad, colourless face. Both his parents had died of a fever when he was but a year old and since then he had been at the mercy of his grasping uncle. The wretched lad had never known tenderness and as he was wholly untutored, he was an ignorant and oft-times bothersome lad but I grew to love him nonetheless. He had real need of me, you understand, and I gladly did what little I could to ease his suffering.

"I spent the best part of eighteen months with him, for much of that time confined to a fetid chamber with only the boy and some mice for companionship. I had my liberty to roam the manor, of course, but I cared not to leave Geoffrey on his own for too long lest he take fright and fall into a fit in my absence. The other servants at the manor shunned me for the most part, wanting no truck with Sir Stephen's hired ruffian which was what they truly took me for.

"The thrice-cursed cowardly hypocrites! Not a one of them, save mayhap the dull-witted oaf who turned the spit, would piss in the wind to aid the boy yet they held themselves better than I! Until I arrived, there was no more pathetic and lonely a soul than Geoffrey Plaincourt in the whole of Christendom but I was able to change that. I loved him as my son and he cared for me as the father he never knew. I was there to hold his head when he puked and see to his soiled linen but more important than this, I gave him laughter and a reason to fight his illness. If he could make it through to manhood, how different then his life would be. May God forgive me, I taught the poor lad to hope.

"As the months passed by, it must have occurred to Sir Stephen that far from hastening Geoffrey's death I was in fact prolonging it. Strangely, he seemed not to care that his fiendish plan had failed and left us alone to enjoy our existence as best we could. In truth, the only change that occurred in our circumstances was one that proved to be entirely for the better and I give hearty thanks to the Almighty for the miracle that He sent us.

"There came to the chamber one April day a woman by the name of Mistress Blanche, a waiting woman newly arrived at Plaincourt. She told me she had leave from Sir Stephen to tend to the boy now and then, being reputed, so she said, for her knowledge in the healing arts. For all that Mistress Blanche was the most wondrously fair female I had ever beheld, yet I was loath to let her minister to my Geoffrey for fear her intentions were base. With hair as black as the ink on Master Caxton's printing press, tumbling in loose curls nigh on to her tiny waist and with eyes the hue of spring violets set in an oval face as smooth and pale as a dove's downy wing, she was lovelier than living flesh has any right to be.

"I trusted her not and bade her begone, back to the devil whence she came. She just laughed at me and with an audacity I could scarce believe, stood high on her dainty feet and planted a fleeting kiss, right here on my ill-figured cheek. 'Give this to the boy,' she whispered in a honey-sweet voice, placing a small greasy package in my callused hand. I made to fling the packet back at her but she had already turned on her nimble feet and vanished from the passageway like a startled sprite.

"Geoffrey was lying abed as usual and he called me to him, bidding me show him what the strange woman had left behind. I opened the cloth-wrapped package and uncovered a large square of gingerbread, fresh baked by the smell of it and moistly sticky to the touch. Geoffrey's eyes grew round with longing, for treats of this nature were infrequent for the boy. He was fed well enough but mostly on naught more tempting than pottage and similar slops, Sir Stephen having declared that richer fare was more than his delicate state could manage.

"Thus I understood the lad's craving for the rare sweetmeat all too well but refused to give any to him until I

34

had broken off a sizeable portion and eaten it myself. 'Twas not selfish gluttony on my part, as Geoffrey fretfully accused, but a precaution I deemed needful to ensure the food was untainted by any poison. Several hours later, when I had suffered no ill-effects, I considered it safe to give Geoffrey leave to devour what remained of the delicacy. He did so with obvious relish though he remained sullen and resentful towards me for the rest of that day.

"After this first visit Mistress Blanche took to calling upon us on a daily basis. I mistrusted her still but Geoffrey became fond of her and looked with pathetic eagerness toward her visits. She would bring such small gifts of sweetmeats and delicacies as she could filch from the kitchen and sit with the boy, singing to him in her clear, tuneful voice or teaching him to play chequers. After that first time there was no need for me to taste the edible treats she brought Geoffrey as she always took some of them herself, sensing mayhap that I was as yet uncertain of her and suspectful of foul play. She showed no sign of resenting my hostility toward her and indeed, in time, began to converse with me as amiably as she did with Geoffrey.

"It grieves me to recall how at first I strongly resisted her overtures of friendship since I now know her to be the kindest, truest woman ever gifted to man by God. The exceptional beauty of her countenance is surpassed only by the beauty of her spirit. Suspicious cur that I was, I did her much wrong in believing her angelic soul capable of harming my dear boy. She came to us from simple goodness of heart, having heard tell of the lonely existence we endured confined day in and out in Geoffrey's fusty chamber. All this I came to see in time though it shames me that it took so long.

"When finally Blanche had won my trust, I asked her how it was she had obtained permission from Sir Stephen to spend time with Geoffrey. She answered that it had been achieved with difficulty. At her first request he had bellowed at her for her insolence and threatened to send her from Plaincourt should she persist in meddling in his affairs. Nothing daunted, the blessed girl held firm. Displaying what I consider rare courage for such a slip of a thing, she hinted to the vile man of her high-placed friends who would be deep distressed to learn of Geoffrey's sorry treatment should she be denied her will in this matter. Plaincourt crumbled like three-day bread at this threat, my beautiful and cunning Blanche told me, and thus she had her way.

"My lord, I may as well now confess that I came to love the beautiful Mistress Blanche with all my heart. Moreover, to my unbounding bewilderment and joy, I discovered that she returned my devotion in full measure. It scarcely seems possible that even an ill-favoured woman could feel affection for me; how much more miraculous is it, then, that the fairest woman on earth gives her heart and soul to me? I understand it not but praise the Almighty daily that it is indeed so. Blanche herself tells me that the goodness of my heart shines through the ravages of my poor face and it is the man inside she loves, not the damaged shell that houses him. 'Tis foolish woman's chatter, I avow, and yet 'tis the only explanation I have for the miracle that has befallen me.

"We took pains, of course, to disguise our affection for one another, knowing well what would occur should Sir Stephen come to hear of it. My Blanche would have been expelled from the manor in an instant and I would have been unable to follow her, having sworn to remain at Geoffrey's side until he drew his last breath. And so we conducted our love affair in secret, snatching kisses here and there, content enough in our hearts and minds to be together yet ever hungering for more. It seemed we were doomed to spend long, heavy hours together in the same small chamber without ever once tasting the sweet fruit of our passion. Forgive my bluntness, my lord, but the fire of our desire burned strong and yet we knew no solace, until all unknowingly young Geoffrey gave us the chance to finally satisfy our yearning.

"It happened that whilst Blanche and I had been growing ever more deeply attached to one another, my sad young master suffered a dreadful weakening in his already frail condition, developing a hacking cough that in its ferocity and persistence left him quite exhausted. I watched my precious charge struggle with this fierce affliction and longed to wrest the demon sickness from his wasted body with mine own two hands. The nights were the worst for Geoffrey; sleep eluded him and none of my fussing and finicking brought him any comfort.

"I knew that I was losing him and the knowledge seared my soul as agonisingly as the flaming torch had once seared my face. Useless dolt that I am, all I could do was rail at fate and pray. It was left to my clever little Blanche to hit on a way to relieve the lad's suffering and mayhap even preserve his life a short while longer.

"Using her woman's knowledge of herbs and grasses, she concocted a potion that would help Geoffrey sleep peaceful as a babe throughout the night, granting him the rest he so sorely needed to combat the sickness inside him. I shook with terror the first time Blanche gave Geoffrey a draught of the potion, mixing it into some strong ale to hide the taste of the strange-looking liquid. I was afeared lest aught go amiss but to my unending relief, it worked much better than I had dared hope. For the first time in many days Geoffrey slept deeply from sunset to sunrise and awoke feeling rested and happy.

"When we realised how soundly Geoffrey slept with the aid of her potion, my angel and I knew that we could consummate our love in his chamber without fear of awakening and alarming him. Somehow my darling contrived to locate a spare key to the chamber and, by means of this, was able to enter and leave at will without drawing attention to herself. I know 'tis true we sinned in the eyes of God by lying together without the blessing of Holy Mother Church but I'll not feign contrition where none is truly felt. In any case, no mumbling dotard of a priest could have made our union more holy and more wonderful than it was on that first night or any night thereafter, come to that.

"Pardon me, my lord, if I dwell over much on the glory of

my love for Mistress Blanche but I am reluctant to leave that happiness behind and move on to the part of my tale that fills my heart with horror whenever my thoughts turn to it. And yet it must be told. Blanche and I had been lovers for upwards of fourteen nights. Every night my young charge slept a little longer and with every passing day I felt certain that he must be recovering his strength thanks to Blanche's physic. All was well, and then disaster struck.

"On this dreadful evening, Blanche came to the chamber at her usual time and stirred the draught into Geoffrey's bedtime ale. She hugged him as he drank it down and promised to bring a sugared comfit when she came to visit him next morn.

"'You are my darling boy,' she told him fondly, and Geoffrey curled contentedly into his pillows and fell asleep. 'And now, my love,' she whispered to me, 'Sir Stephen has visitors to whom I must attend but I'll be back with you as soon as my duties allow.'

"I caught her to me as she passed towards the door and held her in a passionate embrace. She kissed me tenderly and then I released her, confident that we would share many more such kisses before the night was too much older.

"A few minutes after she had gone Sir Stephen arrived, as was his habit, to lock Geoffrey and I into our chamber for the night. I smiled to myself as I heard his key turning in the lock for I knew that my dearest girl would let herself in using the spare key that Plaincourt had so foolishly left lying about for her to discover.

"I awoke next morning with a head as thick and woolly as a ram's backside. My senses were all awry and it took me several minutes to realise that I was lying in a sprawling heap, face down on the cold, hard floor. My left temple throbbed most damnably and a sticky substance, blood as I later discovered, glued a lock of hair across my eye. Before I had time for further thought, the chamber door was flung wide and Sir Stephen strode in, accompanied by his two most vicious henchmen.

"'God's blood!' he exclaimed angrily when he found me on the floor, 'is this what I pay you for? To roll about like a drunken hog half the morn whilst your young master languishes abed! Rouse yourself at once, man, and look to the boy.'

"I made to utter a few words of explanation for my condition but could find none for I was much bewildered by it, and knew not how to defend myself. In any case Plaincourt disregarded my mumblings and walked towards the bed, calling to Geoffrey to bestir himself. As I struggled to regain my feet a savage kick from Sir Stephen caught me off guard and I collapsed once more to the floor. 'You miserable wretch,' he hissed at me, 'you have done my poor nephew to death!'

"This wild accusation sobered me more suddenly than a visitation from the Archangel Gabriel could have done. Unmindful of my head injury, I leapt to my feet and lurched towards the bed but Plaincourt's bearded henchmen grabbed my arms and held me firm. 'Geoffrey!' I remember shouting, 'Geoffrey, speak to me! For the love of Christ, lad, speak to me!'

"But there was no reply from the motionless figure in the bed. With one almighty effort I pulled away from my captors and ran to Geoffrey's side. I caught his frail body in my arms and shook him in a desperate attempt to rouse him, all the while knowing in my heart that it was futile. Geoffrey was dead. A sob rose in my throat but I caught it there and buried my head against my poor boy's bony chest.

"'What the.....? Master, look at this!' exclaimed one of Plaincourt's lackeys in a voice laden with meaning, but I ignored him and continued to cradle Geoffrey's fragile corpse in my arms. Then I felt Sir Stephen's strong hands shaking me roughly so I looked up, intent on knocking the irritant away, but instead my attention was fixed by the evil gleam I beheld in his eyes.

"'Pray what explanation have you for this?' he sneered, jerking his head disdainfully towards a heavy pitcher lying on the floor, close to where I had been sleeping. I gawped at the pitcher, not understanding its relevance, ignorant of Plaincourt's meaning, conscious only that my happy world had come crashing down about me with the death of my crippled, luckless charge. 'Geoffrey,' I crooned, 'Geoffrey, my poor boy, what have they done to you?'

"Plaincourt's laugh was loud and brutal. 'It's no use pretending ignorance, Yorke, it's what *you* have done that the justices will be interested in. It all becomes clear to me now! You became sodden with drink last night and set about my nephew in a drunken rage, whereupon he tried to defend himself with that pitcher.

"'No,' he jeered, forestalling the interruption I was about to make, 'do not trouble to deny it. There is blood on the rim of the pitcher and I see you have a fresh cut above your eye. Geoffrey must have struck you with the pitcher using all the feeble force that he could summon, causing you to fall back upon the floor unconscious. Then, weakened by his sickness, he succumbed to the injuries you had inflicted upon him and expired.'

"I saw here how I might defend myself at last. 'Where are these injuries you say I inflicted? Look for yourself, there's not a mark upon the boy! Anyway, all know that I love him and would never do him harm. Ask any of the servants, they all know the truth of it.'

"I saw Plaincourt ponder the truth of this for a moment.

"'Then how does he come to be dead?' he asked me in a more reasonable tone.

"'Truly, I know not,' I groaned. 'I can only guess that mayhap his condition worsened in the night.'

"Sir Stephen seemed to be considering what I said but then his countenance darkened and he frowned.

"'No more than a few days since, you yourself told me my nephew was sleeping longer and as a result his condition was improving,' he shouted. 'Why should he suddenly die when he has been faring so much better? No, no, it makes no sense at all.'

"He moved closer to me and crouched low over the bed, smoothing Geoffrey's hair with a gesture that struck me as oddly tender coming from a man who throughout the lad's short life had dealt him naught but cruelty. Mayhap he finally felt remorseful, who can say? He remained next to me for a few seconds, stroking the dead boy's lifeless face and endeavouring to wipe away what I took to be a speck of dribble from the corner of his mouth.

"The speck refused to move and Plaincourt peered at it more closely, bending over Geoffrey's body until he was nearly touching it. Clamping hold of the lad's stiffened jaw with one hand, he used the other to prise Geoffrey's lips apart and withdrew a small white feather from his mouth.

"The servants in the room gasped in wonder as they saw what their master held in his right fist and I flinched as he rounded on me in anger. 'Suffocation! That's how you slew him. I see it now. You took this pillow and placed it over his face. In his desperate struggle for breath Geoffrey managed to grasp the pitcher and dash it against your skull but the blow did little harm to one as hell-hard as you, you stinking cur. Your grip remained firm until the boy breathed his last and then you slumped to the floor in your drunken stupor. Murderer!'

"My world turned as he all but spat this last at me. I tried to find the words to refute the charge but was given little chance. All at once the henchmen were upon me with stout ropes and my legs and arms were tightly bound. I struggled with all my might and could perchance have made some headway but Plaincourt rounded on me with venom in his eyes and struck me full under the chin with a blow of surprising force. As I was dragged from the chamber, dazed with grief and desperate to refute these false accusations, I did briefly wonder how it was that Plaincourt's men came to have the restraining ropes so conveniently to hand.

"The foul cell they locked me in was tucked away at the back of the manor, well hidden from the prying eyes of the villagers. A thin layer of dirty straw upon the earthen floor

41

comprised my only comfort; there was no bed nor stool and not the smallest shaft of sunlight pierced the enveloping gloom. Yet on my immortal soul I swear I cared nothing for my discomfort but thought only of Geoffrey and the dreadful thing that had been done to him. In the long, dark hours that I spent alone in my prison, I examined my conscious most keenly, straining to recall the events of the previous evening that I might unravel the mystery of my poor young charge's death.

"Even as I berated myself for failing to protect him, I knew as surely as I know my own name that I was innocent of the fell charge laid against me. There were many questions that remained unanswered but I was fully satisfied that I stood unjustly accused. In my misery, this was one of the two thoughts that consoled me. The second was that Blanche would never believe in my guilt. Sweet Blanche, who knew my love for the lad to be genuine and knew also of my habit to drink but little! She would know for a falsehood the assertion that I had smothered Geoffrey whilst in the grip of a drunken rage. Even now, when the bright happiness of my recent life had been snuffed out with Geoffrey's death, a flicker of gladness still remained in the memory of Blanche's fond affection.

"I was dwelling on these thoughts and others when the narrow door of the cell opened slowly and by a gleam of candlelight I saw a hooded figure move silently towards me. 'So now it ends,' I thought, believing that Plaincourt had sent someone to slit my throat and silence me forever. I could defend myself, I knew, for my bonds had been untied as I was flung into the prison but I remained impassive, ready to accept without a struggle the kiss of cold steel against my skin.

"A kiss I did indeed receive, but one of warm and lovely living flesh against my unshaven cheek. Her perfume filled my nostrils and my overwhelming love for her filled up my heart. For the second time that day I felt that I could cry as copiously as a virgin on her wedding night. 'Blanche!' I managed to gasp, before her soft sweet mouth descended on my own and silenced me. Yet all too soon she drew away from me.

"'We have little time,' she whispered, 'so you must listen to me and do exactly as I say.' I gazed at her in astonishment. 'But how come you to be here, sweeting?' I enquired. 'Did Plaincourt let you in?' She hushed my words with an impatient gesture of her hands and tied a belt containing food and water around my waist. 'There's no time now for your foolish questions,' she said, smiling up at me to lessen the sting of her words. 'There is a horse waiting for you outside, you must be gone with all speed. Plaincourt has sent to Lincoln for the King's justices, you're to be tried and hanged as soon as they get here.'

"'But I did not harm Geoffrey, I swear it on my sacred love for you,' I told her. 'You must believe me.'

"'Muttonhead!' she laughed then. 'Of course I believe you, why else do you think I am here? Do you imagine I would aid the escape of dear Geoffrey's murderer? Now come,' she urged, 'no more talking. You must flee forthwith.'

"I followed her from the dismal cell into the blackness of the night outside. Blanche snuffed out her candle and we were eaten up by darkness. I could see nothing before or behind me but Blanche grasped my hand and led me unerringly across the grass to where the horse was saddled and waiting.

"The speed of events had addled my wits and I floundered like a stricken fish against the shoals of her audacity. 'Where am I to go?' I asked her. 'I have no friend in all England but for you.' She paused for a moment, leaning her gorgeous silken head against my breast. 'I have a thought,' she said after a long moment. 'If all you have told me of your past is true, there is one person who not only has the influence to help you now but will do so gladly in gratitude for your past services to him.' As I said, my brain was working slowly and I gaped at her most stupidly. 'Sharpen your wits, Will,' she hissed, 'your life depends on them! You must ride with all haste to Richard of Gloucester and throw yourself on his mercy.'

"I gaped at Blanche, gradually remembering how, one evening when I had been nestling in her sweet arms, I had related to her the old story of your flight to the Low Countries, my lord, and the part I had played in the adventure. She was the first living soul to whom I had confessed my true identity since my return to England. It had been, nay, still was, my intention to leave Will Fielding dead and buried but I knew I could not accept Blanche's generous love whilst keeping such a secret from her. She agreed without hesitation that I should remain incognito and swore to speak to no one of the matter, although she ventured to suggest that Sir Stephen must have some knowledge of it since he had once mentioned in her hearing that the ruffian Will Yorke had friends in curiously high places.

"At this I was much perplexed until I recalled that during my very first meeting with Plaincourt, when I had been hoping to win his favour, I had attempted to impress him by speaking of an old association with the Duke of Gloucester. I had given him no particulars and he had asked for none; in fact, he had seemed manifestly disinterested in the tale and had sneered at my shameless swaggering.

"Now I realised that my dearest Blanche was right. I had never thought to see you again but my only hope of salvation lay in reaching you and putting my story before you. 'Ride to Middleham,' Blanche commanded me as I swung up onto the mount she had provided. 'And ride fast.'

"'Aye loveday, that I will, for it makes more sense than aught else I can think of,' I whispered back to her, 'but what of you? How will you fare once I am gone? Will you not be blamed for my escape?'

"I felt rather than saw the defiant shrug of her pretty shoulders as she made her brave reply. 'What can they do to me, Will? If they guess I aided you, I shall tell them I know you to be innocent and see no crime in freeing you. I can take care of myself, Will, have no fear.'

"I did fear for her, most dreadfully, but she would brook no further argument and after one last kiss laid a smack on the horse's flank that started me on my way to Middleham. And so I stand before you, my lord Duke, a fugitive from those who would accuse me of young Geoffrey Plaincourt's murder. Before Almighty God, I tell you that I am innocent and I beseech you to intercede and help me show the world that I am blameless."

Chapter 3
Embarking on a Journey

I scratched the last few words with frantic haste across the sheet of parchment and tossed my quill aside with undisguised relief. There was an intolerable ache in my right arm and the tender stretch of skin beneath my eyes felt as weighty as an ugly maiden's dowry. I yawned noisily to fill the silence that had continued after Fielding's final words. If I did not reach my bed within the next few minutes I feared for my reputation as the comeliest man at Middleham. My lord of Gloucester glanced at me and smiled, guessing correctly that I was eager for my bed.

"You have given me much to muse on," he said to Will "but now the hour grows late. I see you are a hair's breadth from exhaustion. Get you some rest at once and we shall speak again on the morrow.

"Francis," he turned to me, "I would be obliged if you would stay with me awhile to discuss some other business."

My dear friend Dickon could be heedless of my comfort when the occasion called and it seemed that this was one such time. I knew full well there were no pressing matters to discuss and he knew how I longed for sleep but he wanted my opinion of Fielding's account and would have it whether it suited me or no. The only person who could have rescued me then was the Duchess Anne and she, sensible lady, had long since retired to her bed. Since there was to be no escape, I revived myself with a draught of Gloucester's finest Rhenish and focused all my attention on the task in hand.

A sleepy page, hastily summoned, led Fielding away to his billet and when he had gone my lord fell at once to examining his story.

"Well, Francis, do we believe this improbable history? That is to say, do we believe Fielding is innocent of the murder of this tragic child, for I see no reason to question the rest of his tale."

I moved my head in tired agreement.

"The account of his supposed death in a tavern brawl fits well with what your lady mother was told. I find it passing strange that any sensible man would spurn the chance of a generous reward from the King's own mother and yet there was undoubted sincerity in his voice as he described his feeling of unworthiness. I am inclined to agree with you, that part of his tale is true, my lord."

As I concluded, Gloucester shot me a glance of ill-concealed impatience.

"How many times, Francis, must I ask you to call me Dickon when we are alone? Why must you make me ask it again on each successive occasion? All this my lording prevents us from speaking freely, friend to friend. Come, Francis, you are my equal tonight. Share your thoughts with me."

I was tempted to tell him then, as his equal, that I was in sore need of sleep and would share my thoughts on this other matter in the morning but my well-developed sense of self-preservation stayed my tongue. Besides, I was, in all honesty, as intrigued by the mystery as he. Flashing the Duke a look of injured innocence, I returned to my dissection of Fielding's story.

"I can credit it all up to his arrival at Plaincourt Manor. After that, the tale plunges deep into the realms of purest fancy. He avers that Sir Stephen hired him to torment the boy and drive him to despair but has not a shred of evidence to support the allegation.

"Next, he introduces to his improbable yarn an earthly angel who is goodness and purity personified but who nonetheless fornicates with our unwholesome hero in the chamber of their tender charge while he is sleeping.

"Then, on the morn that the boy is found dead, despite his protestations that he drinks but little our Pretty Will is discovered dead drunk on the chamber floor. When questioned he can recall nothing about the events of the preceding evening that will help explain the circumstances of the hapless lad's death. Why, Dickon, 'tis a tale that would stretch the credence of an addle-witted virgin. None but a fool would believe it."

This was audacious of me, I'll admit, but sometimes I found it diverting to bait my noble master, to test whether the ties of our boyhood friendship would stretch sufficiently to shield me from the famous Plantagenet temper. As I finished speaking I watched him closely to see if he would react as I had supposed. I was not to be disappointed. My lord of Gloucester flushed slightly and twisted one of the rings on his middle finger, then fixed me with that intense grey gaze of his.

"But I believe him, Francis, as you well know. Am I then a fool?"

It was a reasonable question and the obvious answer was yes, if you accept Fielding's story, then yes my lord, you are a fool. Only, I had known Richard of Gloucester intimately all my life. He was a stubborn man and was not to be shifted once he had determined on a course of action. Swift and decisive in matters of justice, generous and considerate towards his retainers, nevertheless on the field of battle his enemies knew him as a fierce and relentless opponent. For his family he felt a burning devotion and loyalty that manifested itself most strongly in the shining adoration he felt for his brother, King Edward. He was a kind and loving husband and the best friend a man could ever have. Above all, he was no fool.

"Dickon," said I, feeling somewhat chastened by the tone of mild reproach with which he had asked the question. "Dickon, if your instincts lead you to put your faith in the veracity of Fielding's anecdote then I accept it also. You well know that there is no man in the land whose judgement I trust better than your own. But even supposing it is the truth, have you considered the greater implications of meddling in this affair? Fielding, or Yorke as he now styles himself, is wanted by the King's men. If you give him succour you could be accused of committing an act of treason against your royal brother. Think how your enemies would feast on that!"

I paused for a moment to draw breath and Gloucester leapt into the breach. Dolt that I was, I was blissfully unaware of the trap he was smoothly setting before me.

"You speak wisely, Francis, as ever. Were it put about that Pretty Will was my guest here at Middleham, it would not look well for me. And yet, I think it safe enough, for who is to know that he is here? Only the Mistress Blanche and she, having affected his escape in the first place, is unlikely to betray his whereabouts. No, I am quite decided on the matter. Will remains at Middleham until his innocence is proven."

Quick as a beggar falling on scattered alms, I pounced on the obvious flaw in his reasoning and thus tripped headlong into his snare.

"Ah, but Fielding is known to have links with you!" I crowed, delighted to have out-thought the Duke for once. "By his own admission, the fool once bragged to Plaincourt of his close connection to you. He is not known to have any other connections in all of England. For sure, his pursuers may suppose he will head for the coast and take ship to the Low Countries but I'll warrant they'll also send men here. And what then, Dickon? What then?"

So delighted was I with my cleverness that I did not at once notice the sly smile adorning my lord's face.

"Quite right, Francis," he grinned, "I should have thought of that. How lucky I am to have you to protect me from myself."

There were times, and this was one of them, when I could have cuffed my sardonic lord and master clean between his princely eyes and not known a second's remorse.

"So it seems I may not keep Will with me," he continued, graciously ignoring my embarrassment. "Therefore, I must send him into hiding somewhere else, a place not too far from Middleham, to be sure, for I may wish to send messages to him from time to time. As it happens, I have the very place in mind."

Well, that is a surprise, I thought, but wisely kept the words unspoken.

"Of course, I can hardly take him there myself, Francis," he concluded, trying to look at me with a guileless expression on his face and failing damnably.

"You want me to escort him to this handy bolt-hole?" I suggested, and was rewarded by the full radiance of the ducal smile.

"This man saved my life once," he told me seriously, "and though in truth I can conceive of no viler offence than the callous murder of a helpless child, yet I owe it to him to do all that is possible to prove his innocence. Besides, I know full well the soft heart that beats inside that toughened carcase. He is no murderer, I'll stake my soul on it."

I confess I was moved, in spite of the prejudicial feelings I harboured towards the bothersome oaf.

"If we are to avoid prying eyes, it's best we make an early start," I said rather gruffly, "so with your leave, I think it best that we retire now."

Side by side we made our way to the doorway and then Gloucester stopped me.

"We must talk some more before you set out, Francis, for I confess there is another boon I'd ask of you."

Another earnest, almost pleading glance was directed towards me but I was ready for him this time. My friend would spring no further surprises on me this night.

"When do I set out for Plaincourt?" I enquired.

Gloucester's laughter accompanied me along the narrow passage of the Northwest Tower and up the winding staircase to my chamber.

***

I slept sound that night, much sounder than I would have done had I known where Gloucester intended me to journey on the morrow. Where my lord thought to hide Will Fielding I knew not, except that it would be no more than a hard day's ride from Middleham. My curiosity on this point was negligible; what really tugged at my fancy was the prospect of

51

the journey into Lincolnshire to meet Sir Stephen Plaincourt. As Gloucester had never encountered the fellow it seemed probable that he rarely visited Court although I realised that since the Woodville clan had risen to prominence, the same could well be said of my lord. There was no reason why Plaincourt and Dickon's paths should have crossed but I regretted that they had not, since it would have been useful to have had an unbiased opinion of the man.

Plaincourt interested me. Fielding had described him as comely and elegant, a smooth and plausible liar. It occurred to me that much the same description could be applied to myself, certainly by those who were envious of my good looks and easy charm. Could it be possible that Fielding disliked Plaincourt for no better reason than that the one was irredeemably ugly and the other was not? Judging by the fellow's hostility to me earlier that evening, the supposition was entirely plausible.

I was also intrigued by the notion of Mistress Blanche. A virtuous and handsome woman, so far gone in love with the loathsome Fielding that she coupled with him in a stench-ridden sick chamber, the very idea was beyond belief. Even King Edward's capering fool could not have concocted a more ridiculous suggestion had his worthless skin depended on it. Blanche, I felt sure, must be a boot-faced hag who had succeeded in blinding Fielding to her imperfections by granting him sexual favours. Either that, or she was a diseased harlot in need of a protector after contracting the pox. My flesh crawled at the very thought. Sweet Jesu! If that was the case, even Pretty Will was too good for such a one. I fell asleep pondering the horrors of the French pox, appreciating more than ever the blunt advice once given me by the late Earl of Warwick.

"There'll be times, my boy," he had said, "when you'll be tempted to plunge your meaty sword into any tasty pudding you find on the street. You must resist these urges, lad, and take care to besport yourself only with virtuous maidens. Wanton trulls oft leave a more lasting memory than the pleasure of the brief tumble you take with them. Be sure to have a care."

It was sound advice which I had always followed, having made myself a solemn pledge to frolic with ladies of none but the most unblemished reputation. Surprisingly enough, the resolution proved much easier to accomplish than I had supposed and over the last three or four years several seemingly virtuous maidens had shown themselves more than willing to learn the rites of passion from me before settling down to respectable domesticity with old and flatulent spouses.

In the morning, I dressed myself for the coming adventure with a little more than my customary care. Over a linen shirt I donned my new blue velvet doublet, cut in the Burgundian fashion with long, tight sleeves and flattering high neck. Over this I placed my favourite crimson jerkin, fastening it about the hips with the handsome jewelled girdle my lord had presented to me on the occasion of his marriage. With black hose, a fur-lined cloak of midnight blue and tall buckled travelling boots completing the outfit, I knew I cut a magnificent figure.

I dallied for a moment over my choice of hat but settled at last for the simple black felt, removing with some regret the silver and ruby brooch that customarily adorned the upturned brim. No point in making myself a target for every scurvy villain on the road, I told myself, as I placed the bauble into the folds of an embroidered kerchief and tucked this for safekeeping into the pointed toe of an old pair of shoes. Vastly pleased with my appearance, I fairly swaggered down the winding staircase and entered the great hall with a mighty flourish.

"By all the saints!" the Duke exclaimed as he caught sight of me in the doorway.

"Look, Anne," he called to the Duchess seated by his side, "here's a pretty fellow come to visit us! Who can he be, I wonder? For sure, when I heard the footsteps I had expected to see the musician Francis Cranley walk through that door but this gentleman is so grand and fancy, 'tis plain he is no humble minstrel.

"Sir, are you by chance related to my royal brother's kin by marriage, the worthy Woodville clan? By the Blessed Virgin, if your hair was fairer you could be Earl Rivers himself for I'll swear his tailor turns him out in nothing finer than your garb."

This morning Gloucester's humour was as heavy as a prior's breakfast but all the same the loyal Duchess smiled faintly at his words.

"Dickon has told me something of your mission, Francis," she said in her gentle, low-pitched voice, "and truly it seems to me that if you are to get this Will into hiding, with none aware of his connection to us here at Middleham, then you had better travel incognito. My lord is unkind to tease you for your finery, which you know becomes you greatly, but I feel you would be remarked much less in something more, well, in something rather more commonplace."

I loved the Duchess Anne well-nigh as much as I loved my lord of Gloucester. Even as a tiny child she had been able to bend me to her will with her tender reasoning and funny little smile. Too frail and wan for any claim to beauty or even prettiness, nevertheless those that knew her well revered her as though she were the fairest of her sex in all the land.

Gloucester at once dropped his jesting tone and touched his wife's hand in a gesture that was both protective and approving.

"Anne as ever speaks with wisdom, Frank. You cannot hope to escape notice dressed like that. I suggest you fly back to your peacock's nest this instant and return in something more akin to the woodcock."

The Duchess kept her face a study of tranquillity but her shoulders gave a gentle heave and I thought I heard her stifle a gulp of laughter as I turned on my heel and made an undignified exit from the hall. It would have been too much for my prickly hide to bear had Fielding also been present to witness this humiliation but the uncouth gawk was nowhere to be seen and that I counted as a blessing.

In my own chamber once again I disrobed in haste, muttering to myself all the while about the duplicity of princes who encourage a man to dress himself finely on the one day and mock him for so doing on the next.

My anger was fuelled by the knowledge that the Duke and Duchess had the right of it. If I was to go unremarked upon the highway it would be best for me to dress as plain as I could contrive. Rummaging through my coffer, I selected an old black fustian doublet that had decidedly seen better days and this I surmounted with the dun-coloured, hip-length gown I customarily wore for sword and archery practice. The tall boots I kept but the jewelled girdle I removed, albeit with no small regret. After a moment's reflection I determined that the splendid blue cloak would also have to go. In its place I reluctantly selected a dingy brown affair at least twenty years out of fashion, with a thick rabbit fur lining that was moulting but had the advantage of being warm. At the last, a spirit of rebellion moved me to conceal a spare linen shirt and breeches within the folds of my cloak.

Fielding was with the Duke when I returned to the hall and I took comfort from the knowledge that however plain my appearance might now be, I would be several months dead before I looked as grim as he. I greeted him with a curt nod and summoned a hovering page to serve me bread and ale. As I ate, my lord of Gloucester explained to the sour-faced fellow the plan we had devised thus far.

"It is unsafe for you to bide at Middleham until your innocence is clearly shown, so until that can be achieved you must of necessity go into hiding. I have many friends in these parts who have reason to be grateful to me and it is to one of these that I am entrusting you. I have writ a letter here that will ensure you are kept in comfort and in safety. Master Cranley will ride with you to this place, staying only to see you settled, and then will journey on to Plaincourt to uncover the truth of this sorry matter. What say you to this plan, Will? Does it not put you in mind of another adventure many years since?"

Pretty Will scowled in a manner most unpretty as the scheme was unfolded before him and I tried to guess which part of it displeased him. Of course, I should have known.

"My lord," he growled, "I appreciate right well the trouble that you take for me and if you say I must go into hiding, then so be it. But damned if I need this grinning coxcomb to coddle me along the way. And think you that Plaincourt will unburden his evil heart as soon as ever this mincing fool rides though his portal? My lord, I beg you not to underestimate Sir Stephen. He is as cunning as a dog fox and as merciless as a hawk. If he suspects Cranley of having aught to do with me he'll not hesitate to destroy him."

I kept my countenance bland but made a notch in my memory to repay him some day for his kind description of me. Grinning coxcomb was pardonable but I felt a burning resentment for the mincing fool part. It seemed I was not alone.

"I'll thank you to hold your tongue, Fielding!" Gloucester barked. "You'll be well advised to learn some respect for Francis Cranley. Do not be deceived by his light and easy manner for I warn you, if you fall foul of him you'll have reason to regret it."

My lord passed a weary hand across his brow and moderated his voice a little.

"Will, think you that I'd entrust your life to some lady-pleasing good-for-naught? To know a man, you must learn to look below the surface. In a fight, there's none I would sooner have at my side than Francis Cranley and be very sure of this, his wits are every bit as sharp as the keenest blade you ever used to smite a foe. Francis will ride into Plaincourt Manor disguised as a passing minstrel. If his charm is as steady as ever, he'll be invited to stay on awhile and if that happens, you may be sure he'll tread as lightly as a moonbeam in a forest."

I endeavoured to appear menacing and charming all at once but mayhap just succeeded in looking as if my morning ale had turned sour inside my stomach. As it did, just a short moment later.

"Now you must go," the Duke instructed. "Here, Francis, take this letter and give it to Master Pennicott by way of explanation."

I stared at my friend Richard, Duke of Gloucester, in absolute dismay.

"Master Pennicott?" I repeated dully. "Master Pennicott, the wool merchant of York?"

"Yes, yes," my lord replied, "you know him well. Old Pennicott whose sister's boy fell foul of my brother of Clarence and would doubtless have ended badly, had I not intervened and seen justice done. The old man has a goodly house near the Micklegate, with space aplenty in which to conceal our Will. What ails you, Francis? You look as if you wish to puke."

With great difficulty I composed my shattered thoughts and made a stern attempt to pull myself together. In company with the Duke and Duchess, Will and I quit the hall and strode across the courtyard to the stables. My mind was still in turmoil and it was some seconds before I noticed that the Duchess was tugging furtively at my sleeve.

"Your lute," she whispered when once I turned my head in her direction. "You forgot your lute but you will need it for your disguise. I picked it up as we were leaving the hall," she smiled, retrieving the concealed instrument from under her cloak and passing it to me in one deft movement that went unnoticed by the others. How I blessed the little Duchess then, for I would have reaped a rich harvest of scorn from friend Fielding had I forgotten to bring the lute with me on the journey.

"So much," I imagined him jeering, "for the much-vaunted sharpness of your wits."

With her gentle intuitiveness, the Duchess had somehow perceived my sudden distress and although she was unaware of its cause, she strove to protect me from the damage it was at that moment inflicting on my troubled mind. A wonderful lady, Anne of Gloucester, and never better loved by any than she was by me on this occasion.

At the stables, my lord of Gloucester spoke a few more words to Will and to myself but for the most part we mounted in silence and rode away from Middleham with the minimum of farewells. This abrupt leave-taking was in keeping with our plan to draw as little attention as possible to our undertaking but it also suited me right well for once to remain close-mouthed.

Had my temper been fairer I might have bid farewell to Fat Nell, formerly Fair Nell, my old wet-nurse who was recently arrived at Middleham to help with the Duchess's lying-in when the time came. Aged about five and forty, Nell had long since lost the pink-cheeked, flaxen appeal that had once earned her the accolade of being fair. Nevertheless, since she was the closest thing I possessed to a mother I chose to ignore her alarming girth, multiple chins and irascibility and concentrated instead on the childhood memories that her warm, musky smell evoked. Since her arrival at Middleham, it had become my custom to visit her lodgings once or twice a week, taking her a basket of apples, a skinned rabbit or some other trifling gift.

Not that she had ever shown me all that much affection, ever seeming to save her caresses and honeyed words for my noble playmates. Yet it had been she who patched up my boyish injuries, mended the rips in my linen and on one gloriously memorable occasion, lashed out at George when he jeered at me for being a bastard nobody. It was not much of a substitute for motherly love, to be sure, but the starving man gobbles up crumbs as eagerly as comfits.

Knowing I would be gone from Middleham for an unknown period, I did briefly think about calling on Fat Nell to tell her I was heading abroad on the Duke's business, just in case the greedy old dame was counting on me to keep her stewpot full. I was prevented from doing so by imagining the scorn Fielding would heap on me if I delayed our departure in order to visit my old nurse. In any case, my spirit was too subdued for me to care overmuch about anything save the awkward fact of my current destination. For me, the adventure had lost all its spice since I had learned of Gloucester's intended hiding place for Pretty Will.

My problem was simple. Old Master Pennicott had an attractive young wife whom I had hoped most fervently to avoid for the rest of my days. Margaret was her name, a joyful and vivacious creature whose laughter had once caught at my heart and brought sunshine to my soul. Margaret, whose kisses tasted of the sweetest wine and whose body intoxicated me as no wine ever has done. Margaret, the girl I had loved with all my heart but known it not until she was lost to another.

Fielding and I rode for the best part of that day in a cold, uncompanionable silence. We did not bother to stop for a noonday meal and paused only once to water and rest our tiring horses. It was well that we left Middleham when we did for I discovered later that the King's men had arrived at the castle a scant few hours after our departure.

When asked if he knew aught of the whereabouts of a fugitive named Will Yorke my lord had been able to answer with perfect honesty that he had never been introduced to anyone of that name. I frequently had occasion to reflect that if the Duke had not been born of royal blood he would have made a first rate lawyer since his sharp wits and keen grasp of affairs made him a formidable opponent in an argument. He rarely used this talent to his own advantage, believing it beneath the dignity of his position to engage in petty disputes on his own behalf but he would not hesitate to do so for any common petitioner seeking justice.

Since the integrity of the Duke of Gloucester was known throughout the land, the justices saw no reason to question my master's word when he avowed that the fugitive they sought was not at Middleham. They apologised profusely for their presumption but excused themselves on the grounds that they had been given strong reason to believe they would find Yorke at the castle. It was not made clear who had led them to this conjecture and my lord deemed it wisest not to press the point but after the men had ridden back towards Lincoln he became most uneasy in his mind. As he later told me, he had wished then for some means of sharing with me the intelligence that someone at Plaincourt had been certain Fielding would seek shelter with him. Most of all he feared it augured ill for Will's lady love since it was she who had suggested Middleham as a place of safety.

Will and I were unaware of these developments as we rode towards York. He was likely engaged in sombre musings of his own while I, try as I would to deflect the thoughts, could concentrate on nothing other than the bitter-sweet memory of the last time I had held Margaret in my arms. My skin still tingled with the thrill of her silken cheek pressed against my own, her shapely form warm and yielding in my embrace. When her soft, sweet lips had brushed the nape of my neck the downy hairs there had sprung up in astonished delight. They did so again as I relived the moment in my mind, surrendering to the blissful recollection like a love-struck imbecile.

Lost in these thoughts and awash with trepidation at the prospect of encountering Margaret once again, I did not immediately hear Fielding as he started to address me.

"Your pardon," I said with polite disdain when I realised he had been speaking to me for several moments. "My thoughts have been elsewhere this last while. I did not hear what you said."

My companion shot me one of his wolven stares and I tried to conceal the tiny shudder of repugnance that his countenance summoned from the base of my spine.

"I was saying, Cranley, that I must ask you to forgive the rudeness I have shown you. 'Twas not meant personal against you, you understand, I just have a natural aversion toward your type. 'Tis more than likely born of my own foul looks and manners. Whatever the cause, I have never been able to stomach pretty looks and fancy ways in a fellow, they rob him of all manliness in my eyes."

He paused for a second and coughed mightily, ejecting an impressive stream of steaming green phlegm onto the ground. May the good Lord preserve me for all time, I prayed, from such exhibitions of manly behaviour.

"But I've been pondering," he continued "and must say in fairness that 'tis hardly your fault how you look. I am glad of your help and regret I have behaved churlish to you. I'm a mean and surly fellow and in general do not care too much for the company of others but I'm willing to try for friendship with you if you've a mind."

It was an awkward little speech and I wondered how two such disparate characters as Fielding and I could ever hope to forge any semblance of a friendship but the sentiment behind the words was honest enough. I leaned across and placed my hand unflinchingly upon the man's greasy shoulder.

"I'll gladly be your friend, Will," I replied, "for my lord of Gloucester values you high and his opinion is good enough for me."

It was exactly the right thing for me to say, as of course I had known it would be. Fielding's face broke into a delighted grin that was even more repulsive than his habitual scowl. Fortunately, I was spared further familiarity with my newly acquired friend by the advent of the city of York. It was nearly dark by this time and I needed to concentrate in order to negotiate our way into the city before the gates were shut for the night.

"Best remain silent," I hissed to Will from the side of my mouth. "If you say nothing there's less chance of some curious soul recalling you later on. And muffle your face with your cloak," I added carefully. "Looks such as yours are not easily forgot."

I feared I might have offended Fielding with these words but apparently his hide was tough enough to rebuff any such hurt. He nodded his head in cheerful acquiescence and followed me as I steered my horse along the cobbled streets of York until we reached the Pennicott's house. There, without pausing for further thought I flung myself from my horse and rapped my knuckles sharply against the massive iron-studded door. A slight commotion could be heard from within and then there was a brief delay before the door opened slowly and candlelight flooded out onto the street. A thick waisted serving wench stood in the doorway with an irritable look upon her broad peasant face; behind her, picked out from the shadows by a halo of flickering light around her loose hair, stood the mistress of the house, Margaret Pennicott.

I lay that night in the small loft above the Pennicott's stable, listening to the whickering of the beasts and the song of the wind as it beat against the wooden structure of the building. My stomach was warm still from the delicious fish stew I had devoured with Will, and my body was encased in a snug fleecy blanket loaned by Master Pennicott. The first part of my mission was now complete. After reading and then most carefully burning the letter I brought from my lord of Gloucester, Pennicott had shown us every hospitality and had readily agreed to conceal Fielding for as long as would be needful. He accepted that Will was an old and trusted friend of the Duke's, forced by unhappy circumstance to flee from those that wished him ill. He forebore to pry into the exact nature of Fielding's problem and I was grateful for his discretion.

Indeed, I had much for which to thank good Master Pennicott. Aside from feeding me and assuming responsibility for Will's safe-keeping, he also offered to provision me for my forthcoming journey, an offer I accepted with alacrity. Pennicott kept a handsome table and I looked forward with relish to consuming the victuals that had been wrapped and placed carefully in my saddle bag. The honest merchant was quite unaware of my erstwhile relationship with his bride and accorded me much greater honour than my modest position as the Duke's minstrel necessitated. He was in truth an admirable old fellow and I wished that I could like him. Instead, I yearned to close my hands tight about his scrawny old neck and squeeze with all my might until his face turned blue and his rheumy eyes bulged from their sockets.

I wanted poor, harmless Pennicott dead so that never more would I be haunted by the vision of Margaret's beautiful, clean white limbs lying alongside his withered, ancient frame. I had been offered a cot in the guest chamber that Fielding was to stay in for the duration of his visit but I declined abruptly, maintaining that as I intended to depart at first light I would be more sensibly billeted in the stable from whence I could leave without disturbing the rest of the household. It was a flimsy excuse but Pennicott and Fielding accepted it readily enough.

Only Margaret suspected my real reason for choosing to bed down above the stables. I knew she understood that I could not stomach to lie under the roof she shared with her decent, decrepit husband. She gazed at me long with her deep, dark eyes and I tried to read her inner feelings but if she still retained any store of tenderness for me she buried it deeper than a miser hides his gold. I slept little that night and quit the Pennicott house before even the meanest skivvy was astir. Forget Mistress Pennicott, I told myself as I took the Lincoln road, and turn your wits to Plaincourt and the adventure that awaits you there.

Chapter 4
A Useful Encounter

Plaincourt Manor lies in a rural backwater some twelve leagues north east of Lincoln. I was mounted on a fine smooth-gaited palfrey, strong and well cared for as were all the horses in the Middleham stables, but even so the journey took longer than I had anticipated. It rained incessantly, the cold, dispiriting December rain that chills the bone and depresses the humours. In truth, the foulness of the weather was in perfect harmony with my temper.

Less than one day's ride from Plaincourt I stopped at a wayside tavern and paid the landlord a generous sum for the indefinite loan of one of his sorry rounceys and the stabling of my own handsome mount. Mine host was a shifty looking fellow with greasy hair and malodorous breath and in normal circumstances I would not have entrusted a three-legged donkey to his care, much less one of my lord of Gloucester's finest palfreys. Yet it was vital to the success of my endeavour that I should be accepted at Plaincourt Manor as an itinerant minstrel somewhat down on his luck, and therefore it was wise to swap my lordly mount for something more suited to such a fellow.

I had grown fond of the palfrey and misliked leaving it but happily found I was able to relieve my low spirits by roundly cursing the miserable landlord and explaining to him in careful detail the violence I would inflict on him should my horse come to harm whilst in his care. Conscious that the inn was perhaps too close for comfort to Plaincourt, I also instructed him to concoct a credible story to explain the presence of such noble horseflesh in his mean stable, should anyone's curiosity be aroused by it. By the time I left him I could tell that my combination of threats and bribery had bought the man's co-operation. While he was without a doubt dishonest, he was no fool and understood that his best interests lay in following my instructions to the letter.

Having concluded these arrangements, I bade the

landlord a courteous farewell and continued on my way. This was the morning of the fourth day since I had left the Pennicott house. The rainfall gradually began to ease off and after I had been riding for an hour or so a glimmer of sunshine appeared on the horizon, heralding the advent of a glorious rainbow somewhere to the east. My spirits rose at last as I shook a cascade of droplets from my sodden cloak and stretched my neck to receive the benediction of the blessed rays. I journeyed on for several miles, glorying in the rare December sunshine and humming a merry tune as I rode.

All good humour vanished in an instant as a sharp bend in the path revealed the unwelcome sight of a body, a man by its size, sprawling in the dirt a few paces ahead of me. I jerked my beast to a halt, dismounted and gazed about in caution, wary lest there should be knaves of malevolent intent skulking in the hedgerow. With one hand on my dagger I knelt to inspect the dead man - or youth, as I quickly established - keen to discover the means of his demise.

Having given him a fleeting examination I could find no signs to indicate that the lad had been set upon by robbers. Rather, it seemed that some misadventure had caused his neck to break, judging by the unnatural angle at which his head lolled in the dust. A fall from a horse was the most likely cause of such an injury, and yet I doubted that the young man had been astride a horse in his life. They say that in heaven all men will be equal and mayhap it will be so but for this life at least, the many must toil in misery while the fortunate few live in splendour. From the evidence of the victim's ragged and humble attire and his blistered, work hardened hands, I surmised swiftly enough that he belonged to the former category. During his life he would have marvelled at his luck had he owned a decent-fitting pair of boots, never mind a horse from which he might one day fall and break his neck.

For all his poverty, however, he had been a fine, strapping lad, broad shouldered and tall enough to earn himself the kind of ironic nickname that often amuses the common sort – Small Sam, perchance, or maybe Little Tom. Fixing my scrutiny on the lad's face I noticed that he had surprisingly unblemished skin, a soft, well-shaped mouth and lashes so long and silkily black as to have inspired poetry had they belonged to a highborn maiden. There was something curiously child-like about these features and though his eyes were closed, I guessed that had they been open I would have recognised the vacant gaze of a lackwit. At once I felt a sense of sadness for the boy's premature death and though I have never been a pious man, some instinct compelled me to mutter a prayer over his mortal remains.

Just as I turned to leave, fully conscious that a matter more pressing than the demise of a peasant boy demanded my attention, a clammy hand snaked out and fastened about my wrist.

"Had thee there, didst I not, master? Thee didst think I were cold as old King Harry, thee did. Go on, thee knows thee cain't deny it!"

Shocked beyond measure by the corpse's sudden transformation into a living being, I crossed myself rapidly, simultaneously jerking away the hand that clutched at me still.

"What foul trick is this?" I demanded, raising my dagger to the lackwit's throat. "State your business, scum, and make it good. I've had a hard ride and am in no mind to tolerate insolence."

My tone was harsh, justifiably so I believe, and in case the youth was too slow to comprehend my anger, a sharp kick to his shins helped deliver the message. As I moved, my blade shifted a fraction and lightly nicked the yokel's neck.

"Steady, master, steady!" he implored, pressing a grimy finger to the scratch. "Thee needs not be so vexy, 'twas nobbut meant as a jest."

Calmer now, I resheathed my dagger and looked again at his baby face.

"Here, use this," I commanded curtly, handing him my kerchief. He looked at it dumbly, unsure what use to make of the fragrant linen.

"For your cut, dolt! Press it to the cut!"

As understanding dawned, he looked at me and smiled, a peculiarly engaging smile. For the first time I noticed his eyes and realised that whilst all else, his behaviour included, might proclaim him a lackwit his blue eyes told a very different tale. They were alive and bright with intelligence, the eyes of one who sees all, understands much and strives to make sense of the rest.

"'Twas nobbut meant as a jest," he repeated, his voice sounding a little sad, and this time I felt obliged to speak to him in a gentler fashion in spite of my irritation at his tomfoolery.

"My name is Frances Cranley," I told him abruptly. "What do they call you?"

"Matthew, master," he replied. "They dost call me Matthew the kitchen boy."

That explains the blisters on his hands, I thought. Turning the spit wreaks havoc on the skin.

"Well, Matthew the kitchen boy," I explained, "it was a cursedly ill-thought trick to play, and others less sweet-tempered than I would beat you soundly for such foolery."

"Aye, thee's right enough there, master," he agreed cheerfully. "Sir Stephen'd whip me to ribbons for't, the sour bastard. That's why I dost make sure he knows naught of it, nor any others.

"But see, 'tis a gift I dost have and 'tis all my own, for there's none other I knows can make like they've just bin cut from the gibbet, with their neck all floppy like mine. 'Tis a gift, I says, but I dost never have the chance to use it. And then there I were picking nettles for Jem Flood and I didst hear the clip-clop of hoss hooves and I just couldst nowise stop from having a little jest with thee, for all I didst know I should not. I didst never mean thee no harm, master, afore God I swear I didst not."

I marvelled silently that the poor lout should risk a beating or worse for the pleasure of trying out his only talent, and such a dubious talent at that. It occurred to me that the life of such a one must be mired in misery, and thus perhaps it was understandable that he took his enjoyments where he could. In any case, my interest had been piqued by something he had said.

"Who is this Sir Stephen whose name you use so impudently?" I asked.

"Why, bless thee, master," Matthew replied, his face ablaze with merriment at my ignorance. "Sir Stephen Plaincourt's the lord of this fine manor, as surely all dost know. Why, folk dost say he's the greatest lord in all of the county."

I knew for a certainty that this Plaincourt was by no means the greatest lord in Lincolnshire, nor even the third of fourth greatest come to that, but I let the matter pass. Such exaggerations are common amongst the lower orders and who can wonder, since to them even the meanest knight with a crumbling manor to his name and naught to ride but a broken down rouncey has a life deserving of envy. There was no gain to be had in disputing with the lad.

"Then this must be the manor of Ringthorpe," I ventured, knowing full well it was not.

As expected, Matthew shook his head in violent disagreement.

"Nay, nay, master," he laughed. "That dost show thee's some out of date with the news of these parts. This here village is Plaincourt and Sir Stephen's now its master, by right of inheritance since the sudden passing of his nephew Geoffrey, the poor bairn."

I allowed a look of surprise to show on my face.

"Young Geoffrey Plaincourt is dead, you say? When did this grievous event occur? And what was the manner of his dying?"

"Why, it were no more'n a few days since," my helpful informant answered. "As to the manner of his passing, now there's a question many'd like the answer to. He were murdered, that's for certain sure. Most say 'twas Pretty Will, the young lord's body servant, what killed him and p'raps they dost have the right of it."

Matthew's forehead furrowed and he gazed at the dirt for a moment, idly kicking a stone with his foot.

"But that dost make no sense to me," he continued, "for Will didst truly care for that poor cripple boy, leastwise that 'tis what I always didst think. And he had no reason to want the lad dead, for his job here didst depend on Geoffrey being alive. So why should he take it into his head to want to kill him, can thee answer me that!?"

As he spoke, he glanced up at me and again I noticed his eyes. The merriment of a few moments before had vanished, to be replaced by something that looked remarkably close to belligerence. Confusion, fear or anxiety, these emotions I might have expected to see reflected in the eyes of a lowly kitchen boy whose young master had recently been found murdered, but surely not anger.

As I registered these thoughts, something tugged at the shadowy edges of my memory. When Fielding had been relating his sorry tale to my lord of Gloucester, he had mentioned something that had pertinence to my current situation. As quickly as I could, I ran through his discourse in my head, watching Matthew closely all the while.

First I studied his face, which under my scrutiny had lost all trace of intelligence and reverted to that of a blockheaded peasant, and then swept my gaze over his well-made frame, strong, muscular arms and large hands, blunt-nailed and blistered. The hands of a kitchen boy. At once, I seemed to hear the uncouth voice of Fielding in my head, raging at the Plaincourt servants who shunned him yet dared show no kindness to their young master. What was it he had he said?

"Not a one of them, save perhaps the dull-witted oaf who turned the spit would piss in the wind to aid the boy.

Those were his very words. I had hardly heeded them before but now I recalled them with great clarity as it seemed they might carry some importance. They suggested that Matthew was the one inhabitant of Plaincourt other than

Fielding who had shown compassion for young Geoffrey, and that made sense of the anger I'd seen in his eyes when speaking of the boy's murder. It occurred to me that Matthew might have been a useful ally for Fielding in his efforts to improve Geoffrey's lot, but the obtuse idiot had dismissed him as feeble-minded and thus of no account. I had been inclined to think the same when I'd first met him yet now I'd spoken with him a while I'd happily wager my best beaver hat that Matthew's wits were considerably keener than most, including the man who'd named him a dull-witted oaf.

Swiftly reaching a decision, I leaned from my saddle and extended a hand to Matthew.

"Ride with me a while," I commanded, "I have need of further speech with you."

This startled the youth and he made at once to shy away from me but I grabbed his forearm and held firm. He was a big strong lad but fortunately I was stronger, or else his reluctance was feigned.

"Leave me be, master," he grumbled. "I dost want no trouble, and thee look to me like trouble a-plenty."

I laughed at this, for his assessment of me was astute enough.

"Aye," I answered, still holding his arm in a merciless grip, "trouble I may well be. But I'll tell you what else I am. I am justice, God willing, and perchance I am vengeance."

Then I took a gamble and let go of his arm. Surprised by the suddenness of his release he stumbled backwards and then turned his gaze upon me. This time I read determination in his remarkable eyes. He nodded once, then reached towards me.

"Right thee are then, master," he said simply. "Best help me up if thee'd be so kind. I didst never sit on no hoss afore today."

***

For a short time we rode in silence as I debated how much

to take the kitchen boy into my confidence and Matthew, as far as I could tell, concentrated on not falling off the horse. When the track to Plaincourt Manor came into view, I turned the beast's head away from it and kept riding. Arriving at my destination with the manor's kitchen boy seated behind me would serve no useful purpose and would be certain to arouse curiosity. Therefore, it were best we were not seen together, yet I very much desired to speak further with Matthew before making myself known to the good folk of Plaincourt.

Although I did not communicate my thoughts, he seemed to guess my mind for after we had journeyed on about half a league he nudged me in the back as we drew level with a tumbledown cottage. The walls still stood but the roof and door were gone and through the gap where it should have been I spied a rich tangle of greenery and a dispiriting mound of loose timber and broken sticks of furniture.

"Take the hoss round the back of here, master," he instructed. "This were old Lynet's house afore she didst get catched, and folk dost rarely come here now on account of her being a witch and all. I dossent think we will be troubled here." I followed his direction but snorted at the mention of an old witch. I fear witchcraft and the black arts as much as any man but simple reason tells me that witchery is not proven every time an ancient crone who lives alone is found to have a fondness for cats.

Alas, in my experience simple reason is rarely considered when a series of misfortunes strike a village. I have seen it all too often. A first disaster occurs – some cattle are struck by a murrain, say. The villagers will be worrying over this when another calamity happens, something like a child being born with a hideous disfigurement. Now everyone starts murmuring about the ill-fortunes that are plaguing the village. And then the third blow falls. Perhaps the blacksmith, a man known by all to be strong and healthy, shows sudden signs of fever and drops dead before the day is out.

These events, or ones of a similar nature, cause the

villagers to become uneasy for they show the random nature of misfortune. In their unease they turn to the village priest, asking why God has allowed these disasters to befall them. The priest scratches his head, troubled by their questioning and unsure how to answer. So he throws the problem back at their feet.

One of their number, he asserts, has been ungodly and this is the Lord's way of bringing the ungodliness to their attention. So now the villagers must root out the wrong-doer in their midst. Very soon, someone recalls that the harmless old crone who helps out at birthings often takes a path past the cattle whilst gathering herbs. This prompts another to remember the ill look the old dame gave the blacksmith when he jostled her roughly on his way to the tavern. Since no one wishes to accuse a more useful member of their community, they declare the crone a witch and hound her to her death. Then they bend their knees in church, thanking God for their deliverance from evil.

Climbing from the saddle, I asked Matthew if this was the way of it with old Lynet whose ruined house now offered us a convenient place to talk away from prying eyes.

"Like that, aye," he agreed amiably, "save that Lynet weren't no harmless old crone. She were a witch right enough, that one. No denying that, she didst herself confess to her guilt. She were caught fixing to put a spell upon old Sir Thomas, him that were father to Sir Stephen, to bring about his end."

Despite being irrationally disappointed that this ignorant kitchen boy shared the prejudices of his kind, I found myself intrigued by what he said and pressed him for the full story.

It was a sorry enough tale if it was to be believed. As a comely young woman of Plaincourt village, Lynet had caught the eye of Sir Thomas and had been badly used by him. When he had done with her no village man would take her for his wife. Even her own family felt shamed by her presence, though she had been blameless, so they built her a house some way from the village. She was far enough away that they did not have to see her every day and be reminded of their failure to save her from their lord, but close enough so they could see she did not starve.

In time Lynet's parents died, her brothers took wives and soon there were too many mouths to feed. When the food stopped coming Lynet learned to survive on her wits, creating and selling potions to cure freckles and spells to help a maiden win her true love. The village folk did not truly believe her a witch or even a wise woman. Most were motivated to buy her concoctions from a sense of charity rather than any conviction that they would be efficacious. All the same, one day a careless tongue wagged to Sir Thomas about the witch who lived nearby. Curious, he rode out to her house and was surprised to find a handsome woman of middle years instead of the hideous hag he had been expecting. He failed to recognise her as the girl he'd ravished repeatedly many years ago but forced himself upon her all the same.

After this, Lynet stopped taking care of her appearance and soon she looked very much like a witch. Her downfall came when she was caught in the church of St Oswald's, muttering as she searched for hairs beneath the bench on which Sir Thomas regularly snored his way through mass. The priest who apprehended her demanded to know what she was doing and in her terror she at once confessed her intention of making a potion to wreak revenge on Sir Thomas.

"Poor foolish creature," I murmured when Matthew reached this part of his story. "What fate befell her? Not the rope, I pray."

Matthew grinned at me, merriment and mischief dancing in his eyes.

"Nay master, old Lynet didst not hang. Truth to tell, I cain't say for sure that she dossent live yet."

The impudent lout then laughed aloud at the confusion on my countenance. A gentle nudge from me brought an end to his mirth and a resolution to his tale.

With the woman's confession ringing in his ears, the

priest had hastened her from his church, intent on bringing her before Sir Thomas to answer for her crime. Yet on the way he was apprehended by a crowd of villagers who demanded he hand Lynet over to them, as they had their own way of dealing with witches. Frightened by the size of the mob, the craven priest put Lynet into their hands and retreated to the safety of his church.

They took the woman to her house where she was held roughly as the angry villagers smashed and stamped on her meagre store of possessions. She was beaten, but not severely, and told that witchcraft was an abomination the God-fearing people of Plaincourt would never tolerate. Then she was told to begone and never return.

"And that was it?" I asked, incredulous that her life had been spared. "She had confessed to attempted witchcraft at the very least, why was she not hanged?"

In reply, Matthew held up one grimy finger.

"Old Lynet were one of us," he intoned.

A second finger was raised.

"Old Lynet were crazed, and with good reason."

A third and final finger arose.

"Old Lynet didst only seek to work witchery on that Sir Thomas that didst her wrong. All folk knew she didst never work no harm on no other."

In time I would have good reason to recall this sad tale and the reasons Matthew had given me for the villagers' leniency. For now, however, it seemed naught but a distraction from my pressing business at Plaincourt and so I steered our discourse towards my mission to uncover the real culprit behind young Geoffrey's murder.

Chapter 5
Arrival at Plaincourt

Dusk was fast approaching when I finally rode up to Plaincourt Manor, passing myself off at the gatehouse as a travelling musician who had lost his way. Gesturing vaguely at my lute, I said that it would be my pleasure to pay for a night's shelter with music and song. Following this little speech I was ushered with sufficient courtesy through to a cobbled courtyard and instructed to wait there while the gatekeeper's lad was despatched in search of authority. Excited as I was at the prospect of meeting the master of Plaincourt, common sense told me that he was unlikely to hurry out to greet a nobody such as I and in all probability my first dealings would be with the household steward.

Dismounting from the tired rouncey, I used the waiting time to take note of my surroundings. My attention was drawn first to the handsome stone manor house which stood at the far end of the courtyard, facing towards the gatehouse. Its walls were neatly white-washed and the windows expensively glazed. On either side of the house, a series of neat buildings ran down to the gatehouse wall, creating the square, enclosed courtyard in which I now stood. To my left as I faced the house were stables and kennels while to the right I spied a granary, dairy and hen house. It was a pleasing scene, for all appeared well-ordered; the courtyard was tidy, free of dung and the air smelt fresh. Not a soul was to be seen but a gentle hum of activity came from the various buildings and from the vicinity of the dairy I heard an indistinct rumble of conversation interspersed with short bursts of laughter.

Thus my first impression of Plaincourt Manor was that it was a prosperous place with servants who attended well to their duties and had leisure to discourse with one another. This was of a piece with my view of Plaincourt village through which I had been obliged to ride on my approach to the manor house. The thatched houses lining the village's sole thoroughfare seemed tidily kept and although they had the usual confusion of livestock and ragged children roaming around outside, I could detect none of the sense of hopeless misery that pervades many such places. The few peasants I passed directly stopped what they were doing to study my progress, their faces alert with curiosity. One soul, perhaps braver than the rest, called out a polite greeting to me which I returned in kind. From this exchange I gratefully surmised that while the appearance of strangers might not be an everyday occurrence in Plaincourt, it was not such a startling event that the residents felt moved to pelt me with muck and stones, as I had heard sometimes happened to hapless travellers in remote locations.

The last building I had passed before reaching the bridge that crossed to the gatehouse was a fine church of medium size. Its dominating feature was a large and very beautiful window which depicted several scenes from the life and death of some obscure saint. In the central section, the saint was wearing a crown and holding aloft a chalice. Since I know regrettably little of these matters I failed to recognise him but later learned that the crown and chalice identified him as St Oswald, a king of ancient times who sought to bring the teachings of the Church to all his people.

Fielding had described Plaincourt as a 'fair manor' and it seemed that, in this at least, he had not been exaggerating. Lying at the foot of the Lincolnshire Wolds, to one side it had rich arable farmland from which, I guessed, the manor drew much of its apparent prosperity while to the other, so Matthew had informed me, was coastal marshland leading to the sea less than four leagues distant. I felt it probable that such close proximity to the coast must also prove advantageous to the Plaincourts from time to time. Certainly, before ever I had set foot under Sir Stephen's roof, I had gained a sense of his wealth. Everything I had seen so far, the orderly village, the magnificent and costly church window, the attractive exterior of his house and the ordered calm of his courtyard, all spoke of a liberal application of gold over many years.

Such reflections were banished by the return of the gatekeeper's lad, accompanied now by a young woman of tiny stature whom I guessed at once must be Fielding's Mistress Blanche. I had just enough time to conjecture ruefully that even the steward considered himself too fine to greet me, and then she was upon me. For a moment she looked me over without speech, apparently decided I seemed respectable enough and then turned on her heel and walked back in the direction of the house, indicating with a flick of her wrist that I was to follow. At once, and without a word of instruction being uttered, a groom emerged from the stable block to see to my horse. I realised I must have been under cautious surveillance from that quarter the entire time I had been waiting.

Walking a few steps behind Mistress Blanche I had the opportunity to admire her graceful figure and elegant bearing. She skimmed across the cobbles on feather-light feet, moving purposefully yet giving no outward appearance of hurrying. I could see little of her hair which was coiled up on the back of her head, but an escaped lock which danced beneath her headdress showed it to be as black and curly as Fielding had stated. Knowing her to be a waiting woman of no great rank, I was much surprised by the richness of her figured velvet gown and fashionable heart-shaped headdress, and likewise by the fact that she had been deputed to receive me.

Crossing the threshold of Plaincourt Manor I followed Mistress Blanche into a small antechamber which gave way into a vast hall, brightly lit even at this hour by dozens of torches. Glancing upwards at the high vaulted ceiling, I noticed a musicians' gallery which ran along the left side of the hall. The sight gladdened me, for my task could be made that much easier with a convenient vantage point from which to watch and listen.

As we walked, I noticed that the floor was covered with decorative patterned tiles and the plastered walls were painted with wheat sheaves, which I knew to be the heraldic device of the Plaincourt family, as well as fish, bees and flowers. Along one wall was arrayed a goodly selection of bows, swords, shields and pole arms, indicating to me that the manor would be able to defend itself should the need ever arise.

I was led to the upper end of the hall where a large table rested upon a dais. In the centre stood an impressive carved chair flanked on either side by oaken benches. To my astonishment, my silent guide took possession of the great chair and nodded at me to be seated on a bench. The moment we were settled her reticence disappeared and in a soft, cultured voice she welcomed me warmly to Plaincourt Manor in the name of its master. Sir Stephen Plaincourt, she explained, was away at the present but was expected to return within a few days.

A clap of her small white hands brought forward an ancient retainer who had been shuffling in the shadows.

"Bring refreshments," she ordered peremptorily, and the old man went about his business as quickly as his hobbling gait would permit. Conscious of my travel-stained appearance I would have welcomed the opportunity to wash my face and hands before drinking but knew that mentioning it would highlight my hostess's deficiency in not thinking of it herself.

"And now," she said, turning to face me fully for the first time, "I would know your name and where you are bound. The boy told me you have lost your way and crave shelter for the night. Here at Plaincourt we pride ourselves on our hospitality and since my lord is from home and his steward is attending him, it falls to me to act on his behalf. Yet I believe it would be folly to give you leave to stay without knowing something of you and your business."

I noted that this last was said with a small, playful smile that asked me to forgive any suggestion of suspicion inherent in her words. I made to answer her but to my chagrin discovered that I was temporarily struck dumb, my senses awry, giddy with surprise and confusion.

The truth was that I had been wholly unprepared for the startling beauty of her face. Even though Fielding had described her as womanly perfection, and the little I had seen of her as she led me into the hall had chimed with his description, still the reality of her countenance was far from what I had expected. Without question, she was by a long way the loveliest looking woman I had ever seen, not excluding my beloved Margaret. Her large bright eyes truly were the exact hue of spring violets, her complexion a flawless milky white with just the right amount of delicate flush on her cheeks. How such an exquisite beauty had ever consented to have carnal relations with a brute like Fielding was beyond me, yet oddly enough, the fact that he had been entirely accurate in his description of her physical charms encouraged me to believe for the first time that the rest of his tale might also be true.

Yet even more perplexing to me than her beauty was the way in which she behaved as though she were lady of Plaincourt Manor. She had welcomed me to Plaincourt in Sir Stephen's name, and spoke with confidence of acting on his behalf, but how could a lowly waiting woman have such authorisation? Then again, why would a lowly waiting woman be so richly decked out in costly velvet and amber beads, and why would the manor servants rush to obey her commands? Especially since, according to Fielding's account, she had risked her master's wrath in order to release him from captivity. Had her part in his escape not been discovered?

I realised now that in my hurried conversation with the kitchen boy the name of Mistress Blanche had not once been mentioned. In truth I had done little more than inform Matthew of my mission to uncover the facts behind Geoffrey's death before making him swear a solemn oath to help me as much as it should be in his power to do so. Now I cursed myself most soundly for failing to ask him about Fielding's lady love when I had had the chance. Frustratingly, here were many puzzling questions for which I lacked the answers.

It was fortunate for me that Mistress Blanche was well accustomed to the effect her beauty had on men, for she paid no heed to my long hesitation, taking it, no doubt, as tribute to her manifest loveliness. When finally I did manage to pull my wits sufficiently together to speak, her sympathetic violet gaze told me she thought she understood the cause for my confusion.

"My name is Francis Cranley," I told her truthfully, having decided it was safe to use my real name as I was far too obscure for the people of Plaincourt to have heard aught of me.

"I am a musician, as you see," - here I indicated my lute case - "and am lately come from York where I was in the employ of a respectable merchant blessed with overflowing coffers and a comely wife."

I ventured an audacious wink at this point. My reward was an amused smile from Mistress Blanche and a toss of her dainty head. I took this as an invitation to continue my wholly fabricated tale.

"It was a comfortable sojourn and I was well content to linger until word reached me through the usual servant tattle that a certain northern nobleman was hiring musicians for his Christmas festivities. I have long hankered for a place at Court and, knowing that this noble stands high in royal favour, I fancied that if I pleased him with my playing, he might be minded to give me an introduction to Court. Thus I bade farewell to my merchant, who was none too pleased and cursed me roundly for deserting him at such a time, and made haste to the nobleman's home.

"Alas for the sorry welcome I received! I was told, none too kindly, that I had come too late! His lordship now had all the musicians he required and more besides. News of his hiring had spread far and wide and thus for several days every half-competent minstrel within forty leagues had been beating a path to his door. The best had been selected and the rest sent on their way. I ventured to say that I came well recommended and begged his lordship to spare a few moments to listen to my art. Sadly, a vicious boot to my backside convinced me I was wasting my time.

"A sorry predicament I then found myself in, with no

snug post at this inclement season. And yet, trust me, fair mistress, despair is not in my nature. I pondered on my situation and decided my best course was to hasten down to London, there to seek out an old comrade who once boasted of a useful connection at Court. So to London I am bound, or so I was until some fool ostler gave me the wrong direction and I found myself gone astray."

When I had finished, Mistress Blanche laughed and leaned forward to give my arm an affectionate pat. As she did so, I noticed a large and uncommonly ugly silver ring on the middle finger of her right hand. It had a crest, which I could not for the moment make out, but what drew my attention was the incongruity of such a crude object on her small, fine-boned hand. Then she laughed once more and her easy, familiar manner took my breath away, so at odds was it with her cultured voice, rich apparel and apparent status.

"I hope you have greater skill at playing than travelling," she joked. "You must know you are some way distant from the London road. It is lucky for you that you happened upon Plaincourt. Had you missed us, you might have journeyed on until you fell into the sea!"

I laughed with her this time, as was expected, and took a sip from the cup of wine which the servant had set before me. She sipped also, and my eyes widened as I noticed that her own vessel was of enamelled silver-gilt. A singularly valuable cup for a waiting woman, I thought. Then she addressed me once again.

"Well, Francis Cranley," she stated, "you may stay at Plaincourt Manor tonight at least, and mayhap somewhat longer. My betrothed returns anon and then we shall see."

At mention of her betrothed, I clenched my cup tightly to prevent it slipping from my fingers. Fielding had made no mention of his beloved being betrothed to another. Had I had been mistaken in identifying my present interlocutor as his Mistress Blanche? Now I thought of it, I realised I had never been told the name of my fair hostess. Realising this needed to be rectified at once, I rose and swept her an extravagant bow.

"Gracious lady," I murmured, "you are as good as you are beautiful. Pray excuse my boldness but I beg you give me your name, so I may thank you properly for your kindness."

At this, she raised both hands to her mouth in an altogether charming gesture of dismay. "What a mannerless goose I am!" she exclaimed, "I have not introduced myself to you, have I? Well, let me put that to rights this very second. My name, Master Cranley, is Blanche St Honorine du Flers."

So saying, she extended to me a smooth white hand for kissing, in a gesture that was one part regal lady and three parts saucy doxy.

Then you are Fielding's Mistress Blanche, I thought, as I duly bent my head and pressed my lips to her knuckles. A deep, oversweet scent of roses filled my nostrils and I felt a strong urge to snatch my head away. Instead, I fought the impulse and lingered a moment longer than was strictly necessary, taking the opportunity to make careful note of the peculiar crest stamped roughly onto the central cartouche of her crudely wrought ring. As I straightened, my senses drowning in cloying, rose-scented confusion, I made a stern effort to gather my wits together.

"It is a name nigh on as lovely as the lady who bears it," I told her, unashamedly dripping honey since instinct told me that flattery was the quickest route to winning the trust of this exquisite little coquette.

"And who is the thrice-blessed gentleman to whom you are betrothed?"

"Now surely you are jesting with me," she replied, speaking a shade more haughtily than before. "Since I greeted you in his name and offered you the protection of his house, I should have hoped it were plain to you that I am the betrothed of Sir Stephen Plaincourt."

She stood abruptly and drew away from me, as if aware for the first time that there might have been some impropriety in her manner.

"We have had an understanding these last few months but

chose not to speak of it until I felt fully settled here at Plaincourt. However, when Sir Stephen rode off two days ago he told his people of our impending nuptials, that they would harken to my command in his absence.

"He returns soon to spend Christmas at Plaincourt and then after the Yuletide festivities we are to be married without delay," she finished, before sweeping from the hall, pausing only to exchange a brief word with the servitor.

Just before she exited she stopped and cast a penetrating glance over her shoulder at me. What the glance meant I could not think, save that when her eyes connected with mine I thought I read in them a flash of uncertainty or deep anxiety.

***

When she had gone the shuffling retainer escorted me to my chamber and then left me, mumbling that supper would be served in the hall presently. Now I took stock of my accommodation.

By presenting myself as an itinerant minstrel of no account I had fully expected to be given lodging of the most basic kind. A straw pallet in a draughty loft was the best that I had hoped for, so my amazement was equal to my relief when I was ushered into a small but comfortably appointed apartment situated at the end of a wide passageway above the hall.

There was a high wooden bed, thankfully large enough so that my long legs need not dangle off the end. The coverlets were red embroidered worsted which looked worn but clean and the pillow was plump with feathers. In the grate a small fire had been made ready and a lit candle had been placed in the sconce affixed to the bed frame. Much of the floor was covered with an old rug of blue and white linsey-woolsey. At the foot of the bed stood a small painted linen coffer and on the wall was a cupboard for my few personal possessions. Peering beneath the bed I found a tin basin,

85

intended for a pisspot, which I immediately put to good use. Across the room was a small shuttered window which overlooked the kitchen garden and fishponds at the back of the house. As I sank gratefully onto the bed I discovered that the servant had left me with a spare candle. Smiling, I gave silent thanks that Plaincourt hospitality spared even unimportant guests the weakling light of rush dips.

In truth, based on my treatment thus far I could scarce direct any complaint at Plaincourt hospitality. Before taking his leave, my shambling guide had taken care to point me in the direction of the Necessary, and then grunted that I should join 'my lady' for dinner once I was comfortable. Since they gave such tender care to a nobody, I wondered idly what treatment they would lavish on a person of real consequence.

That there were bigger, better appointed apartments than mine I was well aware, for we had passed several large and ornately decorated doorways on the way to my simple chamber. I had ventured to ask old Shuffler if one of them was where Sir Stephen slept but he had shaken his head and answered that the master's solar was reached by a different staircase.

I had left the hall through an archway near the main entrance. It gave on to two passageways, one of which led to the staircase that had brought me to my chamber while the other, if I guessed correctly, led to the kitchens. Now I recalled having seen a second staircase at the top end of the hall, near the dais, and I realised that it must lead up to Sir Stephen's private quarters. I wondered if he shared them with the delightful Mistress Blanche, or if she was playing the virtuous maiden until after her nuptials.

Mistress Blanche! Lovely as she was, the thought of her filled me with deep unease, for without doubt there was something very amiss about her. Perchance she was being forced into marriage with Sir Stephen against her will but the pride she had shown when identifying herself as his betrothed told me otherwise, as did her avowal that she had been promised to him for some time. And from her demeanour she certainly gave no sign of being a lovesick girl pining for a lover on the run from a false accusation of murder. No, what I had seen and heard led me inescapably to the conclusion that delectable Mistress Blanche had played poor Fielding false. As to why, already I had begun to comprehend and the idea of it filled me with a cold revulsion that threatened to blunt my appetite. Yet if I was to solve this mystery as my lord of Gloucester wished, I could linger no more in my chamber. Supper and Mistress Blanche awaited.

Chapter 6
Mistress Blanche

When I sat down to supper I found myself seated on the dais in company with Mistress Blanche and a pinch-faced priest who was introduced to me as Father Gregory. He tended the flock at St Oswald's, the church I had seen as I passed through the village. From something he let slip I gathered that he was an infrequent guest at the manor table and had been greatly surprised to be summoned thence that day by Mistress Blanche. Why she wanted him there I could not say for sure, but I imagined she was aware that her earlier manner with me had been too free and mayhap she believed she would show greater decorum in the presence of a priest.

If that were the case, it was a pity for her that poor Father Gregory was so sorely afflicted with the toothache that he could scarce chew a mouthful of the salted fish set before us, such was the severity of his pain. Before much time had elapsed, Blanche became exasperated with his audible sighs and extravagant winces and tersely ordered him home to his bed. The brusqueness of her tone was softened by an offer to despatch a servant with a hog's bean plaister of her own devising to relieve his suffering, for which Father Gregory thanked her effusively before scampering from the hall with more haste than dignity.

Now I was alone with the mysterious Mistress Blanche, save for approximately twenty household servants and retainers who sat some way distant at a lower table. Studying their faces, I saw a few I recognised including the gatekeeper's lad, the groom who had taken my horse and the old fellow I identified to myself as Shuffler. I was sorry not to see my new friend Matthew at the tables but comprehended full well that the nature of his duties would tie him to the kitchen. Yet it would have heartened me to see his good-natured face, for despite the comfort, order and plenty of Plaincourt Manor, to me there was a sense of wrongness about the place, a feeling of something rotten creeping outwards from the hidden

89

corners like a vast malignant shadow.

My unease came in part from the sudden realisation that thus far none save Matthew had made any mention of poor Geoffrey, even though the lad had been in his grave less than a fortnight. The boy had been master of Plaincourt, in name if not in fact, so I would have expected at least some small acknowledgement of the manor's recent bereavement and yet there was none.

The servants I could excuse since I had spoken little to those with whom I had thus far come into contact, but Sir Stephen's lovely betrothed was a different matter. It struck me that when she had allowed me to shelter at Plaincourt, she should have informed me that her intended's nephew was recently deceased, believed murdered, if only to ensure I conducted myself with sombre respect. Already more than half convinced that she had played a role in the poor lad's demise, I found that her failure to speak of him only served to stoke the flames of my suspicion.

Further study of the servants revealed that there were scarcely any women amongst their number. This was not in itself surprising since houses such as Plaincourt were often exclusively male preserves apart from the lady of the manor and her attendants. Therefore the current unmarried status of Sir Stephen explained the dearth of females about the place but it did not explain why Mistress Blanche had come to be there in the first place. It struck me as a most unusual state of affairs.

Excepting Blanche, the only other woman present at supper was a pale, thin serving girl with hair the colour of bleached straw. The timidity of her manner as she proffered dishes told me she was unaccustomed to serving in the hall. In fact, the greasiness of her garb led me to suspect that she must be some sort of kitchen skivvy, summoned to the hall so that Blanche should not be alone among the menfolk.

Despite the pallor of the wench she was pretty enough for me to throw an admiring glance her way, which she noticed and responded to with a small gratified smile. Blanche noticed too and bridled somewhat, from which I guessed that she was not pleased to be sharing my attention with another. Yet though Blanche was ten, nay twenty times fairer than the serving wench, if what I suspected of her was correct I should sooner lie with my old nurse than with such as she.

For now though, it was important that she should think me smitten so I removed my gaze from the serving girl and began to ply Mistress Blanche liberally with flattery and wine. Thanks to our earlier conversation I already knew she had a weakness for the former and from the greedy way she kept gulping from her cup, it became clear that she had a strong liking for the latter. Seeing my opportunity, I feigned a desire to repay some of the kindness she had shown me by waiting on her myself. This simple device permitted me to refill her cup far more often and more fully than the serving girl would have done.

"But surely you shall repay me later, Master Cranley," she whispered, inclining provocatively towards me and allowing her velvet-clad shoulder to brush against my arm.

"I shall?" I questioned, uncertain of her meaning but willing my eyes to look meaningfully into hers all the same.

"Why of a certainty," she laughed, "for when we have done here you shall play for me. I am all eagerness to hear you sing and see how you handle your lute."

"Then I shall still be in your debt," I countered, "for it will be my great honour and pleasure to play for you, fairest lady. How could it not be so? But now," I leaned forward and once again poured a generous measure of the ruby liquid into her cup, "will you not tell me something of yourself?"

"What would you know?" she asked, raising the wine to her lips and drinking deeply. When she wasn't holding her cup, she had a habit of rubbing one of the glossy amber beads of her necklace between her fingers.

"I would know everything about you," I ventured, flicking my gaze from her violet eyes to her flushed cheeks and then down to her bosom which, though concealed by the high, v-shaped neck of her gown, could be seen rising and falling with delightful rapidity.

"For now though, dearest lady, I implore you to tell me where you come from. Since you, alas, are betrothed to another I feel I must hasten without delay to your home town in hope of discovering others possessed of similar beauty in the vicinity."

As the words left my mouth I was sure that in my eagerness for information I had overdone the fulsome adulation. By lucky chance, however, Blanche was already too far gone in wine and vanity to notice my clumsiness.

"You'll find none like me in St Honorine du Flers," she chuckled and then, responding to the questioning tilt of my head, explained that this was the name of the rural French backwater from whence she came.

"You are wondering that the name of my home town is also my own name. Well, it is easily enough explained. You see, I consider it a sight prettier than the vulgar name with which I was born. And when my mother placed me in the care of a noble English lady prior to taking the veil, I decided that since I was having a new life and family forced upon me, I might as well take a new name as well."

She stopped abruptly, as if faintly embarrassed by her own candour, but I was intrigued by her words and begged her to continue. It was all the prompting she needed to pour out to me an account of her childhood, a story that might have touched my heart with pity had I not already been convinced she was a cold-hearted whore.

I learned that the exquisite Blanche St Honorine du Flers was born Blanche Le Taverne, the only child of a lovely, pious woman called Fayette and Claud, a fat, good-humoured innkeeper who owned the biggest and best tavern in the town of St Honorine du Flers. Located in a remote corner of Normandy, the town though undistinguished was prosperous enough and pretty too, in a general way. In any case, when Blanche was a small child she thought it the centre of the world. Her father was uncouth and smelt of ale and sweat, she confessed to me, while her mother was refined and lavender-scented. Yet it was only from her father that she received the affection and attention she craved. Though usually busy with tavern affairs he always had time to stroke her under the chin as he passed by, or scoop her up so that she could ride in splendour on his shoulders. Sometimes - the best times, as Blanche recalled - he would sit her on a barrel in the backroom of the tavern and tell her fantastical stories as he worked.

Her beautiful mother did none of these things. Although Fayette was a dutiful parent and far from unkind, she always maintained an emotional distance from Blanche, never enfolding her child in motherly embraces or giving her kisses, even when she hurt herself in childish accidents or fell sick from eating too many cherries. The child took this lack of maternal affection in her stride, accepting it as her lot to have an undemonstrative mother even though she knew, from observing other families about the town, that this was a far from normal state of affairs.

What was also unusual, Blanche noticed, was the freezing hostility with which her mother treated her father. Much of the time she behaved as if he didn't exist but when she was compelled to notice him, she spoke to him as though he were the meanest of her servants rather than her spouse. The observant child also noticed how her mother shunned the day-to-day running of the tavern, choosing instead to spend her hours working on her embroidery in the pleasant courtyard garden behind the tavern or on her knees at the *prie dieu* in her bedchamber.

Curiously, Claud never seemed to resent his wife's coldness or her refusal to set her dainty foot in his tavern, and he seemed well content to clothe her in costly silk and velvet while he himself wore the serge and fustian suited to his rank. At the time Blanche never thought to question why her mother had such fine ways but in later years, she told me, she had come to believe that Fayette had been a highborn lady forced through some ill circumstance to marry the rough tavern-keeper against her will.

When Blanche was aged five or six her father suffered a seizure in the tavern; one moment he was making a ribald jest as he served a customer, the next his face turned puce and he fell to the ground with a hairy hand clutching at his chest. He died minutes later, expiring on the muddy rushes of the tavern floor.

Though her father was dead, for some time Blanche's life remained much the same as before save for the absence of the rough, good-natured man who used to pluck her from her feet and plant onion-scented kisses on her cheek as he swung her around. Unwilling to allow the inconvenient death of her husband to interfere with her daily routine, Fayette promptly hired a capable man to manage the day-to-day running of the tavern. Thereafter, she continued to spend her days in the garden or on her knees.

Blanche blithely assumed that this way of life pleased her mother and she therefore expected it to continue indefinitely. Thus she was in no way prepared for the drastic way in which her life changed when she was eight years old. It started with a summons to attend Fayette in her chamber. There, she received the news that her mother could no longer tolerate living in the world and intended to retire to the cloisters. Before Blanche could utter a word, her mother announced that she had sold the tavern in order to pay for her life of comfortable seclusion.

"But what about me, Maman?" the startled child had asked. "Must I also live with nuns?"

Even at that tender age, said Blanche, she had known she was a thoroughly worldly creature. A life of prayer and contemplation was far from the exciting future she imagined for herself so when she learned that she would not be sharing her mother's religious seclusion she had been shocked yet deeply thankful.

"I know you, my child," Fayette had told her, "I know how you love gaiety and music and food and laughter. Indeed, how could it be otherwise, my pretty greedy one, when you have grown up in a tavern such as this? So I know that the abbey is no place for you. You would be miserable and in your misery my peace would be destroyed.

"So this is what I have arranged for you. Before I turn my back on the world I am taking you to Calais. There I will deliver you into the care of Mistress Cecile. Her aunt is the Abbess of the religious house in Caen I have chosen to enter.

"Mistress Cecile is waiting woman to a fine English noblewoman who has been residing these last few weeks at Calais Castle. Now the lady is about to return to her home in England and at Cecile's request - and in return for a handsome stipend, for this lady currently has great need of funds - she has graciously agreed to take you into her household.

"Attend me well, my daughter! This is a wonderful opportunity for you. You will be brought up in the household of a great noblewoman where you will learn to be genteel. Cecile will keep an eye on you, and ensure that your new mistress keeps her word to raise you as she would a high born maid-in-waiting.

"You must be willing and obedient, of course, but there will be no rough work for you, for you are to be more than a common servant. You will meet many important people and if you are always virtuous and clever, who knows but you may find a husband far above your station. Yes Blanche, I pray you will always remember that your mother has done well for you in securing Jacquetta, Dowager Duchess of Bedfordshire as your mentor."

Throughout her story, Blanche had shot occasional glances at my face in order to see how I was reacting to her words. She did so again when she came to name Jacquetta of Bedford as her noble benefactress but this time she paused, placed her dainty white hands flat upon the table and gave a slight but perceptible toss of her head before fixing me with her startling violet eyes.

Clearly she expected me to register some kind of amazement at the auspicious company she had been keeping and I was in no mind to disappoint. For one thing, I wanted to keep her sweet as I was eager to hear the rest of her story. For another, I was every bit as astonished to discover her connection to the Dowager Duchess as she had hoped I would be.

Jacquetta of Bedford was an exalted personage indeed. Her daughter Elizabeth was now the crowned consort of our liege lord King Edward but even before this illustrious marriage had taken place, Jacquetta had been an extremely high-ranking and well-connected woman with the blood of several European royal houses flowing through her veins. It was extraordinarily advantageous for a young woman from a lowly tavern background to have been given a place in her household, and Blanche's animated manner told me she was well aware of the fact.

Look at me, I fancied her eyes were commanding me, I was a tavern-keeper's daughter but see how far I have risen, and how much further I might yet rise. In the face of such desperate eagerness, I easily found the eloquence required to express my surprise and admiration at her good fortune. Satisfied, she continued with her tale.

Parting company from her mother had apparently been no great agony for Blanche since Fayette's extreme piety had always been a barrier to any real closeness between them. Even so, she was initially devastated to be uprooted from all she knew and cast amongst strangers in a foreign land, but she rapidly discovered that her new life was very much to her taste.

She had spent her first years in England at the Dowager Duchess's manor of Grafton Regis in Northamptonshire. Before leaving France she had learned that although her new mistress retained the courtesy title Dowager Duchess on account of her first marriage to the late Duke of Bedford, she was now married to Lord Rivers, formerly plain Sir Richard Woodville.

While complicated English politics were beyond the grasp of the child, she understood that her new family was allied to something called the House of Lancaster. Unfortunately, it seemed that the opposing House of York currently had the upper hand and indeed one of their staunchest supporters, the Earl of Warwick, had been holding her mistress captive at Calais Castle when Blanche had first encountered her. The release of the Dowager Duchess had been secured after the payment of a substantial amount of money - at least some of which had come her way via Blanche's mother - but her husband and oldest son remained in captivity for a further six months.

Naturally enough, this unsatisfactory state of affairs meant that the mood at Grafton was initially subdued when Blanche arrived there. Even so, she found that her education was taken in hand and her days were spent in comfortable surroundings with people who seemed content to have her in their care. To be sure, she had duties to attend to but all these amounted to was a little fetching and carrying for the ladies of the household, and gently brushing the tangles from their hair and soothing their temples with her small, cool fingers when their heads ached from too much wine.

With ill-placed pride Blanche confided to me that she had been a quick-witted child who enjoyed observing her superiors without their knowledge. She had found it easy to fit in and be useful, and with her vivacity and prettiness she charmed the entire household.

As she grew older she was even asked for by name by the regal Dowager Duchess whenever her spirits were low and she wished to be amused. The first time this had happened Blanche had been terrified in case she failed to please her mistress but she had screwed up her courage and determined to do her best. She had a talent for mimicry and remembered that it never failed to make Cecile and her other companions laugh whenever she imitated the uncouth behaviour of the clientele at her father's tavern.

Now those same antics worked their magic on the noble Jacquetta, who found herself sobbing with mirth at the sight of the slight girl pretending to be a blacksmith with an enormous belly, surreptitiously reaching into his underclothes to scratch his private parts. The great lady called for more, so Blanche obliged by transforming herself into the chaste parish priest who turned cross-eyed in his desperate attempts not to ogle the ample bosom of the serving wench. One by one, Blanche brought the tavern folk vividly to life and when she had finished, the Dowager Duchess had quite recovered her spirits.

Thereafter, the girl would be summoned regularly to sit with Jacquetta and her older ladies. Gradually, her stock began to rise within the more elevated ranks of the household. When she had first arrived at Grafton, though her treatment had been kind enough, she had been regarded as too insignificant to merit much notice. Despite her charm and prettiness, her inferior background had meant that there was no need for anyone to curry favour with the girl. At Grafton, as in many noble households, friendship was a valuable commodity, a gift to be bestowed only in the expectation of a worthwhile return. Since Blanche was known to have no fortune or useful connections there was nothing to be gained by cultivating her friendship.

At once the situation had changed. Since the Dowager Duchess had made a pet of her, the girl from the Normandy tavern had become a person worth knowing. At the same time, the fortunes of Jacquetta's family were decidedly on the up following the clandestine marriage of her oldest daughter Elizabeth to the handsome young King. Once the match was made public, Grafton suddenly seemed to become the hub of the world with messengers riding in and out several times a day, illustrious lords arriving to pay their compliments and a seemingly unending flow of beautiful ladies coming to wait on the new Queen's mother.

The astute among these newcomers swiftly discovered that showing kindness to the pretty maid-in-waiting called Blanche would often pay dividends. One lady who gave her a cast-off gown, a handsome, richly figured confection with only a small rent in the skirt, found that her petition for help from Jacquetta in securing an advantageous post at Court met with success beyond her expectations. Another, who showed Blanche how to repair the rent and helped her cut the gown to fit her diminutive frame, was delighted when her husband was asked to hunt with Lord Rivers and the King. This trade in favours was conducted with the utmost discretion but the message was very clear all the same: Blanche was a nobody still, but she was a nobody with a very important patroness.

Around this time, Mistress Margery, one of the Dowager Duchess's older waiting women, approached Blanche with a proposal that was to make an enormous impact on her life.

"These cackling geese seek to buy your favour with gowns and fripperies," the rather austere lady had said, "but if you have the wit, you will let me give you something infinitely more valuable.

"Have you ever asked yourself why I am allowed to remain as part of my lady's household? As you can see, I am no ornament and since my poor father was of little account there was no inducement for anyone to overlook my plain face and marry me. By rights I should have been sent home in disgrace years ago for failing to make a good match, yet my place here is assured for as long as I wish because I am useful. For is it not me they all turn to when they are sick?

"Let me be your tutor, my child, let me teach you all I know. I can show you how to treat almost every ailment known to man and tend all manner of wound. Aye, and I do it better than most physicians, too, for I had my training from a wise woman steeped in ancient lore.

"Now it is your turn to learn from me, girl! Then, when all your beauty goes for naught and you fail to catch a husband, as I predict will happen, they will know you to be useful and your future will also be assured."

Compliments and presents had made Blanche giddy and forgetful of her low birth but Mistress Margery's words brought her back to reality. While she resented the woman's assertion that her beauty would not be enough to find her a husband, she had enough sense to recognise a good offer when she heard it and so she readily agreed to the proposal.

Then began a long apprenticeship in herbal lore. Standing by Mistress Margery's side she learned how to stifle her revulsion when holding a basin to catch a patient's vomit and how to keep her hands steady when applying a poultice to skin charred by flame. As time went on, she found the work increasingly satisfying for she knew that the more skilled she became, the less likely she was to lose her place in the household.

Once, when she returned to her bed after helping Mistress Margery clear putrid flesh from a festering wound, one of her more delicate companions asked how she could stomach such gruesome sights. Blanche had simply laughed and answered that she did so willingly and would bear a great deal more in order to stay close to the noble Jacquetta and her kin.

As she told me this I fancied I caught sight of a grimace briefly marring the perfection of her face but this may have been naught but my imagination.

By now Blanche was far gone in her cups and even though I had not drunk nearly as much, I had nevertheless taken a deal more than is my habit. Realising that she might soon be incapable of further speech or that I might be incapable of heeding what she said, I bade her finish her story with all speed.

Thus I heard that as Blanche reached womanhood her usefulness, gaiety and good-nature continued to guarantee her place with the Dowager Duchess yet nevertheless she began to fear for her future. As I well knew, there had been much turmoil in the country during the last few years with uprisings led by the traitorous Earl of Warwick and the King's own brother, George of Clarence. My lord of Gloucester had suffered most painfully when Warwick, to whom he had always been strongly attached, betrayed Edward and he had scarce been able to credit the fact that their own brother was party to this foul treason. I, on the other hand, had found it all too easy to believe since I had always known Clarence for a bully and a fool.

During this period of bloody insurrection, Jacquetta's

husband and one of her sons had lost their lives. Not long after this most grievous blow, the entire household had been forced to claim sanctuary in Westminster Abbey while the King fought to regain control of his throne.

These events had sorely afflicted the health of her mistress, Blanche confided to me, and all at once the great lady seemed to become old and querulous, complaining ceaselessly of aches and agues. Blanche did what she could to ease the discomfort of her mistress but she knew very well that the real cause of the problems lay beyond her powers. The old lady was gravely wounded by the loss of her husband and son John and could not be reconciled to the brutal manner of their death. Dragged from hiding in the Forest of Dean, they had been taken to Kenilworth where they were beheaded on the orders of Warwick, her old adversary, their heads afterwards mounted on spikes.

When she learned of the defeat and death of Warwick at the bloody battle of Barnet Jacquetta's health had rallied but the improvement had been short-lived. Her prolonged sojourn in the damp quarters of Westminster Sanctuary had done her great harm and Blanche was too skilled in medicine not to know that her lady's allotted time on earth was drawing to a close.

Now she was forced to confront a future without the patronage and protection of her well-connected mistress. How would she manage when the Dowager Duchess was dead?

For years, Blanche admitted to me, she had been secretly yearning for a home of her own, a place where she would be mistress and not forever reliant on the goodwill or favour of others. Yet though she had waited anxiously, she found that Mistress Margery's stark prediction had come to pass, her beauty had not been enough to elicit a single acceptable marriage proposal. Of course, there had been no shortage of admirers eager to take her to their beds – she rebuffed them all, she assured me primly - but her unfortunate tavern background and even more unfortunate lack of fortune deterred men of standing from wanting to make her their wife.

While Jacquetta still flourished Blanche had been able to brush aside her failure to find a husband. She told herself that she was young and exceptionally comely and there was still time a-plenty. Then the unexpectedly rapid decline of her mistress put a different complexion on the matter.

Such was her closeness to the Dowager Duchess that she felt confident of being provided for in her will, though she doubted that any legacy would be sufficient to buy her the life she craved. She was too cautious to say as much to me but I suspected that having lived amongst the Woodville clan since she was a small child, she was wise enough to know their reputation for avarice was well-founded. Any bequest to her from Jacquetta would have to be small indeed to pass their jealous scrutiny.

Nothing if not a realist, Blanche knew that when her mistress died she was going to have to petition for a place in the Queen's household where she would have to prove herself all over again. The prospect held little enchantment for her.

"Yet in the end I need not have fretted," she trilled delightedly, her wine-flushed cheeks a becoming cherry red, "for amidst her own concerns, my dear mistress had not neglected to plan for my future.

"She summoned me to her sick chamber one day and informed me that she knew her end was coming. Before she died she wished to fulfil the promise she had made long ago to my mother to provide for my future. To that end she had found a splendid new home for me.

"And thus I came to be here at Plaincourt," she concluded, a considerable shade too hurriedly for my liking.

The tale had been long in the telling and I sensed that Blanche had greatly relished recounting it to such an attentive audience. I found it vexing, therefore, that now she had reached the crux of the matter she seemed determined to say no more. I wanted to question her further, to find out if her understanding with Sir Stephen had existed from the moment she arrived at Plaincourt. If such was the case, Jacquetta of Bedford must have offered an irresistibly powerful incentive to secure such an advantageous match for her protégé.

Much as I desired to discover the nature of this incentive, however, I held my tongue. Instinct warned me to tread carefully. Much of an intimate nature had been divulged to me in the course of the evening, certainly more than was proper considering my short acquaintance with the lady and her elevated status as future mistress of Plaincourt. Were I to push for yet more, she might become suspicious. In any case, her increasingly slurred diction gave me reason to suspect that soon she would be wholly incapable of further speech.

Alone in my chamber, after Blanche had with great difficulty bid me a dignified goodnight and apologised prettily for being too tired to hear me play, I went over the last part of her tale in my head. My intention was to fill in the missing parts with conjectures of my own.

Since the dying Dowager Duchess of Bedford had been able to find a place for her young waiting woman at Plaincourt Manor, it followed that there must be a connection between the Woodville clan and the Plaincourts. The precise nature of that connection interested me, for my noble friend Dickon was always eager to know which men of rank were friendly with the Woodvilles. Such knowledge made it easier for him, as he often wryly observed, to identify potential enemies.

On the surface it appeared that the presence of Blanche at Plaincourt was indicative of an alliance between the Woodvilles and Plaincourts. How deeply-rooted that alliance was I had as yet to ascertain. I felt sure that Blanche's betrothal to Sir Stephen was crucial to the matter I was investigating, as was the fact that it had been kept a secret until after Geoffrey's death.

By agreeing to take the unimportant girl as his wife, had the ambitious Stephen Plaincourt simply found a way to ingratiate himself with the matriarch of a very powerful family? Surely not, for he would see that as insufficient reward for missing the opportunity to increase his fortune with another fat dowry. How then had the wily old woman persuaded him to overlook Blanche's poverty? Not by giving the girl a fortune herself, her rapacious children would never have tolerated that. But if not money, then what?

I was also troubled by the disparity between Fielding's version of Blanche and her present status as the future lady of Plaincourt. According to Will, she had of her own free will indulged in carnal relations with him and had risked her own safety to release him when he was being held for Geoffrey's murder. At the time he had believed her to be no more than a lowly waiting woman yet all the while she had been secretly betrothed to Sir Stephen.

My task was to make sense of this conundrum and I knew that in the fullness of time I would do so. At that moment, though, it was making my head ache abominably – or perhaps that was just the effect of too much wine – so after staring into the darkness of my chamber for several minutes, I flung off my shoes, wrapped myself in the woollen blanket and waited for sleep to claim me.

It was as I was about to drift away that an errant thought unconnected to my earlier musings made my eyes fly open in amused surprise. When Blanche had been recounting the litany of troubles that her aged mistress had encountered during the final years of her life, she had unaccountably neglected to mention a notable event that had held the nobility and commons fascinated for weeks.

During Warwick's rebellion, shortly after the death of her husband and son, the imperious Dowager Duchess had been taken from her home and put on trial for witchcraft. It had been talked about everywhere and from potboy to prostitute and vintner to varlet, the consensus had been that having done away with her husband, wicked Warwick was now attempting to find a way to dispose of Jacquetta. It seemed likely to me, for he was known to detest all Woodvilles, blaming them – probably correctly - for his loss of influence over the King. As he was a vengeful man I could well imagine that he would relish finding a legal way to end Jacquetta's life, yet in the end he had seemed to lose his nerve and let her go free. Not long afterwards, Edward regained control of his kingdom, Warwick was vanquished and the Queen's mother was fully exonerated of all charges.

As I thought of all this, I wondered why Blanche had failed to speak of the witchcraft trial as it must surely have been a dreadfully anxious time for her mistress. It then occurred to me that Blanche had genuinely loved Jacquetta of Bedford and loving her, had found the episode profoundly painful. She would have known that if found guilty of witchcraft, her mistress would most likely suffer an agonising death. The very best she could have hoped for would have been permanent incarceration in a dismal, distant castle. Not so very long ago this had been the fate of another royal duchess, Eleanor of Cobham, when she was found guilty of practising witchcraft. Now I understood Blanche's reticence to mention the matter and I liked her the better for it. I remained certain that she was a manipulative little whore but perhaps her heart was less cold than I had at first believed.

Chapter 7
A Short History
of the Plaincourt Family

Next morning I woke early as was my habit, in spite of all the wine I had imbibed. Having taken little of the plentiful but dull Advent fare offered at supper, I felt in urgent need of sustenance so I made my way to the kitchen where I hoped to scrounge fresh bread and something to quench my thirst. If luck was with me I might also hear some manor gossip.

In my eagerness as I entered the room I collided with a heavy-set, red-faced washerwoman carrying a basket full of dirty linen. I begged pardon for inconveniencing her but she made no reply although her jowly face registered shy pleasure as she exited into the passageway.

In the centre of the kitchen stood a vast deal table and at its head was a powerfully made man of about forty years. He was at that moment employed in readying herrings for dinner and his sleeves were pushed back, revealing arms bristling with thick red hair that matched the wiry bush on his head.

Deducing that this must be the manor cook I called out a cheery greeting and made my way towards him, announcing my desire for a bite to eat and friendly conversation if he had time to spare.

The man looked up at me then, regarding me with alert, crinkly hazel eyes that stood out in a face liberally splattered with orange freckles.

"Now then, Master Cranley, sit thee down," he instructed, "and by all means break thy fast. The lass here'll fetch thee some victuals," he nodded towards the pallid wench I had spied at supper the night before, "but as for conversation, I misdoubt I can entertain thee half so well as did Mistress Blanche last night."

Whether intentionally or not, he spoke Blanche's name with palpable loathing. Since it was apparent that my lengthy tête-à-tête with her had been reported to him, I realised that it was critical for any hope I had of befriending the man to dispel the notion that I was smitten with her.

"Sweet Jesu, that woman can talk!" I cried, rolling my eyes ostentatiously and slapping the cook heartily on the back as I lowered myself onto a three-legged stool.

"'Tis a pity that such a fair creature has so much to say for herself, and scarce a word of it of interest. For my part, I prefer a woman a little less handsome and a lot more silent."

To my relief, the man guffawed at this ungallant sally but he was not yet prepared to let the matter drop.

"Cuckoo here said thee seemed plenty interested in what the mistress was saying, didn't thee, lass?" he snickered, casting a cursory glance towards the serving girl.

"Said thy heads were bent so close thee were thick as thatch, and thee did keep refilling her wine cup and gazing at her like thee could eat her up."

It was pointless to deny any of this since every servant in the hall could attest to my shameless flirtation with their mistress. What they did not know, and I could scarce reveal, was that my sole purpose had been to elicit information.

"Well what do you expect, man?" I countered, feigning indignation.

"She's a vain little trollop if I'm not mistaken, and I'm a man in need of a comfortable billet this Yuletide. What of it if I hoped by my fawning to win an invitation to bide awhile at this pleasant place? Do you know how cruelly the December wind cuts into a man's bones when he has no roof over his head? I say without shame that I'll choose flattery over freezing every time, as would any man who's known the sky for his roof in winter-time."

It seemed my angry words convinced the cook for he ceased his chopping and sat down alongside me.

"Hush now, Master Cranley," he soothed, "don't thee go getting mardy like, I never didst mean no offence. Truth to tell, Mistress Blanche is little liked round these parts and it could be that dost make us a deal too cautious with any that dost share fair words with her. But by Christ I'd as leave feast on Old Nick's turds than begrudge any honest traveller a warm bed on a cold night.

"I'm Jem Flood," he announced, holding out a large hand slimed with herring juice, "and thee's welcome in my kitchen.

"Cuckoo thee've met," he added, "and yonder," he pointed over my shoulder, "is Matthew, my kitchen lad. He's a good fellow and though he dost look mazed much of the time, yet he dost have more gumption than most I dost know so mind thee dossent fall for his backward act."

When I had first entered the kitchen I had spied Matthew warming his buttocks in front of one of its two great fireplaces but had deliberately refrained from acknowledging him. Now I turned to greet him, hoping he would remember my admonition to reveal no sign of our previous meeting.

Studying his pleasant, impassive baby-face, I saw no sign of the vital spark that had encouraged me to believe the youth was possessed of unusually sharp wits. I was beginning to doubt my instincts when a corner of his mouth twitched upwards and for a short moment his expression was alight with intelligence. Then the moment was gone and his dullard countenance returned but it was enough to restore my confidence in him.

"Good day to you, lad," I called to him genially. In reply he mumbled something indiscernible and idly scratched his behind.

At a signal from the cook, the girl Cuckoo came to the table and set before me a clay beaker which she filled to the brim with barley ale.

"Try that," Flood commanded, "and tell me if sobeit thee's ever tasted better."

I had, and in any case I much prefer fine Rhenish wine over home-brewed ale but good manners dictated that I should heap praise on the manor's provender, warranted or not. Flood drank also, and beckoned to Matthew to come forward and claim a cup. Only Cuckoo did not drink, so I asked her gently if she was not thirsty.

The wench blushed, and her wan face looked better for the colour it brought to her cheeks.

"I'll take some if Pa dost say I might," she answered, looking anxiously at Flood.

She is his daughter, I thought with some surprise. I had not discerned a resemblance between the small pale girl and the strapping, gingery cook, nor could I see evidence of paternal affection in the way he spoke to her.

"Drink then," Flood ordered surlily, "but see thee dossent take all day about it."

Turning to face the fireplace at which Matthew had been standing, I saw two pallets covered with fustian blankets lying close by. Flood followed my gaze.

"'Tis where Matthew and the lass dost bed down of a night," he informed me.

"And what of you?" I enquired. "Is there not a cosy spot at the fireside for you to rest your head after your labours?"

"There is not," Flood laughed, "and God be thanked for it. I dost have a tidy house of my own in Plaincourt village, and a bonnie wife to go home to when my work here is done. 'Tis sometimes hard to make my way across the moat in the dark but I've lived in Plaincourt all my days and my feet dost find the path well enough."

"So you and pretty little Cuckoo spend your nights alone together here," I said to Matthew with a suggestive gleam in my eye. "That must be passing pleasant for you."

It was an idle remark, meant as a harmless jest, so I was unprepared for the vehemence with which all three of the kitchen folk rounded on me in denial of any loose behaviour.

"There's nowt of that sort going on, thee may be assured of that, Master Cranley," Flood said firmly, while Matthew spluttered incoherently and Cuckoo declared with indignation that she was yet a maiden pure and untouched.

It was plain that I had touched a sore place with my careless remark and I marvelled a little at their reaction. I knew that the other household servants slept in the great hall but it was not uncommon for kitchen staff to lie down next to their own fires where they were guaranteed warmth and an unusual degree of privacy.

What was peculiar was for a young unmarried girl to sleep alone with a lusty youth, especially when her own father went home to a house in the village. I concluded that the bonnie wife Flood had mentioned might not be the girl's mother. If that was the case, it could be that she was unwilling to share her roof with a grown-up step-daughter, although Flood did not strike me as the sort to suffer a shrewish, domineering spouse, however comely she may be.

Putting the matter from my mind, I returned my attention to the task in hand. In order to bring Mistress Blanche back into the conversation, I asked when she was likely to rise from her slumbers. Flood pulled a disgusted face.

"That vicious piece dost oft-times lie low in her pit half the day," he sneered.

"She's made a snug nest for herself in an apartment over the buttery. And having heard tell how much of Master's best Gascon she didst guzzle last night, I dossent expect her to leave it anytime soon.

"For which," he added with a shudder, "I dost confess I am nowt but thankful. The longer she dost stay out of my way, the happier it dost make me."

Matthew and Cuckoo nodded their agreement. Oh Blanche, your gift for making friends has failed you here at Plaincourt Manor, I thought. You would seem to be universally loathed.

"I see you have a high opinion of your master's future bride," I jested, hoping to encourage him to speak some more of her. Yet I was destined to be disappointed.

"'Tis not for me to like or mislike Master's future wife," he commented shortly, perhaps regretting having spoken so freely in front of me. "If Master dost want her, I daresay she'll serve well enough."

Realising that Flood was not willing to be drawn further about Blanche I abandoned that tack and turned instead to Sir Stephen himself.

"What manner of man is the master?" I enquired, explaining my interest on the pretext of sounding out my chance of securing permanent tenure at the manor. "Does he treat his servants fairly?"

To my relief, this line of questioning met with greater success.

"Sir Stephen, he dost have his merits," Flood opined carefully. "Mind, I dossent say he's a good man but serve him well, keep thy nose out of his affairs and he'll give thee no cause for complaint. And to my way of thinking, that dost make him a better master than his father, may the evil old bugger burn in hell's fiery furnaces for all eternity."

My interest was roused by hearing the cook speak of the old master with such open hatred. Sensing a story, I asked what fault there had been with the old master.

"Sir Thomas didst cleave to the ancient view that he didst have the right to force himself on every comely lass in the village, maid or married, whether she didst want him or no," he answered in a voice rich with bitterness.

At once, I was reminded of Matthew's story about the witch called Lynet who had been repeatedly raped by Sir Thomas and then all but cast out by her family.

"He didst start as a young 'un, soon as ever he didst know what his cock were for, and never didst stop 'til the day he dropped dead. Plaincourt's littered with his bastard bairns, though he didst never recognise them as such, oh no, not he. Our wives and daughters didst bear his bairns and we didst have no choice but to care for them as our own or watch them starve. Even I dost have a cuckoo in my nest!" he spat angrily.

A whimper escaped the kitchen drab's lips and finally the significance of her odd name dawned on me.

"I see thee has it now," Flood growled. "Aye, Cuckoo's called my daughter but in truth the girl were fathered when the shameful old devil didst force open my poor Letice's legs at knifepoint. Even when he were old and feeble there were no slaking his prodigious lust. He didst die not long after and I didst gave thanks for it, may the good Lord forgive me.

"I never didst blame Letice for what happened, nor should I in fairness blame the girl but I cain't help it. The very fact of her being is like a sore that dossent heal. She's allus there to remind me of what that old goat didst to my wife, and how there were nowt I couldst do about it.

"My Letice is a goodly soul and she dost love the brat in spite of all; 'tis for her sake I didst agree to raise Cuckoo as my own but God forgive me, I cain't learn to like her. As soon as ever she were old enough to work I didst say she must leave my house and bide here at the manor. Leastways now, though my days are blighted by her presence in my kitchen, I find a smidgen of peace when I dost lie under my own roof at night."

I felt an overwhelming sense of pity, mostly for poor Cuckoo who had stood limp and dejected throughout Flood's tale but also for the man and his wife. Much as I deplored his hostility to the hapless girl I could well understand his inability to forget the vile circumstance that had led to her birth. At least her mother loves her, I thought, let that give the wench some consolation.

Glancing at Matthew, I saw that he too was moved by Flood's story. This I found surprising since I felt it could have been no secret to him. He saw me looking at him and smiled sheepishly.

"When thee didst hear tell I share the same bedding down place as Cuckoo, thee didst think there must be mucky goings on 'twixt she and I," he muttered, "and I dossent blame thee any for it. But Letice Flood dost know full well her lass's maidenhood is safe from me for Cuckoo is my sister. Half-blood sister, that is, seeing as her and me dost not have the same ma.

"My ma were a bad girl that didst live near a place called Mablethorpe Hall. I didst never go there but I dost know 'tis by the coast. Old Sir Thomas didst take a fancy to her one time when he was visiting with the Fitzwilliams up at Mablethorpe, and he didst carry her home across his saddle. He didst give her a house here in the village and didst visit

113

her regular until she didst fall for me.

"Then he didst stop his visiting and Ma didst make shift to earn her bread helping Dulcy the washerwoman. When I was birthed she didst plain bleed away and die, Dulcy didst say there was nowt to be done to save her. Dulcy didst think I looked lusty enough, mind, so she didst pick me up and carry me along to the manor for Sir Thomas to see. He weren't interested though, and didst bid her be off afore he didst put his fist in her ugly face. 'Tis not me calling Dulcy ugly, you understand, master, 'tis what Sir Thomas didst say to her. She herself didst say so many a-time.

"At first Dulcy didst think that the Lord meant for me to die since there were none to suckle me. But she didst pray on it some and then it didst come to her that Letice Flood had just birthed a bairn, so she didst take me along to Jem's house. Letice didst say she had milk enough to nurse me along of her own babe but Jem didst say as how he didst not have the stomach to raise another of the master's by-blows.

"So I didst bide with the Floods only 'til I were weaned and thereafter Dulcy didst arrange it so that all the villagers didst take a turn at raising me. Every family didst have me for a spell for Dulcy said bastard or no, it were their Christian duty to keep me alive if they couldst. Before I didst become a burden to any I would be passed on to the next family, and so it continued until the day I were old enough to start work here in the manor kitchen."

As he finished speaking the thought came to me that Matthew and I had a common bond. Like me, as a babe he had been left motherless, though the cause of his abandonment had been natural death rather than unnatural indifference, and like me his survival had been brought about by the charity of strangers. Indeed, I could have found myself in Matthew's place, had not the good Duke of York felt moved by an obligation to my dead father to care for me. The thought made me shudder. I was already disposed to like the kitchen boy for the compassion and intelligence that lurked beneath his bovine exterior but now I felt for him a surge of something akin to brotherly affection. I resolved that when my business at Plaincourt was completed, I would do whatever I could to improve his lot in life.

We had been sitting in idle conversation a good while and when Matthew's story drew to a close Flood became aware of it and jumped to his feet.

"Well, Master Cranley," he said as he fetched a sack of oats from a cupboard in the corner, "thee dost know our secrets now. As cook-master I am king of this kitchen yet of the three of us that labour here daily, 'tis me's the only one as dossent claim kinship with the noble Plaincourts. The bastard maid I am obliged to call daughter dost share no blood of mine but that of my master, and so dost my lowly kitchen boy. Come now, what dost thee think of this merry affair? If nowt else, it'll give thee a jolly story for the next fine lords and ladies thee dost play for."

I made to answer but before I could speak he cut me short abruptly.

"Another time, master, another time! Thee's welcome to sup ale with me again for I dost like thy face and thee've a pleasing way, but now thee must leave us to work in peace else there'll be no dinner to serve."

At that I had little option but to murmur my thanks for the food and drink and retreat to the courtyard.

***

Mulling over the stories I had heard in the kitchen I came to the conclusion that while they were sad and regrettably not that uncommon, they brought me no further forward with my mission. I was fast becoming frustrated with my lack of progress and felt there was something sinister in the way no one spoke of the very recent death of young Geoffrey.

Flood struck me as a level-headed fellow and during my conversation with him I had badly wanted to ask his opinion as to who might have engineered the boy's death. Alas, there had been no opportunity to do so without raising suspicion since I, as a stranger to the manor, could not be expected to know anything of the murder. The only soul who had mentioned it to me since my arrival at Plaincourt had been the kitchen boy. Since I preferred to say nothing of my prior encounter with him in the interests of securing a secret ally, I could hardly name him as my source of information. I found it most damnably annoying. If only someone other than Matthew would speak of Geoffrey's murder I could begin asking questions but until then I must feign ignorance of the entire affair.

Unsure how to proceed next, I decided to while away a few minutes by visiting the stable to see how my borrowed nag was faring. Of course, Plaincourt hospitality being what it was, I should have known that the beast was being cared for better than it ever had been in its miserable life. I was tempted to toss the stable lads a few coins as reward for their diligence but desisted just in time, remembering that a down-at-luck minstrel would not distribute largesse like a man of means. Instead I contented myself with thanking them fulsomely for their trouble and headed back to the great hall.

As I entered from the anteroom I encountered the servitor I had privately dubbed Old Shuffler. He was struggling to manoeuvre a heavy bundle of firewood into the hall, with little success so far as I could make out. Feeling sorry for the poor old fellow I plucked the burden from him, carried it across the floor to the fireplace and set it next to the remaining stash of logs.

Rather than thanking me for my kindness, the ingrate huffed that if I wanted to be useful there was plenty more kindling I could fetch. Stifling an urge to cuff the wretch for his impudence, I forced a pleasant smile and ventured to make a bargain with him. I would finish his task in return for some information about the master of Plaincourt Manor. Hastily, before he could register suspicion, I trotted out the tale that I found Plaincourt much to my liking and thought to seek a permanent position. It would be helpful to learn what manner of man the master was, I said, that I might know how best to please him.

This must have struck the decrepit retainer as plausible, or else in his eagerness to shift his duties onto me he didn't much care what questions I asked. In any event, he readily agreed to my bargain. Thus, when I had made short work of hauling the wood into the hall I joined Shuffler who was busily arranging the new logs into neat stacks. He now seemed warmly disposed towards me and informed me that his name was Alan Rolf. His sister, he said, was Dulcy Rolf, the rotund, red-faced washerwoman I had spied earlier.

Whilst I had been toiling I had reached a decision to risk bringing up the subject of young Geoffrey's death. I had spent time that morning both in the kitchen and the stable and if Old Shuffler – or Rolf, as I must now think of him – asked how I had learned of the matter I would simply say that I had overheard talk of it somewhere about the manor. As it turned out, I need not have worried for Rolf registered no surprise when I broached the subject.

"'Tis clear that this is a goodly, prosperous place," I began, "yet I gather until but recently the master was a delicate lad confined to a sickbed. Well, poor boy, if naught else he was fortunate in his steward for the man has kept the manor in prime condition."

"That dost show how little thee knowst then, master minstrel," the old man said rudely.

"It were not the steward as looked after Plaincourt for young Master Geoffrey, it were his uncle Sir Stephen, him that is now master in law as well as in fact. And I'll tell thee summat else,'tis no wonder he didst make a good fist of keeping the land fat and the coffers full, for getting rich and living high is what Plaincourts allus didst best."

He stopped then and looked at me expectantly. I wondered if the old fool wanted money to continue but then I realised that he was of the garrulous type who like to show off their knowledge in front of an audience but need to have it encouraged from them little by little.

Sighing inwardly, I hurried to oblige.

"Pray don't stop there," I implored, "for I would gladly know more about the Plaincourts if I am to become part of their household."

"Bah!" he spat, "'Tis a mystery to me why any man of sense dost give good money to hear songs and all that foolish folderol. And I dost know not why a strapping, hearty fellow like thee dost choose to mince thy way through life 'stead of earning thy bread in a way that's good and manly.

"Yet Sir Stephen is like to take thee on, Master Minstrel, sobeit thee is skilled," he continued, "for 'tis known he dost have a fondness for music and such doggerybaw. Not like his old father! That tough old bugger didst have no truck with owt of that sort. No, of a certainty Sir Stephen didst have it from his lady mother. She were from London where they dost go in for all manner of strangeness, I dost hear tell.

"Ah, I'm an old man now and there's much in the world today I dossent comprehend. Mind," he chuckled, "in some ways the new master dost carry on like enough to his sire. He dost know that if a man hopes to protect what's his he dost need to be strong and ruthless. And if he dost wish to add to what he has, why then he dost need cunning and plenty of it.

"Aye, cunning! There's summat the Plaincourt men dost allus have. The family didst come here in the time of the first William, they dost say, granted the land as payment for fighting in his army. Rough folk they were, no better'n thee nor I. But they didst fight mighty fierce for old King William and he didst need to reward them in consequence. So he didst give them a parcel of land at a place finer folk didst reckon the arse-end of nowhere. It didst keep Plaincourts happy and got them out the way at the same time, dost thee see?

"There weren't no manor house here then, of course, and no village to speak of neither but that didst not stop the Plaincourts. They didst set to at once, cultivating the land and striving to make rich.

"Over time the rough soldiers didst grow into noble knights and then they didst find an easy way to increase the manor's fortune. Plaincourts have allus been blessed with sons, see, and sons dost need wives. Unlike most families of their sort, the Plaincourts didst go a-courting amongst the merchant folk, hunting for rich girls with fat dowries, or fat girls with rich dowries come to that. They didst not care a swine's fart who they took to wife so long as she didst bring gold or land or both.

"That 'tis what has made Plaincourt Manor the rich place it is today. Plaincourt heirs are allus born knowing 'tis their duty to wed a fortune, and none didst know it better than old Sir Thomas."

Rolf paused and I knew I was expected to prompt him once again.

"Sir Thomas?" I enquired. "He that was father to the present lord of Plaincourt?"

"The very same," he replied, "and some dost say the cleverest Plaincourt of them all. He didst surpass all previous matches by fixing for his bride the oldest lass of the richest goldsmith in London.

"Alice Lambert, that were her name," Rolf remembered. "Old Sir Thomas, he didst well for himself bringing that one home to Plaincourt, and not only on account of the riches she didst bring with her. Her father didst have powerful friends at Court. It were said he didst regular turn a blind eye to the huge debts run up by jewel-hungry nobles and in return they didst whisper to him things that he could use to his advantage. When clever old Sir Tom didst wed this gold grubber's daughter, he didst too begin to benefit from these whisperings.

"Sir Thomas were a hard man but he were gentle as a lamb with his Alice. Oh dear me, I dossent reckon no Plaincourt man didst ever before cosset his wife half so much as Sir Thomas didst cosset Lady Alice. He didst know her worth to him and treated her accordingly. Didst treat her better'n a queen if you dost ask me! Why, after she didst give him two sons he didst even leave her in peace, if you dost take my meaning, for it were said she didst much mislike that part of married life. Yet that were not well, as it happened, for there's no denying old Sir Thomas didst have a powerful lust."

"Ah yes," I interrupted, "I have heard something of that, and also that he had a habit of slaking it in the village."

I kept my voice free of any reproach but Rolf regarded me closely all the same.

"Aye, well," he mumbled, "that's true enough, I cain't deny. I didst hear tell that when the heat was on him there was nowt any man couldst do to stop him having his way. Some might say that didst make him an evil man deserving of punishment in the hereafter. I say he didst take his punishment in this life, in the heavy cares his oldest son didst place on him.

"William his name was, and he were the sire of young Geoffrey, him that didst die so recent, God rest his poor soul. William didst look like a Plaincourt sure enough but there was allus something different about him. Folk said by nature he was more Lambert than Plaincourt and it is true he were strong attached to his mother and didst take on most fierce when she didst die.

"She were not long in her grave when it didst come time for him to wed. Then what dost the naughty lad but spurn his father's choice of bride, a girl from Lincoln with a face like the bleached flannel from which her old pa hadst made his fine fortune. Far as the old master were concerned, her face didst not come into it. What didst matter were the riches she would bring when the match were made.

"But William, he didst insist he would not have her! Instead, he didst swear none would do for him but Philippa Braunche. How old Sir Tom didst rail at him then, naming him a disgrace to the family and no true son of his."

The disloyal servant cackled gleefully at the memory of this familial discord.

"What was so amiss with this Philippa?" I asked, drawn into the tale even though I doubted it had any bearing on the matter I was investigating.

"Why nowt," Rolf answered acidly, "save that she were

penniless and of no account. Her father were Sir Ralph Braunche and he didst once own the manor of Ringthorpe that borders Plaincourt to the west. The Braunches were an old family of higher blood than the Plaincourts if truth be said, but over time they didst lose their fortune.

"Proper knights they were, living only to wage war for their King. Across the sea they didst go, with all their destriers and armour and men-at-arms eating into their gold. Much good didst it do them! By the time Ringthorpe come to Sir Ralph he were weighed down in debt and in time didst have no recourse but to sell up. It were Sir Thomas that didst buy it from him, and being the cunning dog he were I dost know for certain the price he gave were niggardly.

"When young William didst come to him saying he didst wish to marry the Braunche lass the old man didst strike him hard in the face and forbid it. So the disobedient lad didst go behind his father's back and didst wed her all the same. I can tell you Master Cranley, it didst nigh on kill Sir Thomas to have his heir tied to the penniless daughter of a disgraced knight! But the marriage were done proper and consummated afore he learned of it, so there were nowt he could do. That was when he didst sign away the manor of Ringthorpe to his younger son, Stephen."

"For what reason?" I asked, although I had already guessed the answer.

"Why to punish William and his wretched new wife, of course. The old master didst believe the girl had snared his heir in order to regain her family home. If he couldst do nowt else he'd make certain he didst thwart her plan. Stephen were despatched to make the place fit to live in again, and a pretty sum of money were paid out to get him a knighthood. All his father didst require of him in return was to swear afore the priest that he'd never suffer his brother's wife to set foot in his house."

"Poor lady," I commented, "I can see how grievous something like that would be to a soft-hearted girl. And her husband, he must surely have resented losing part of his rightful inheritance to his brother."

Rolf grinned delightedly.

"Aye, thee'd think so, would thee not? But not a bit of it! The daft devil were too moonstruck over his lady to care about owt much save pleasing her. And as it turned out she didst give not so much as a tinker's belch for her old family home! No, William and Philippa were happy as couldst be. At first even the daily jibing of Sir Tom didst not lift the shine off it.

"Yet after a year of marriage and no bairn to show for it, the old master didst start abusing Lady Philipppa for being barren as well as penniless. Then she didst take to weeping and that didst not sit well with William. One day he didst go out hunting with his father and didst return with the old man's corpse. There'd been an accident, he didst say. Sir Thomas didst fall off his hoss and hit his head on a rock.

"There were those that didst whisper it were a mighty lucky fall for William and his lady but Sir Thomas had not been well-loved, not even by Sir Stephen, and anywise none didst know how to prove it had happened other than what William claimed. So now there could be peace at Plaincourt with no more insults to affront the Lady Philippa. It were all she didst need to quicken with child. Soon enough she didst show a big belly and in the fullness of time young Geoffrey were born.

"Ah, but he were a sorry scrap even at that age! Small and maungey, all didst think him like to die but against the odds he didst make it through his first twelve-month. Then for the lady nowt would suit but she and her husband must away to Lincoln to give thanks at the cathedral for the boy's survival. Poor pious fools! While there they didst catch a fever and were dead afore they knew it. Only Geoffrey didst survive for he'd been left here at Plaincourt with a nurse."

"A tragic tale!" I exclaimed, for so it struck me. The young couple had scarcely had a chance to enjoy their lives free from the malign influence of the old man before death had claimed them.

"What happened next?"

Rolf took his time answering, sensing perhaps that I would be less willing to bide so companionably with him once his story was told.

"Just so soon as word didst reach Ringthorpe that William were dead, Sir Stephen didst up and ride to Plaincourt and didst make plain his intention to set himself up as Geoffrey's guardian. He didst think to have it all his own way, mind, but he didst forget the Lamberts, his mother's kin in London. Within a matter of weeks their lawyers didst come to Plaincourt with demands to see the infant master and inspect the arrangements made for his care.

"According to Gervase Root – him that's steward here at Plaincourt - the Lamberts didst fear Sir Stephen meant to do away with his nephew so that he could claim Plaincourt for his own. But by sending in the lawyers, they didst tell him they were watching. He didst know then that questions would be asked should the boy come to ill."

At these words I pretended to be greatly shocked and asked Rolf if he seriously believed Sir Stephen to be capable of killing a child, and his own nephew at that, for material advantage. Before he could reply, a loud commotion issued from the courtyard and then a breathless boy rushed into the hall. Gasping for air, he brought word that the master was arrived home. What's more, he brought with him a fine lord accompanied by several attendants, all of whom would be wanting bed and board.

Grimacing, Rolf rose to his feet as swiftly as his creaking bones would allow. The divers tasks that now awaited him would, I felt sure, drive all thought of my last question from his mind. Yet I was wrong.

"Be the master the murdering kind?" he whispered. "Thee'd best judge for thyself, minstrel. No doubt thee'll be meeting Sir Stephen soon enough."

Chapter 8
Plaincourt
Receives a Mighty Guest

At once, the erstwhile peace of the hall gave way to frenetic bustle as a stream of dusty menials tramped inside, their arms aching from the weight of saddlebags and travel chests. All looked to Rolf for instruction. He had begun directing them when a messenger boy burst in, shouting that the master desired dinner to be served the minute he and his honoured guest were rid of the dirt from the road.

"They've rid hard and fast," the lad said, "and dost have a mean hunger upon them. Master dost say he's not of a mind to wait at cook's convenience."

Rolf groaned and looked at me imploringly.

"T'would be doing me a service, master minstrel, if thee didst get thyself to the kitchen rightaways and relay to Jem Flood Master's order for dinner without delay. I cain't go myself, thee dost see how I'm fixed here."

I did indeed see that the poor old devil had his hands full directing the new arrivals. I wondered that the steward had not yet shown his face to order affairs, or Mistress Blanche come to that. But then, she was most likely still sleeping off the terrifying quantity of wine she had imbibed at supper yesterday. Deciding it was no hardship to be helpful, I agreed to carry Rolf's message and much relieved, he thanked me kindly before returning to the business in hand.

I found the kitchen staff already appraised of the master's return but not of the presence of a noble guest. Flood was contentedly bringing forth the herring dish he had been preparing earlier and he cursed angrily when I told him of the need for finer fare.

"And how dost Master imagine I am to fashion a fancy Advent dinner at a moment's notice?" he bellowed, his brow furrowing alarmingly. The girl Cuckoo, cowering a few paces from him, turned paler than I would have thought possible.

Only Matthew seemed to have his wits about him. Having anticipated Sir Stephen's need for hot water, he was at that moment filling a basin from a cauldron over the fire.

"They'll want clean cloths as well," I remarked, and he nodded, indicating a stack of linen set ready on the table. Grabbing them, he carried the filled basin to the door and exited as quickly as he could manage without spilling the water.

Flood may have been a competent cook but I could tell he was not the sort to cope well when faced with a challenge. He stood at the table, flailing his arms as he expostulated about the impossibility of providing a fine dinner without prior notice. Cuckoo stared at the floor, shuffling helplessly from one foot to another. I saw that in the absence of any real authority - where in sweet Jesu's name was the steward? - I would have to take charge of the situation.

"Cuckoo," I ordered firmly, "stop your dithering and listen. Quick as you can, you must rouse Mistress Blanche. Tell her she must hasten to make herself presentable, for the master has returned with fine company and he will be desirous of her presence."

As she fled the room, I turned my attention to Flood.

"Be calm, master cook," I said firmly, raising a hand to silence his bawling, "there's no call for this commotion. With your skill and my wits, I warrant we'll make a dinner the King himself would relish.

"Let us have the herrings baked in sugar to begin. Then pluck a fat pike from the freshwater vats I spied out yonder, and prepare for it a galantine. To follow... have you pickled sturgeon? Aye, of course you do. Then it will do very well if you dress it with a verjuice. And to finish, a simple dish of sweet raisins, dates and figs will be most pleasing. "

Flood's scowling lessened somewhat and he leapt to follow my suggestions yet I had the feeling the touchy churl resented my intervention.

"I know not how we didst ever manage without thee, Master Cranley," he threw sarcastically at me as he set to grinding spices with a pestle.

Shrugging, I took my leave and strolled outside. At the corner of the courtyard nearest the kitchen I found a cosy nook in which to conceal myself whilst observing all the hubbub.

As grooms and valets darted to and fro, a pair of richly dressed men stood in conversation outside the stables. Straining my ears, I managed to gather that they were delivering detailed instructions to the grooms about the care of a particularly magnificent destrier. One of the two had his back to me but the other faced towards the manor house and thus I had a clear view of his features.

From the authoritatively familiar way in which he issued his commands I guessed that this must be Sir Stephen Plaincourt. I was glad at last to have a chance to look upon his face, and to do so quietly and unobserved by others. After studying him closely for a short while, noticing his mannerisms as much as his features, I felt I had the measure of the man.

"Good fortune, Mistress Blanche," I whispered softly. "You're as like to find contentment with that one as I am to wed Master Pennicott's mule."

Although of no more than average height, the erect bearing of the master of Plaincourt Manor made him seem taller. He was sleek and well fed but had as yet no hint of fat or dissipation about his person. His face was handsome and haughty with slate grey eyes that from my vantage point appeared as full of warmth as the winter ocean. Yet I noticed he had a well-shaped, full-lipped mouth that hinted at a sensual nature. Here, I thought, is a proud man with little compassion and an appetite for the good things in life. He enjoys luxury and plenty but will suffer discomfort readily enough if it suits his purpose. What manner of welcome, I wondered, will such a man offer to a humble musician supposedly down on his luck?

Then his companion turned around and I almost yelped in surprise for here was one I recognised immediately.

Plaincourt's guest was a man of some thirty-two years, spare of frame and possessed of a soldier-like bearing. A helmet of fair curly hair grew back from his high forehead, beneath which were large, expressive green eyes. Sharp, prominent cheekbones dominated his face. The man's wide mouth was at that moment set in solemn lines but I had seen his smile and knew that it transformed his countenance from sombre and forbidding to warm and merry.

I marvelled at my stupidity in failing to identify his voice while he had been speaking to the grooms. It was deep and smooth and I had heard it many times before, albeit always from a distance. Stephen Plaincourt's honoured guest was no less a personage than the King's brother-in-law, Earl Rivers. Anthony Woodville, as I still thought of him, was the Queen's beloved brother, a Knight of the Garter and close confidant of the King. Few men in the kingdom were possessed of more influence than he. Discovering him here at Plaincourt, the arse-end of nowhere to borrow Alan Rolf's colourful epithet, was a shock for which I had been in no way prepared.

I knew Rivers had the reputation of being a very learned man with a formidable brain. According to my lord of Gloucester, the man also had an unfortunate appetite for scheming and my royal friend was rarely wrong about these matters.

Rivers' presence at Plaincourt disturbed me greatly, not least because I feared he might recognise me as a member of Gloucester's household and give the lie to my travelling minstrel disguise. Yet after a moment's reflection I considered that though I had seen him many times when accompanying my lord of Gloucester to Court, it was unlikely that he would have taken special note of me. My origins were far too obscure for me to have been called to his notice and in any case, whenever I was with Dickon at Court I made it my habit to disappear into the background.

Moreover, I had never exchanged so much as a word with Rivers. At the very most I had encountered him once or twice in a passageway at Westminster, at which times I had pressed myself against the wall until the great lord had passed me by, as befits a man of no account. I could think of no occasion when I might have given him cause to remark me and thus considered myself safe from recognition.

Feeling a degree of certainty that he would not know my face, I then set to worrying lest he knew my name. Perhaps after all it been a mistake to give my real name when I arrived at Plaincourt. Yet after some thought I dismissed this notion also, chiding myself for being so vain as to imagine that the powerful Earl would even have heard, much less remembered, that the Duke of Gloucester had an insignificant boyhood friend called Francis Cranley.

Even so, the Earl's arrival made me uneasy for it proved that the association between the Woodvilles and the Plaincourts was far stronger than I had anticipated. As the King's close friend, the expectation would be for Rivers to spend Christmastide at Court. That he had chosen instead to spend it at the remote Lincolnshire house of a knight with no known political influence struck me as little short of incredible.

Deep in thought, I was about to leave my observation post when Blanche appeared from the direction of the kitchen with a look of sharp consternation disfiguring her fair face.

""There you are, knave," she shrilled at me, "it's time you stopped loitering about and started earning your keep. Sir Stephen and my lord Rivers will be dining shortly and I believe some soothing music would please them greatly.

"I only hope for your sake that you are capable of providing it!" she added in an angry hiss.

I was amused to notice that the seductive, confiding manner in which she had spoken to me the previous evening had now been replaced by shrewish shrieking. Showing your tavern origins there, my girl, I thought, fully aware that anxiety was making Blanche forget to be pleasant. Plaincourt's unexpectedly early arrival had caught her unawares and set her at a disadvantage.

I noted that while she remained beautiful she was not

looking her best. Beneath those violet eyes there were dark, disfiguring shadows and thick coils of hair were escaping from her headdress. Sniffing discreetly, I again smelt on her skin the cloying scent of roses I disliked so much and beneath that I detected a slightly stale air. In spite of myself I was almost moved to pity her for having to entertain an important guest whilst suffering the ill effects of too much wine.

"I gather your betrothed has returned sooner than you anticipated," I remarked pleasantly, falling in with her as she made her way through the kitchen, into the passage and onwards to her lodging above the buttery, thereby making sure not to encounter Sir Stephen and Rivers as they entered the house from the front.

"Did he not warn you he would be returning in such exalted company?"

"He did not," she snapped, shooting me such a black look that I deemed it prudent to leave off baiting her. Excusing myself on the genuine grounds of needing to fetch my instrument, I ran hotfoot up the staircase towards my apartment. As I passed along the corridor I noticed that the ornately carved door of the largest guest chamber was flung wide.

Peering in, I saw three women hurrying to make the place ready. Two of them I recognised; Cuckoo was sweeping the floor while Dulcy, the old washerwoman, was labouring to place fresh sheets upon the bed. The third, who was sprinkling the pillows with what I took to be rosewater, I had not seen before yet I guessed her identity all the same. A handsome woman who looked much like an older, less downtrodden version of Cuckoo, she had to be Letice Flood, doubtless summoned from the village to lend a hand with the hurried preparations. The three were too absorbed in their work to notice me so I lingered for a few moments, taking in the opulence of the furnishings.

The chamber was dominated by an enormous tester bed hung on three sides with embroidered hangings of green silk. Atop it was a white and green damask bedspread piled high at the head of the bed with velvet and satin cushions. A large arras rug covered most of the floor and rich tapestry hangings brought colour and warmth to the walls. By the fire - which was significantly larger than the one I had been pleased to find in my own chamber - a small table was set with writing implements and a psalter covered in ruby velvet. Lying at the foot of the great bed was a low truckle for the Earl's body servant to occupy.

It was a chamber every bit as fine as that occupied by my lord of Gloucester at Middleham. Struck once again by the opulence on show at Plaincourt, I marvelled that a remote manor house could offer accommodation to rival that of the King's own brother.

Not wishing to be noticed, I tore my eyes away from the scene and hurried to my plainer quarters. Retrieving my lute from its case I made haste to the minstrel's gallery, arriving just in time to see Rivers and Plaincourt take their places on the dais. A moment later Blanche entered the hall and I saw that she had tidied her appearance and was now looking serene and demure. She had imprisoned the errant locks beneath her headdress and fixed a welcoming smile to her face but at such short notice there had been nothing she could do to disguise the dark circles beneath her eyes.

Chapter 9
Dinner with Lord Rivers

I watched with keen interest as Plaincourt greeted his intended with little evident pleasure, bestowing on her cheek a kiss both perfunctory and tentative. Rivers, by contrast, embraced her warmly and with real affection if I judged correctly. It was then I remembered that Blanche would be well acquainted with him, having spent her formative years within his mother's household. I saw him murmur in her ear some pleasantry that drew from her a throaty laugh. Then she spoke softly to both men and gestured towards the gallery. At the sight of me standing ready with my lute, they beamed their pleasure and signalled for me to begin.

The day yet lacked more than two hours to noon, making it full early for the dinner hour. Even so, Rolf had ensured that all was as it should be. A white linen cloth had been spread across the table and over this a sanap had been placed. Fat wax candles, a silver-gilt salt cellar and three richly enamelled and gilded cups stood in readiness on the table.

Demonstrating a finely tuned sense of courtesy, Sir Stephen graciously invited Rivers to take his own chair which now stood beneath a red silken baldaquin decorated with the Plaincourt wheat sheaves. With a shake of his head and a smile, Rivers modestly declined and instead took the place to his right. Immediately a servant I had not seen before sprang forward with brightly coloured cushions to pad the noble backside. Blanche sat to the left of her betrothed and after a short but noticeable hesitation the servant proffered cushions for her, also.

With the important folk seated the Earl's attendants placed themselves down one side of a hastily erected trestle table while the manor servants took the other. As the meal commenced I played and sang softly, caressing with pride the beautiful five course lute which had been a characteristically generous gift from Dickon last Twelfth Night. Sleek, long-necked and curvaceous as an Ottoman's concubine, it had been crafted by a master luthier from a far distant Alpine valley according to the London merchant who had sold it to my lord of Gloucester.

I loved my lute, in truth it was my most cherished possession though I knew it was too fine for my meagre talent. Nevertheless, since owning it I had been striving to improve my playing that I might one day become at least somewhere close to worthy of it. To this end I had recently learned to pluck the strings with my fingertips instead of with a quill. I found that this method, which had been brought to Court by musicians from France and Italy, was better suited to the seductive chansons I favoured. I began playing one of them now, guessing it was the kind of music my audience would find most pleasing.

Fortunately my guess proved to be accurate and more than once I noticed Rivers glance up at me with a look of surprised approval on his face. This granted me the opportunity to study him closely. I saw that despite his lean frame, he looked powerful and in robust health which was no wonder since he was known to be the greatest tournament champion at Edward's Court. Such men could never be weaklings.

His raiment was subdued in colour and fashion but marvellously rich in quality. Around his black velvet jerkin he wore a handsome silvered girdle and on his hand I spied a splendid ring of gold and emerald. As he ate, I saw that he took great pains to be attentive to Mistress Blanche, drawing her into his conversation and smiling fondly at her from time to time. I could not help but wonder how his lady wife would feel if she knew of the unnecessarily elaborate attention her husband was paying to his mother's former attendant.

According to Court gossip, Elizabeth Scales - a baroness in her own right having inherited the title from her father - was something of a virago. She would not expect her husband to be faithful to her, of course; few noble ladies were foolish enough to expect that but good manners dictated that spousal infidelities should be conducted with discretion.

Rivers' attentive behaviour to Blanche was insufficient reason for me to believe that he was tupping her but nonetheless it did give me pause. There would have been ample opportunity for them to begin a liaison while Blanche resided with his mother. Furthermore, if Sir Stephen knew or suspected there was aught improper in their relationship, it would explain his lack of warmth towards his betrothed.

As the meal progressed, sharp belly pangs served to remind me that I'd had naught to eat that day but the mite of bread I'd cadged from Jem Flood. I watched with envy as first the baked herrings and then the pike were set before the company, and by the time the pickled sturgeon appeared my mouth was watering so much I found it hard to sing. Fortuitously, at this very moment a servant arrived with a message from the master. I was to present myself before him without delay.

Descending with alacrity from the gallery, I made my way to the dais and bowed low before my betters. Sir Stephen accepted my obeisance and indicated that I might sit and, better yet from my point of view, signalled to a servant that a place should be set for me at the table alongside Mistress Blanche. I eyed the sturgeon hungrily, yet knew I must stifle my impulse to eat until Sir Stephen had said his piece to me.

To my surprise, he began by paying me a compliment.

"Good man, you play most elegantly and I find your voice harmonious to the ear," he said cordially.

To me this affirmed that the pompous fool knew little about good musicianship. Yet I noticed that Rivers was nodding his head in apparent agreement, and he was renowned as a connoisseur of the arts.

"I am told you intend to make for London," Plaincourt continued, "where you seek a new position. But it would gratify me if you would delay your leaving until after Christmas, for my most noble friend " - here he bent his head in the direction of Rivers - "and I have a fancy for some musical Yuletide diversions and we feel you will do very well. You may be sure that you will be recompensed most generously."

From his tone I could tell he was in no doubt that I would acquiesce to his request. He struck me as the kind of man who rarely failed to have his whims satisfied and this irritated me. For a reckless moment I toyed with the notion of declining his invitation simply that I might have the pleasure of seeing the annoyance such an impertinence would provoke. Happily, however, good sense prevailed. Since my secret work was far from complete at Plaincourt, an invitation to stay was precisely what I needed so I accepted his offer with fulsome thanks.

Having resolved the matter of musical entertainment to his satisfaction, Plaincourt removed his attention from me and began attending to a little speech Blanche was making to Rivers. I listened also, whilst hungrily piling sturgeon into my dish, and was in time to hear her say how honoured she was that the noble Earl had come all the way to Plaincourt for her wedding.

"Although why I should wonder at it I do not know," she prattled, "for your dear lady mother and all your kin were ever most kind to me."

In response Rivers smiled vaguely but made no reply. Blanche tried again, this time stating that his presence at the nuptials would make her feel that she had family present. Still Rivers maintained his silence. By now obviously disconcerted, Blanche gazed at him for a heartbeat, then turned and stared enquiringly at her betrothed.

"Mistress," he began in a tone several degrees frostier than the one he had used when addressing me, "I had hoped to be able to discuss this matter with you in private. Yet now it seems I must explain.

"Out of respect for my poor dead nephew I have with regret decided that our marriage must be postponed. It hardly seems the appropriate time to celebrate a wedding with the lad so newly deceased. I know that when you have reflected awhile you will feel as I do."

As he finished there was a long, uncomfortable silence.

Blanche looked stricken and made as if to remonstrate but checked herself with visible effort. Glancing at Rivers through lowered eyelids I saw that he was regarding Blanche with pity. It was plain that he had already known the wedding was to be postponed. Leaping to fill the awkward pause, he ventured that nothing would give him greater pleasure than to be present at the wedding of his friend and his late mother's lady, and therefore he would do all in his power to return to Plaincourt when a new date had been set.

Smoothly changing the subject, he then spoke a few gallant words in praise of Blanche's beauty, claiming he had never before seen her look better. I assumed this must be untrue; Blanche had looked tired at the start of the meal and now, since learning of her wedding's postponement, she had a face as sour as month-old ale. Yet Rivers appeared not to notice and continued to converse with her as if all were well.

"Though trifling, the private affairs that brought me to Lincolnshire took longer than I had anticipated," he told her.

"Now I am weary, so I have determined to spend a part of the Yuletide season here with my good friends at Plaincourt Manor. I have sent a messenger to convey this news to the King and Queen, and also of course to my lady wife. I doubt not that they will contrive to manage full well without me," he finished, his handsome features assuming a self-deprecating expression.

As was expected, Sir Stephen and Blanche rushed to remonstrate, assuring Rivers that his absence would be felt most keenly by his royal kin. Plaincourt either genuinely meant what he said or else his talent for flattery far surpassed my own because there was the ring of sincerity in what he said. Blanche, however, spoke flatly and as if the words cost her a great effort.

This I could understand for I knew full well how desperate she was to finally throw off the handicap of her humble status by becoming Plaincourt's wife. The unwelcome news of her wedding's postponement had hit her hard. Indeed she probably suspected, as did I by this time, that her betrothed might even be hoping to extend the delay indefinitely. Whatever had prompted him to attach her affections in the first place, there could be little doubt that Plaincourt now wished most heartily to be free of her. The sympathy in Rivers' eyes as he looked at Blanche told me that he was well aware of this fact and cared deeply enough for her to feel sorry.

Almost from my first arrival at Plaincourt I had wondered how Mistress Blanche the humble waiting woman had come to be the master's intended wife. Now, though many of the details remained unclear, I thought I understood how the unlikely match had been brokered. Unlikely not only on account of Blanche's birth but also her dismal lack of fortune.

"Plaincourt heirs are allus born knowing 'tis their duty to wed a fortune," Rolf had told me earlier, yet Blanche St Honorine de Flers could bring nothing to her future husband but her beauty and her wits.

Plainly, she had found some other way to win her man. I remembered that William, Geoffrey's father, had married his Philippa for love. I had wanted to believe that Sir Stephen had succumbed to the same malady when Blanche had been given a place at the manor through the connivance of Jacquetta of Bedford. Improbable as it seemed, I had just about been able to entertain the notion until I witnessed the coldness of Plaincourt's manner with her. Such behaviour was clearly at odds with the idea of a man so besotted that he was prepared to overlook her woeful lack of fortune.

Now I could only conclude that a bargain had been struck before Blanche ever set foot at Plaincourt. She had been sent to Plaincourt to perform some great service for Sir Stephen and in return he agreed to make her his wife. The nature of that service I had suspected for some time although I confess I had been reluctant to think her capable of such heartlessness.

I was considering all this when I heard my name called by Rivers. It was no small surprise to find myself addressed by the great man and my first thought was that he had suddenly recalled having seen my face before. Yet when I looked at him his expression was benign.

"This is a handsome lute that you have, master minstrel" he said, his voice smooth and rich as butter. "I can't think I have ever seen a finer example save at Court."

His interest made my skin prickle but I managed to keep my composure as I answered him.

"As to that I cannot say, my lord, but 'tis certain it cost a pretty penny," I laughed with all the nonchalance I could summon.

"Then how came you by it?" he returned. "Forgive my curiosity and my bluntness but you pique my interest. You dress according to your station yet your instrument was crafted for higher purpose."

Luckily I had been prepared for such a question and had an answer ready to hand.

"You have the right of it, my lord. My poor lute deserves a master far greater than I, and had not my old mother died and left me her pie shop, I should never have afforded it."

On the surface Rivers seemed to accept this, yet still I was aware of his close scrutiny. He knows me, I thought with alarm, it can only be that he knows me.

"So you sold the pie shop to pay for the lute?" he asked. "Whatever would your old mother have said to that?"

"Why, that a minstrel cannot play pastry!" I quipped nonsensically, and to my enormous relief Rivers appeared amused.

"Perchance a fishmongery would have been a bequest more to your liking," he observed, glancing with meaning at my dish which I had emptied of sturgeon at indelicate speed.

"Ah," I countered, "but playing gives a man a great appetite, my lord. Why, when I sat down to eat, I was so famished that I would have gladly devoured anything, even one of mother's miracle pasties."

"A curious sounding delicacy," Sir Stephen interjected. "Pray tell why were they so named?"

"With pleasure, my lord. Because for any that ate them, 'twas no less than a miracle if they survived."

It was a foolish joke but Rivers gratified me by laughing loudly. For a heartbeat I felt safe and then he fixed me again with his alert green gaze.

"The musicians at Court are passing skilled," he remarked conversationally, "yet I feel it is always well to keep things fresh by bringing forth new talent. You have skill and you amuse me, Cranley, so I think I will help you find your place at Court. You will ride with me when I leave for London and I shall see what can be done. Mayhap Her Grace my sister could use you."

Now I was really concerned. Rivers was showing far too much interest in me and it could only mean that I had been found out. I was not for a moment taken in by his offer to get me a position with the Queen. If I was fool enough to leave Plaincourt in company with Rivers and his men, I did not fancy my chances of reaching London unharmed or even alive. More than likely I'd end my days in a roadside ditch with a knife sticking out of my back. Yet why did he toy with me in this fashion instead of revealing my true identity to the assembled company? I could not fathom his motive.

Another worry was that Plaincourt was suddenly glaring at me with evident hostility, all trace of his former cordiality quite vanished. This led me to the suspicion that his earlier amiability had been naught but a ruse to catch me off guard. I had a strong inkling that this did not bode well for my safety.

I was endeavouring to think of a strategy to extricate myself from this mess when Sir Stephen rose, indicating that the meal was over. As he and Rivers retired to the solar for some private discourse, Blanche mumbled to no one in particular that she had matters to attend to in her chamber. I had little doubt that these matters would involve weeping furiously over the blow she had just been dealt.

Out of courtesy I accompanied her as far as the buttery, commenting delicately as we walked that she seemed less indisposed than when I'd seen her earlier.

"You forget my training," she said, sounding weary and low in spirits. "One of the first things I ever learned from

Mistress Margery was how to remedy wine fever with an infusion of milk thistle.

"Now it would please me if you would be silent, Francis," she continued. "In truth I crave solitude for the nonce."

"Then I will bid you farewell," I said, sketching her a small bow and heading back towards the kitchen where I hoped to find some answers. The time for treading daintily had past, now I must find a way to ferret out the truth.

Chapter 10
Cranley in Peril

I found the kitchen servants taking their ease at the table. Cuckoo leapt nervously to her feet when I entered but after glancing up and seeing it was none more important than I that disturbed them, Flood and Matthew remained as they were, legs sprawled out in front of them.

"You dost find us taking a short respite from our labours, Master Cranley," Flood called out to me by way of greeting.

"And why not, for it is most well-deserved. Lord Rivers was exceeding gracious about the pike. I overhead him compliment Sir Stephen on the excellence of his kitchen," I lied smoothly.

I ventured this flattery in the hope that it would encourage the fellow to overcome any resentment he might still harbour towards me for taking control of the dinner arrangements earlier when he had lost his head. Although my quick thinking had saved him from Sir Stephen's ire, I knew better than to expect any gratitude. No cook will suffer gladly to be ordered within his own domain.

As I had hoped, the flattery worked and I was asked to join Flood in a mug of ale. At once Cuckoo raced to fetch it for me, tripping over the hem of her greasy flannel gown as she ran. It struck me that whenever I saw the wench she was either motionless or making unnecessary haste – it seemed there was nothing between the two extremes.

When she placed the ale before me I thanked her for her trouble and, thinking to be kind, remarked that hurrying agreed with her for it had brought a lovely bloom to her cheeks. Her eyes widened and she turned her head away from me but not before I noticed a small smile light up her face. In truth she really was a pretty little thing, or could have been in happier circumstances. Too pale and bony for my taste, yet fairer all the same than many heiresses I knew who were named beauties solely on account of their fat dowries.

I supped my ale in companionable silence for a minute or

two, smacking my lips to demonstrate my appreciation. When the cup was drained, Flood ordered Cuckoo to refill it and to bring more for him, also. Matthew declined a second cup and I was unaccountably pleased to see that the lad was abstemious in his habits.

"You do well to take your ease when you can." I remarked to Flood. "Know you that Lord Rivers has stated his intention to spend Yuletide, or a least part of it, here at Plaincourt? With all these extra mouths to feed and a noble lord to gratify with fine dishes, I fancy you'll have little enough time for leisure. Think you the steward will take on extra hands to help?"

"Rolf dost say that steward's biding at the master's manor of Ringthorpe for the by, seeing to some repairs. But we'll do well enough," he continued comfortably, "the village dost have plenty of lads that'll gladly take a turn in my kitchen for no more'n a full belly and a sup of ale.

"Thee dost not need fret on my account, Master Cranley, 'twas only the unexpectedness of the master's arrival, and with such noble company, that didst throw me and have me a-fluster. Since I didst have time to order my thoughts some I dost know how I shall manage. There are three more days of fish to go and then I dost mean to prepare the finest feast Plaincourt didst see in many a-year. Venison, coney, peacock and partridge, I dost have them all in hand, aye and subtleties too, so cunning and tasty Lord Rivers'll likely think himself back at Court."

His talk of feasting gave me the opportunity to raise the subject uppermost in my mind.

"Will not the recent death of Sir Stephen's nephew put a curb on such festivities?" I enquired innocently. "I heard the boy was full young to die. It seems a tragic case."

"So it were," Flood agreed hurriedly, "so it were. But if thee dost ask me, it were better for him had he died when still a bairn, for all the joy he didst have out of life. Poor Geoffrey never were strong, and as he didst grow older he didst become ever more maungey and didst have to keep to his chamber. I didst hardly see him after that, none of us did, but I didst hear it said his illness made him suffer greatly, God rest his soul."

At mention of Geoffrey's name both Matthew and Cuckoo looked grave and I wondered if this was out of simple respect or because they remembered that the lad had been their half-nephew.

"Who tended the boy if none of you ever saw him?" I ventured to ask.

"An ugly great brute name of Pretty Will," Flood answered, "a stranger to these parts. Master didst take him on to be young Geoffrey's body servant. Will Yorke's his given name but Master didst bid us call him Pretty Will, why I dost know not save that it tickled him to hear the ill-favoured man so-called."

"Who knows why fine folk do anything?" I asked philosophically. "Their ways are different to the ways of ordinary folk like you and I, Jem Flood."

Flood nodded his head in absent agreement but Matthew broke urgently in to the conversation.

"Aye, but we all dost know for why Pretty Will were hired. Master didst think to hurry him into his grave by landing him with such a one."

I looked at the kitchen boy in alarm, concerned that he had spoken too freely and would suffer for it. Yet the ale had unbent Flood and he at once lent credence to the boy's words.

"Matthew dost have the right of it," he said. "'Tis common knowledge that Master were eager for Geoffrey to be gone but it wouldst not do for him to dirty his hands by harming the boy himself. Job didst need to be handled in such a way as wouldst earn him no reproach. I dost fancy it were his notion that a spell of rough-handling from Pretty Will would bring about the boy's end soon enough."

The cook snorted with contemptuous laughter.

"That didst backfire on him right an proper, for it didst turn out that great ugly beast has a heart soft as butter. 'Stead of hastening Geoffrey's death it is my view he didst prolong his life by treating him kinder than the little scrap didst ever get treated afore."

Cuckoo nodded her head in fervent agreement.

"'Tis true," she put in hurriedly. "Only times Pretty Will ever didst talk to any of us it were to seek some comfort for poor Geoffrey.

"No little matter were too small for his attention, he were allus badgering folk with his wants. Old Dulcy were to be sure to air Geoffrey's sheets most careful-like and sprinkle them with the lavender water he didst favour. Pa here, he were told to make for Geoffrey a special kind of strengthening posset. Why even the grooms didst not escape his commands, for they were bid to exercise the pretty brown mare Geoffrey liked 'neath his window so he might look upon it.

"I tells thee, master, we were all sore afeared for Geoffrey when Pretty Will first come to us but we didst never dare say nothing. Then when we didst see that he didst mean him no harm we were right glad for it didst mean that Geoffrey had a friend to look out for him."

It was the longest speech I had heard Cuckoo make since my arrival at Plaincourt. Mostly she just said yes and no; for her to speak out now and at length about Geoffrey must indicate she felt strongly about his murder, I thought. Yet I remembered what Fielding had said about all of the manor servants apart from Matthew seeming indifferent to the boy.

I decided to test if this was a tender spot.

"Did not any of you look out for him, then?" I asked, and the girl had the grace to redden and look at her feet.

"It weren't no place of ours to interfere," Flood interjected angrily. "We didst not like what we saw happ'ning but we didst know there were nowt could be done to help it. It were different for Pretty Will, not being a Plaincourt man he weren't bound to please the master like we are. I dost tell thee, master minstrel, twould've been the worse for us if ever we'd tried to aid young Geoffrey."

I saw that he had a point and in any case realised I would achieve nothing by alienating the man so I made a placatory remark and then continued with my questioning.

"How then did the boy come to die, with such a tender servant to care for him? Did his sickness finally break him?"

"No," Flood replied, "it were not the sickness that didst take him. Geoffrey were murdered most foully in his bed. And Pretty Will, he didst take the blame. Sir Stephen didst have him bound and locked up quick-smart. 'Tis well for him he didst find a way to escape else the poor devil would've hanged for it. I say poor devil for all I didst not care for the man, since none of us at Plaincourt dost believe in his guilt."

"Then who?" I asked eagerly, too eagerly perhaps, for Flood's face took on a wary expression.

"Who can say, Master Cranley, who can say? But I'll give thee some advice as a kindness to thee. At Plaincourt 'tis not healthy to ask so many questions, if thee dost take my meaning. Not if thee's a wish to keep that handsome face of thine."

Disregarding this advice - and unsure as to whether it had been issued as a threat or a friendly warning - I pressed on with my next question.

"What say you to talk I've heard that this Pretty Will had carnal knowledge with Mistress Blanche?" I enquired, incautiously revealing that I had already heard of the man before beginning my questions. Fortunately, what I'd said occasioned Flood so much mirth that he all but choked on his ale and in his distraction failed to note my slip. It was some moments before he could speak.

"Who's been peddling thee that doggerybaw? Whoever 'twas, they didst make jest with thee or else they dost have lost their wits! Why, I'll wager dainty Mistress Blanche would sooner fornicate with old Rolf than with that gargoyle."

He laughed again but I noticed that neither Matthew or Cuckoo joined in. Then Cuckoo spoke up, rushing her words to get them out before the cook could silence her.

"I didst spy Mistress Blanche a-sneaking back to her chamber the night Pretty Will got free. She dost sleep over the buttery, see, and I could not rest easy on account of being troubled about poor Master Geoffrey, so I didst leave the fireside to take some air. I saw her then, and though it were dark I didst know it were she for she didst carry a lantern and I could see her wicked face clear as day.

"Not wishing her to see me, for she dost frit me something dreadful with her strange ways, I didst slip into the shadows as she didst pass me by. Then I didst go back to the kitchen and thought no more of it 'til the alarm were raised that Pretty Will had fled."

Quickly, I asked her if she had spoken to anyone of what she had seen but Flood cut off her reply.

"Hold thy tongue, thee stupid little bitch!" he yelled at the trembling girl. "Thee's said more'n enough already. Wants thee to end like Master Geoffrey, eh?"

The terrified chit sobbed and slowly backed away from Flood. Then it was my turn to be on the receiving end of the cook's aggression.

"Now, Master Cranley, I dost think I've had a bellyful of thy snooping," he snarled at me. "I'll thank thee to be gone from my kitchin for thee's welcome here no longer."

He rose to his feet and moved towards me, as if intent on ushering me out with physical force, then stopped as he caught my eye. He's a big fellow, I thought, not taller but broader than me but I could best him in a struggle and he knows it. Matthew rose also, his fists clenched and his face tense. As he met my gaze he moved his eyes imperceptibly towards the doorway. I realised he was advising me to make myself scarce lest Flood should become more agitated.

I was unwilling to go, for I felt I had made progress and was, perhaps, on the verge of discovering something significant. Yet little would be gained now Flood had his hackles raised. Gathering my dignity, I stood up, filched a handful of raisins from a bowl on the table and then, as casually as possible, ambled from the room whilst bidding them good day through a mouthful of the sweet fruit.

At first I considered retiring to my chamber in order to contemplate all I had learned that day but on reflection decided that some clear air would benefit my thinking. Thus I ignored the passageway leading to the hall and chose instead to go outside to the kitchen garden. There I stood for some time, breathing in the mingled aroma of cabbage and mud and going over in my head the strands of information I had gleaned.

One thing in particular puzzled me. Flood had been speaking freely until Cuckoo mentioned seeing Blanche moving mysteriously about the manor the night of Will's escape. Thereafter he had erupted into anger. I had little doubt the anger had been provoked by fear but of whom was the volatile fellow afraid?

Sir Stephen seemed the obvious answer but even so I was not sure. For one thing, the manor and village people seemed so accustomed to the injustice of Plaincourt rule that had they witnessed their master murder Geoffrey with his bare hands, I believed they would not have thought to speak out against him. I could tell that centuries of dominance had ingrained in them a sense of hopeless resignation. Like dumb animals they accepted that oft-times their Plaincourt masters did evil things. The best they could hope was that those evil things would have little impact on their own lives.

Put another way, even though the common folk knew very well that Plaincourt had desired his nephew's death, they would never directly accuse him of murdering the lad. Sir Stephen would understand this. He would know that he was assured of the villagers' loyalty come what may, in the way that a cruel man who whips his dog knows that when called the cur will always come cringing to his side.

Since he had no reason to question the loyalty of someone like Jem Flood, a Plaincourt man born and bred, I reasoned that Flood surely had nothing to fear from Sir Stephen. Yet the cook was desperately afraid of someone, of that I was certain, and as far as I could tell there were just three possible candidates – Rivers, Blanche, and me.

I immediately dismissed Rivers from my calculations for the Earl had not been present at Plaincourt when Geoffrey was killed. In any case it was scarcely credible that Flood would suspect the King's brother-in-law of skulking outside his kitchen door in the hope of overhearing scurrilous gossip concerning their master. Even I could not think this of him, and I was more than ready to follow my friend Dickon's lead in thinking ill of the noble Earl.

So then, Flood was afraid of either Blanche or me. It was possible, I acknowledged, that my appearance at Plaincourt and subsequent interest in Geoffrey's death might have given the man reason to be suspicious of me. He might well believe that my true purpose in visiting the manor was to delve into the matter but why should that frighten him? I could think of one reason only, namely that he was involved in the murder.

It was possible, that was certain. He was a strong fellow, and he had readily given me his opinion that Geoffrey should have died when he was much younger. The only trouble with this hypothesis was that I thought I already knew the identity of the murderer and it was not him.

So, if not Rivers and not me, then it was Blanche who struck terror into Flood's heart. From something Cuckoo had said earlier I knew that she also feared the master's betrothed. Me too, I thought, me too, for I was now quite convinced that the exquisite Blanche St Honorine du Flers was naught but a black-hearted murderess.

When my nostrils could suffer the stink of cabbage no longer I quit the kitchen garden and headed back into the house. I made my way to the hall, intent on retrieving my lute from the dais where I had left it after dinner. Before I set foot on the dais, however, I was apprehended by a snivelling, ill-nourished urchin who tugged at my sleeve and told me I was needed at once in the stable.

"Who needs me?" I demanded to know but the snot-nosed squirt ignored the question and stupidly repeated his message.

"Thee's to come at once t'stables," he said again, "and be quick wi'it!"

To emphasise the urgency of the matter he pulled at my

wrist and, realising he was not going to say any more, I made to go with him. At once he let go of my hand and shot in front of me, crossing the hall and bolting through the doorway before I had taken five steps.

Grinning at the oddness of his behaviour I followed at a brisk enough pace, wondering idly what emergency could require my presence in the stables. My borrowed rouncey had seemed hale enough the last time I had looked in on it but mayhap it had been eating too richly and had taken a colic. Musing that I was the last person to know what to do in such a circumstance, I had made it as far as the kennels when a massive figure ducked out from a behind a wall and stood four-square in front of me, blocking my way. Thickset, with a ludicrously bushy black beard and granite countenance, this was no one I'd yet encountered at Plaincourt.

Realising at once that I was being ambushed, I turned sharply on my heel only to see with sinking heart that another bearded and thickly muscled brute, the virtual double of the first, had already taken position behind me. Glancing about the courtyard for a friendlier face, I saw the place was deserted save for my would-be assailants.

Deciding that making a run for it was my best option, I made a forward feint and then dodged sideways but the bristle-faced scoundrel in front of me read my intention and grabbed my arms. As he held me, the second delivered a vicious punch to my abdomen, winding me sufficiently so that they were able to manhandle me behind the kennels where they preceded to lay about me with their fists and boots.

So swift and vicious was their onslaught that I found myself wholly unable to retaliate. No sooner did I try to rise to my feet than another blow would catch me on the chin, in the gut or on the rump and I would find myself kissing dirt. As blow upon blow rained down on me I knew extreme pain but even then the real damage was to my pride. Drawing ragged breaths, I cursed my attackers as loudly as I could manage but inside I cursed my own foolishness for falling into their trap.

I know not whether their intention was to beat me to death or simply render me senseless. I was saved from either fate by the ruckus the hounds set up, excited by my grunts of pain, the scent of blood or both. Their barking disturbed the kennelman who from some unknown location across the courtyard flung at the agitated beasts an angry imprecation to be silent. Blessedly, the hounds ignored his command and so some moments later his footsteps could be heard approaching the kennels.

The fellow's advent persuaded my assailants that the time had come for them to leave off my beating, enjoyable as it had so obviously been for them. One last cruel kick to the head sent me sprawling face down in the dust and then they were gone.

When the kennelman discovered me, he swore softly and then quieted the hounds with a few words of reassurance. When they had fallen silent he surveyed me and then, with commendable lack of drama, asked if I thought I could stand. Nodding, I stretched out my right arm and suffered him to raise me gently to my feet. I felt dazed and unsteady but also overwhelmingly relieved to be breathing still.

Gingerly assessing my injuries, I ascertained that I was bleeding freely and would soon have bruises all over my body. Mercifully, however, I detected no broken bones and saw that apart from a few grazes my hands were unscathed. For this I gave heartfelt thanks to Saint Cecilia, the patron saint of musicians, since hands are of utmost importance to a lutenist.

The kennelman offered to walk with me to the house but I declined his help as graciously as my swollen lips could manage. Though he had been my saviour, I sensed in him a reluctance to become further embroiled in my affairs and in truth I could scarce blame him for it. Yesterday when we'd met, Matthew had said I looked like trouble and now I had proved his point. Yet before I released the kennelman there was one question I needed to ask him.

"Did you know the hairy bastards who did this to me?" I

asked hopefully. "I saw their faces but cannot place them. I think they must be newly arrived at Plaincourt for I have not seen them before."

"Sorry, master," the fellow answered gruffly but also, I thought, a touch apologetically, "I didst see no sign of anyone. Whoever it were, they didst scarper when they didst hear me coming. Now see thee dost take my advice, master, and get thyself safe to bed."

Aware that simple self-preservation would likely dissuade the fellow from disclosing the identity of my attackers even if he had seen them, I thanked him again for his assistance and limped back to the house. With no little effort I made it to the dais where I was piteously grateful to find my precious lute unharmed. If someone at Plaincourt wished to injure me, I conjectured they could find no better way to achieve their aim than by damaging my instrument. Luckily, my enemy - whoever that was – had been unaware of this fact. Thanking God and the saints for this blessing at least, I picked up the lute and then made my way slowly and painfully up to my apartment. Intent on further examination of my wounds, instead I found myself seized by such deep fatigue that I lay as I was in my bloodied state and slept.

I woke some while later, stiff and sore in body but sufficiently rested in mind to start considering who might have instigated my beating. Running through a list of possible names in my head, I came to the conclusion that the likeliest candidate had to be Rivers. Having recognised me as a friend of the Duke of Gloucester, the Earl must have wondered why I was peddling a different story about my identity. Either he suspected that my motive in coming to Plaincourt was to stir up trouble for his friend, or he was simply inclined to dislike me for being close to Gloucester. Whichever way, I guessed that he had charged two of his most brutish retainers with giving me a thrashing, maybe to frighten me into an abrupt departure or to kill me outright.

In support of this supposition was the fact that both attackers had been strangers to me. I was wholly certain I had seen neither of them before and this served to convince me that they must have arrived with Rivers. It did strike me as curious that I had not remarked these conspicuous characters sitting with the Earl's other retainers at dinner. However, for much of that time I had been occupied on the gallery, my concentration focused on endeavouring not to disgrace myself with poor musicianship whilst simultaneously paying close attention to the people on the dais. Was it any wonder, then, that I had failed to notice a couple of boorish henchmen who would in any case have likely been seated far from the main table?

Satisfied with my conclusion that Rivers had ordered the attack, I considered the implications to my investigation. Common sense dictated that I should quit Plaincourt with all speed since my life was clearly in danger, yet I baulked at the idea of leaving without a resolution of the matter for my lord of Gloucester. As my mind fussed and fretted with the problem it became apparent that my faculties were not as refreshed as I had supposed and within a short while I began to doze.

I was roused from my slumbers by a loud hammering outside the chamber. Swearing softly, I rose groggily to my feet and threw open the door. Rolf stood before me, the look of comical indignation on his face giving way to shock when he beheld the condition I was in.

"Blessed Saint Oswald!" he spluttered. "What mischief didst befall thee?"

So I look bad enough to startle Old Shuffler, I thought ruefully. That's not reassuring. Without waiting for my answer, the old servant pulled at my bloodied gown.

"What to do, what to do?" he muttered anxiously. "'Tis certain thee didst not ought to be seen in this, yet thee's wanted in't hall this very instant.

"Well, there's nowt to be done, thee must come as thee is and make answer for thyself as best thee can."

"Who wants me in the hall, and why?" I asked, resisting his feeble attempts to tug me from the chamber by my sleeves.

154

"Why dost thee ask such a fool question?" the old man snapped. "'Tis the supper hour, thee's a minstrel and the company dost desire that thee play. Now dost thee come or would thee have me tell Master thee dost prefer to lie abed?"

"Aye, I'll come," I said curtly, "but I'll not bring my lute for I doubt I could hold it to play."

"As thee will," Rolf answered, and then commenced a slow shuffle back towards the hall. I followed, thankful for once for his sluggish pace since it meant that my aching limbs did not need to move more quickly than they were able.

At the bottom of the staircase I paused for a moment to gather my thoughts. I was aware that I might be walking back into danger, though I doubted that Rivers would authorise a public attack, in which case I should be safe enough for the time being. Yet as I approached the dais my theory that the noble Earl had ordered the beating was set on its head.

"What's this?" he called out as he took note of my cuts and bloodied clothing. "Master Cranley, who has done this you?"

Plaincourt, Rivers and Blanche sat at the table as before. I attempted a bow and then winced, whereupon Rivers leapt from his bench and strode to my side.

"Here, man, take my arm," he ordered.

Obeying, I found myself guided to the place next to the Earl's.

"Who did this to you?" he demanded again. "Whoever it was must be punished severely. It is a monstrous affront to Sir Stephen's hospitality, aye and an affront to me, also, for I would hear you play again tonight and clearly you are in no condition to do so."

Well, I found myself thinking, this is passing strange. The very man I blame for my attack seems genuinely offended by it. I knew, of course, that he might have been feigning indignation yet his words and looks struck me as sincere.

Stealing a glance at Blanche I saw that she too looked aghast at the sight of my injuries. Rising purposefully, she walked to me and examined the marks on my face.

"You must return to your chamber at once, Master Cranley," she instructed. "Rolf, you are a sorry muttonhead to bring the minstrel in this condition. Send for a boy to help him back up to his apartment. Master Cranley, I will fetch some things from my still room to alleviate your discomfort. I'll attend you directly."

She swept from the hall on her dainty feet, pausing only to bob a respectful curtsey to Rivers. He gave her an appreciative smile and then turned his attention back to me.

"Now speak, man," he commanded, "tell us who did this to you?"

Before replying, I cast around the hall to see if the bully boys were present. Perhaps unsurprisingly, they were not.

"I saw their faces, my lord, but did not recognise them," I replied. "I was sent word that I was needed in the stables. On my way there I was jumped by two ugly brutes with beards down to their chests. They seemed to have a grudge against me, I know not why."

From the corner of my eye I saw the urchin who had delivered the message disappear beneath his trestle table. He was right to be afraid, for he had no way of knowing that I did not mean to land him in trouble. Very likely he hadn't understood that he was sending me to a beating and even if he had, I could not bring myself to blame him for grabbing the chance to earn a farthing. Further up the same table I spied the kennelman who had come to my aid. His face had reddened and he looked agitated.

"Then something, I know not what, disturbed the ruffians," I said loudly, "for they took off at speed, leaving me in the dust. When I was able, I made my way back to the manor."

Relief flooded the kennelman's face. A slight dip of his head signalled his thanks for leaving out his part in my rescue. Whether or no he had seen my aggressors it was plain he was unwilling to be questioned about the matter.

Rivers now turned his emerald gaze to his host who had not, I suddenly realised, uttered a word since I had entered the hall.

"What say you, Stephen?" he enquired, a little pointedly I thought. "How shall we uncover the guilty parties?"

Sir Stephen looked me over with ill-concealed dislike.

"I neither know nor care why this tiresome man was given a beating. Doubtless he offended someone and was punished for his impertinence. Really, my lord, I do not comprehend your interest in the fellow. Look at him – he's little better than a vagrant! The sooner he leaves Plaincourt the better."

From the expression on Rivers' face I gathered he was as astonished at Plaincourt's words as I.

"Stephen," he said very quietly, "I believe that you should care. It looks very ill that a man staying in your house, at your invitation, should be dealt with so ungently."

He would have said more but Sir Stephen rose abruptly and stalked haughtily from the hall. Silence fell at the lower tables and I knew I was not the only one present to marvel at Plaincourt's discourteous behaviour. I was wondering how this matter would resolve itself when Matthew appeared at my side.

"Come along now, master," he urged. "I'm come at Rolf's bidding to help thee to thy bed."

Cheered enormously by the sight of his pleasant face, I allowed him to lend me his support as I stood up.

"Take heart, Master Cranley," Rivers called to me as I quit the hall. "You'll come to no harm from now on, I vow, for I extend to you my own protection. Your ill-wishers should know that I'll regard any new attack on your person as an attack on me, and will deal with it accordingly."

With those puzzling words ringing in my ears I was escorted by Matthew back up the staircase and thence to the welcome solace of my chamber.

Chapter 11
A Nocturnal Visit

When Blanche arrived to tend my wounds I was more than ready for some answers.

"Who did this to me?" I demanded to know as she began to help me from my raiment.

"That's easily answered. From the description you gave of your attackers I'd say you have Walt and John Tench to thank for these injuries. But perhaps you would be wiser to ask who it was that ordered the beating."

Soon I was standing naked before her. I would have resisted her insistent hands as they pulled away my clothing but I was too far gone in pain and weariness to make the effort. In any case, she seemed insultingly disinterested in my manhood, flicking her violet eyes at and then away from it as if inspecting a tray of three-day old offal.

"Very well, then I will ask you. Who ordered my beating?" I continued, prompting her to make a small, impatient sound.

"Can you truly be such an innocent?" she asked, dabbing a soothing salve onto my cuts.

"This is made from myrrh and yarrow," she informed me though I cared not a whit. "It will ease the pain and encourage the wounds to heal cleanly."

"Aye, that's all very well," I said ungraciously, "but please explain your meaning. In what way am I an innocent?"

Deliberately ignoring me, she produced another concoction which she proceeded to apply with deft strokes to my bruises.

"Leopard's bane," the infuriating woman intoned. "To make the bruising hurt less and fade faster."

"Lady," I hissed through clenched teeth, "I swear if you do not answer me this instant I will call for help and then who knows but Lord Rivers himself will burst through the door and take you to task for tormenting me."

She smiled at this nonsensical idea and then folded her

hands into her lap and watched as I donned my clean shirt and breeches.

"Francis, without knowing it you have arrived at the crux of the matter. You ask who ordered your beating? Very well, it was my betrothed.

"Why should he do such a thing, you will ask next, to which I will answer, how can it be that you are so unworldly? Have you not understood that my future husband and the great Earl are of that curious persuasion of men that love their own sex?"

At these words I gaped at Blanche, too astonished to utter any words, and so she continued.

"Since they met several years since they have had, ah, what should I call it? Well, perhaps the genteel description is a friendship of the most intimate kind.

"It was at the house of the Lamberts, those famously wealthy goldsmiths who are close kin to Stephen. He was making his yearly visit to report on Geoffrey's progress, a visit you may be sure he begrudged most heartily, and my lord Rivers was there to select a pleasing trinket for his jewel-hungry sister. I believe they felt a strong surge of attraction for one another the moment they met.

"For Rivers, you understand, the liaison with Stephen is one of many such affairs. I should know, for when I lived with his lady mother I used often to carry messages from him to his favourites, arranging assignations or delivering little gifts to them. He chose me for this purpose because from childhood I was ever eager to please him and he knew I could be trusted not to spill his secrets. I do believe this is why he feels for me a certain fondness, though it is most likely the fondness a huntsman feels for his most obedient hound.

"Alas for Stephen, his love for Rivers is real and unequivocal. What he feels for him is naught less than a grand passion, a matter that rules his heart completely if not quite his head, for like the true Plaincourt he is, even in affairs of the heart he remains ever alert to the possibility of material advancement. Yet you may be certain that he worships the

Earl and guards the precious crumbs of time he has to share with him as jealously as a mother guards her daughter's chastity."

Recovering a little from the dumbfounding discovery that Plaincourt and Rivers were lovers, I now recalled that I had once overheard some vulgar tattle to the effect that the Earl had small use for the fairer sex. At the time I had paid it little heed for I believe all men have a right to their private affairs, however incomprehensible such affairs might seem to me. Also, I knew full well that great men are always targets for scurrilous stories. Great women also, come to that, for I had once heard a plainly ludicrous report that the pious Duchess Cecily had consorted with a common archer and that was how she got the King. That this was malicious nonsense I was in no doubt but as for the tale about Rivers, I saw now that there had been truth in it after all.

"But I still do not see why Plaincourt should wish me harm," I said stupidly.

In my defence, I had just been severely beaten and perhaps the blows I had taken to the head were impeding my faculties. Blanche realised this and answered me with exaggerated patience.

"Because Lord Rivers has taken a fancy to you, Francis, and Stephen has seen it. You have been asked to accompany the Earl to Court. It is a mark of extreme favour for one of your undistinguished rank and you may be sure he expects a particular favour of you in return.

"Small wonder my poor betrothed is mad with jealousy! Too soon he must watch his idol ride for London in company with you, a man both handsome and charming, if pitifully slow-witted."

"And Rivers knows it was Plaincourt who attempted to kill me," I interjected, eager to demonstrate that I was less feeble-minded than she supposed. "Surely this will anger the Earl. Will he not exact some revenge?"

Blanche laughed shortly.

"You flatter yourself, Francis," she mocked. "Handsome

you may be, but it is no more than a passing fancy my lord Rivers has taken to you. He is angry with Stephen, yes, for spoiling his pretty new toy but he will forgive him soon enough. And you exaggerate when you say he tried to kill you."

"How can you be so sure?" I demanded.

"Because you'd be dead if he'd wanted you so," she replied, but I cut across her words.

"No, I mean how can you be sure Rivers will forgive Plaincourt?" I asked. "I do not imagine that I am of the slightest import to the mighty Earl but I know that such men greatly mislike having their will interfered with. Will that not be sufficient reason for him to punish Plaincourt, if only by ending all intimacy with him?"

No," she said curtly, "it will not. The ties that bind them are too strong to be broken over such a trifling business."

Later I would remember her strange reluctance to discuss the matter further but at that moment the relevance of her intelligence about Rivers and Plaincourt was filtering into my brain. Indeed, Blanche could not have known it but her words were washing over me and soothing my mind just as her unguents would soon begin to soothe my hurts.

Rivers had not, as I had feared, connected me with my lord of Gloucester so therefore it was safe for me to continue with my investigation. The first glimmering of this welcome turn of events had come to me when the Earl's concern for my injuries had struck me as sincere, yet I had been unwilling to take his protestations of protection at face value. Blanche's surprising words showed me that I could, and my spirits soared. I had been dreading riding back to Middleham on the morrow with the matter unresolved, not for any fear of recrimination from Dickon but because I was ever loath to disappoint him. Now I knew I need not.

Then a new thought occurred to me.

"But what of you, Blanche?" I enquired. "How can you contemplate being tied to a man like that, a man with no appreciation for your feminine charms? He'll get an heir on you, no doubt, but there will be no joy in it, no happiness."

Her eyes narrowed and her features took on a stony cast.

"Oh believe me, I'd have happiness enough, for being the lady of Plaincourt Manor would give me all the security and comfort I have ever desired. But I do not believe that is going to happen now. Stephen is never going to marry me, for all that he made a solemn vow at the altar of St Oswald's that he would.

"I sense that his distaste for me grows stronger day by day. Saying he must delay our nuptials because of Geoffrey's death is arrant nonsense since they were only announced after the boy's death! He is merely questing for an excuse, however flimsy, to put off making me his wife. In due course he will find another reason, and then another, and on it will go, on and on, with me living here, hated by his people and hated by him too, if truth be known. I truly believe he would sooner die heirless than suffer me to be his wife."

There was so much emptiness in her voice that even though I suspected her of murder I could not help but pity her.

"Then what will you do?" I asked gently.

"I know not," she said bleakly, before collecting up her salves and ointments and bidding me goodnight.

When she had gone, I lowered myself onto the bed and found that already my aches were receding. My body still remembered the pounding it had taken but Blanche's ministrations had blunted the pain. Against my will I found myself impressed with her skill, dexterity and gentleness. She was a more than competent healer and had shown kindness in coming to repair the damage her intended's jealousy had inflicted on me. I found the thought troubling since I could not reconcile her tender care with the hideous murder I was certain she had committed.

Sighing, I turned cautiously onto my side and surrendered myself to slumber.

I knew not how much time had passed before I was awakened by a furtive scratching at my door. Groggy with sleep, my first impulse was to ignore the sound in the hope that it would cease. It did not. In fact the scratching became more insistent and as my alertness returned I comprehended that anyone who came to my door at dead of night must have a compelling reason for doing so. Reaching beneath the pillow for my rondel dagger, I swung my legs from the bed and rose silently to greet my uninvited guest.

I had opened the door the merest fraction when someone hurled themselves at it, forcing it open just wide enough to be able to push through into the chamber. Since all was darkness I could not yet make out who it was that desired to see me so urgently but a familiar scent gave me a strong clue. Earlier that day my nostrils had detected Blanche's heady rose concoction on another, filched, I surmised, when this individual had delivered a message to her at my behest. I did not like the fragrance and found it less pleasing still when combined with underlying odours of sweat and smoke and unwashed hair.

Lowering my dagger I slammed the door shut and pushed my visitor onto the bed.

"I'm weary, sore and in no mood for games," I said softly, "so you'll indulge me by stating your business without ado, Cuckoo."

Giving a nervous titter, the wench reached up to touch me but I roughly slapped her hand away and bade her keep her distance.

"Thee didst not ought to be like that, master," she whined. "I didst only come to see could I comfort thee some. I didst hear thee'd been hurt, see, and didst think mebbe I could make thee feel better."

Grimacing in the darkness, I told her that was a sweet thought and thanked her for it but said what I needed most at present was sleep. Pretending to take this as an invitation, she patted the bed and cooed at me to lie beside her.

"No, girl," I said sternly, "I mean it when I say I wish for naught but sleep. You had better go."

She giggled then and whispered that she would much

sooner stay.

"Thee likes me, master, I know thee dost. I seen the way thee dost look at me. And I dost like thee plenty, so here I be. I wants thee to have my maidenhead, master."

With a sick feeling I realised that the wretched girl had misread my small acts of kindness to her for lust when in fact they had been motivated by nothing stronger than pity. Now I would have to disabuse her of the notion that I desired her, for the thought of despoiling the poor, pathetic child was truly more than I could stomach.

Not wishing my rebuffal to hurt her feelings I spoke lightly to her.

"I do like you, Cuckoo, but not in the way you think. I think you are a fine, pretty girl, deserving of much more than a quick tumble with a rogue like me who'll be gone from the manor within a few days. And you should put a higher value on your maidenhead, else all too soon you'll find yourself landed with a fatherless child. Now go back to your fireside and, I pray you, put me from your mind."

"Dost thee reckon me not good enough for thee then, master minstrel?" she shot at me with an acerbity I guessed she'd learned from Flood, her adoptive father. "I suppose thee dost think thee's too fine to lie with the skivvy."

I should have remembered that kitchen drab or duchess, no woman likes to be rebuffed.

"You're wrong," I lied, aware that the ignorant chit had come painfully close to the truth, for I was most fastidious about where I took my pleasure. Like most men my age I would gladly lie with any comely, willing woman whatever her station in life, but only so long as I was satisfied she was clean, fragrant and, most important of all, free from the pox.

At that precise moment I did not feel equal to explaining my foibles to the girl so I took a different tack.

"Cuckoo, I cannot lie with you for my heart has been stolen by another and I find it is not in my power to be unfaithful to her."

I had hoped that this sentimental patter would appease

the unexpectedly wanton maid and allow her to leave my chamber with her pride intact. Instead, I saw to my horror that my words had managed to inflame her anger.

"So that's the way of it!" she screeched, lashing out and raking my cheek with her ragged fingernails.

My patience at an end, I caught hold of both her arms and twisted them ungently behind her back.

"Leave now, you foolish baggage, and I'll not report your assault to your betters," I told her in a voice choked with suppressed fury.

Bundling the enraged girl to the door, I managed to control her struggles long enough to shove her unceremoniously into the passageway and then collapsed wearily onto my bed. Perchance I should have dealt more patiently with Cuckoo but I had endured more than enough violence for one day and craved sleep as a starving man craves bread. Yet even after she had gone I was kept awake by the cloying stench of roses which hung obstinately in the air, as repugnant to me as a midden. Eventually I fell into a sleep troubled by dreams of corruption, blood and fire.

I woke next morning feeling little refreshed yet from the weak winter sun pouring in through my window I gathered I had been abed long enough. Rising carefully, I ventured to the hall which I found empty save for Rolf who was occupied brushing cobwebs from the baldaquin over Sir Stephen's seat. I greeted him affably and asked if the master had not yet risen.

"Risen and ridden," the creaky old codger answered. "Lord Rivers and Master, they didst take theirselves over to Mablethorpe where they dost mean to dine with Sir Thomas Fitzwilliam. I misdoubt us'll not see they again afore the morrow."

This intelligence told me that Blanche had been correct in her insistence that Rivers would not long remain angry with Stephen. I could only hope that his protection would hold sway in his absence as I had little wish to find myself preyed on once more by Sir Stephen's hairy bully boys. One thing was certain, I would be ready for them this time but even so I was none too sanguine about my chances of besting them in my current tender condition.

There was an unlooked for advantage, however, in Plaincourt and Rivers' absence from the manor in that it presented me with a valuable opportunity to progress my investigations without fear of interruption. If things proceeded as I hoped, I knew I might soon be able to bring matters to a head. Therefore, having ascertained from Rolf that I would find Mistress Blanche in her still room, I hastened there without delay.

In the small, well-ordered storeroom that served as the manor still room I found Blanche reaching from a stool to retrieve a bunch of dried herbs from the central ceiling rack. Along the shelf-lined walls I spied neatly ordered ranks of flagons and flasks, all in differing sizes and all filled with some kind of physic, standing in readiness for the moment they would be needed. They stood as testament to her industry and efficiency, just as the efficacy of the salves she had used on my injuries stood testament to her healing skills.

Even with the stool increasing her height she was struggling to reach the herbs and I could see she was in imminent danger of losing her balance. Swiftly, to avert such an eventuality, I put one arm about her waist and plucked her from the stool whilst simultaneously reaching up with the other to remove the bundle she required. As my face brushed against her gown I held my breath against the onrush of sweet roses that flooded my nostrils. Setting Blanche lightly on the ground, I was struck by how insubstantial she was, how little effort it had taken to lift her. Truly there was a strangely ethereal quality about the woman.

"Thank you, Francis," she said, "but you should not be exerting yourself in your condition."

"Scarcely exerting myself," I laughed. "Lady, I swear you are not of this world! I vow you are no greater burden than my lute and I trust you'll not expect me to leave off carrying that while my petty hurts mend."

She smiled but made no reply and stood facing me, the enquiring look on her face asking plainly enough why I had sought her out. I saw that today she was wearing a modest, square-necked russet gown more suited to her rank than the figured velvet confection I had seen before. Over it she had tied a linen apron to protect the gown from any still room spillages, and on her head she'd placed a severe linen cap that completely concealed her wondrous hair. She had been lovely in her finery but I liked her better in these simple, workaday clothes as they allowed her sublime features to shine out in sharp contrast to the plainness of her garb. Perhaps also I felt that her attire gave a portrait of the woman she might have been had her heart not been twisted by ambition.

There was a part of me that was reluctant to begin speaking, to say what I had come to say, but I knew that I must if I was to conclude this business for my lord of Gloucester.

"I know it was you that killed Geoffrey," I said without further preamble. "Don't seek to deny it for I am assured of your guilt. Yet I am also certain that you did not act alone. In fact, I believe you were brought to Plaincourt for that very purpose.

"The part you played in the vile affair was crucial yet I do not think you are inherently evil, unlike those that incited you to commit the crime. There is something about you, I cannot say what, that leads me to see the best in you in spite of all. Therefore, Blanche, I exhort you, confess everything to me and I will do all in my power to help you."

Her face had turned ashen as I accused her of murder but when I said I would help her it became contorted with derision.

"You will do all in your power to help me!" she jeered. "Ah well, I can rest easy then. What mighty friends will you call upon to plead for me, I wonder? For if I am as guilty as you pretend to know, I will need friends of passing magnitude to save me. So who amongst his high and noble connections will the rootless minstrel Francis Cranley call upon to speak for me?"

For all that her tone and words were mocking, I heard the underlying desperation.

"Will the Duke of Gloucester suffice?" I asked quietly. "If you confess your crime fully and show true repentance, I believe I can persuade him to look mercifully upon you. With him speaking for you, you may yet keep your life."

As I mentioned the Duke's name Blanche's legs folded and she collapsed onto the stool upon which she had lately been balancing.

"Who are you?" she whispered hoarsely.

"I have not misled you as to my name," I told her, "but in most other respects I have. My master is Richard, Duke of Gloucester and my home is Middleham Castle. I have travelled here at the express wish of my lord to uncover the facts pertaining to a grievous murder charge laid against an old acquaintance of his."

Understanding dawned in those extraordinary violet eyes.

"Will," she breathed slowly. "He sent you to find out about Will's role in Geoffrey's death."

"To prove his innocence," I corrected her sharply.

At this she began to dissemble but I interrupted her.

"Before you lie to me again," I hissed with a savageness born of impatience with the whole sorry affair, "remember that your betrothed is likely at this very moment devising new excuses for delaying your nuptials. He may have pledged to wed you but he strikes me as a slippery fellow and now that you have so obligingly rid him of his nephew he may think he need not hold true to his word.

"I'd say your position here is precarious, nay I'd go even further and suggest your very existence is in jeopardy. Lord Rivers is fond of you, aye, but he will be gone from Plaincourt soon enough and then what good will his fondness avail you? He will be hundreds of leagues away and then all that will stand between you and Sir Stephen's desire to be rid of you will be his villagers. Are you well-loved by them, Blanche? Will any one of them come to your aid when some misadventure befalls you? When you find yourself drowning in the moat, perchance, or suffering a fall from the staircase?

"Do not trouble to answer for we both know well enough that there are none here that would risk their skin to save you. I believe it inevitable that in due course you will meet with some feigned accident. Sir Stephen will relay news of your demise to the Earl as another tragic death at Plaincourt Manor. He will suspect the truth, of course, and will be saddened by your fate but he will take no action against Plaincourt because as you yourself have said, the ties that bind them are too strong to be broken. And it is your own actions that have made those bonds unbreakable.

"Understand this - your only chance of salvation in this world, aye, and mayhap the next also, is to tell me every detail large and small about Geoffrey's murder. I have guessed a great part of it but I must hear it from your own lips. You must tell me how you came to be recruited as the pitiful boy's executioner, and by whom; how you managed the dreadful business and how, for the love of Christ, Blanche, you must tell me how you regret with all your heart your wicked, wicked actions."

When I had finished speaking Blanche's hands flew to her mouth and she began to weep. As she did so I could not help but notice that the crude, crested ring she wore looked all the uglier for its proximity to her pretty red lips. Her sobs continued for a few heartbeats but I was untouched by them and made no move to comfort her. After a while, perhaps realising that her tears were to no avail, she managed to compose herself enough to speak the words I had been willing her to utter.

Chapter 12
She Would Not Cavil

"Very well, Francis, I will do as you demand and tell you everything," she began in a small voice throbbing with contrition. What then unfolded was a story of everyday avarice and mendacity partnered with a cruelty so casual and pitiless as to render it truly monstrous.

Much of what Blanche told me I had already fathomed but even so there were some details that took me by surprise. She started by saying that her first awareness of Plaincourt Manor had come about when she had been summoned to Jacquetta of Bedford's bedchamber a month or so before that lady's death.

Expecting a private audience with her mistress, she had been astonished to find Lord Rivers sitting at his mother's bedside, the more so as she had not been aware that he was visiting. This, he had told her, was precisely his intention; he had entered the house in secret in order to discuss with Blanche a very private matter and he wished few to know he was there. At once Blanche suspected that he had come to seek her help in arranging some intimate assignation and she was only a little surprised that he had chosen to involve his mother in the matter.

She was swiftly disabused of that notion, however, when Jacquetta herself spoke up. Taking Blanche's hand in her own emaciated grasp, the regal old woman spoke with many ostentatious sighs of her regret that she had never succeeded in finding for her young protégé a wealthy husband who would overlook her material disadvantages. Yet now, finally, she believed she may be able to set right this regrettable state of affairs thanks to her son who had come to her with some welcome tidings. There existed a very handsome and cultured knight who was ready to enter into a betrothal with Blanche on Anthony's recommendation. He would, moreover, be fully content with the small dowry the Dowager Duchess was willing to bestow on her.

Though these were words Blanche had long desired to hear, she was no fool and understood full well that there would be a price to pay for this seemingly miraculous reversal of fortune. Sure enough, Lord Rivers then took over from his mother, explaining in meticulous detail what Blanche must do to secure her husband. All the while as he spoke, his cozening words tumbling from his mouth like honeyed wine from a polished carafe, one elegant, finely-boned finger tenderly stroked her face in a circular movement from cheek to chin. Blanche was sure the dreamy repetition of the motion was intended to lull her senses yet every time the thin, tapering finger passed under her chin its gentle caress across her throat felt as threatening as a blade. At least, that is what she told me.

Careful at first to mention no names, Rivers had told Blanche that the knight in question was already in possession of a modest manor and would inherit a much finer one on the death of his nephew, a sickly boy who clung to life with tiresome tenacity. The lad was feeble and unlikely to survive far into adulthood but his obstinate refusal to die sooner rather than later was occasioning his uncle no little inconvenience. Yet desirous as he was that the boy's demise should be hastened, the knight scrupled to sully his own hands with the matter. In any case, in order to avoid arousing the suspicion of some interfering relatives, the affair needed to be arranged in such a way that any blame for his nephew's death fell elsewhere.

Whether she spoke true about this I cannot say but Blanche alleged to me that she had felt sickened at the cold talk of snuffing out a boy's life. She claimed she had voiced her disquiet on this score but Lord Rivers had soothed her conscience with smooth words. The poor lad's suffering was so great, the Earl maintained, that he would undoubtedly regard death as a blessing. I failed to comprehend how these words could be reconciled with his earlier sneer about the boy's obstinate refusal to die but Blanche allowed herself to be persuaded that the Earl spoke truly.

Her next question had shown a far greater regard for her own skin than for the fate of the young lad. Understanding that she was being asked to use her skills to end his life, she asked how she herself would avoid falling under suspicion were she to do as they desired. Realising that he had Blanche hooked, Rivers proceeded to divulge the rest of the scheme, at the same time clarifying his own interest in the affair.

The knight, he told Blanche, was a friend of his who had come to him with an intriguing tale. Some while ago he had hired a grotesque ruffian to serve as his nephew's body servant, anticipating that the unsavoury character would chase the boy to his grave through fear, careless handling or downright ill treatment, he cared not which. Unluckily, in this the knight's hopes had been disappointed and he had been on the verge of dismissing the man when a chance recollection stayed his hand. At their first meeting, in his eagerness to convince him of his fitness to tend his nephew, the fellow had boasted of a close association with the King's beloved brother, Richard of Gloucester. At the time the knight had paid little heed to the story since he was more closely interested in the man's brutish appearance and manners than in details of his former service. Nevertheless, he now remembered the tale and though it seemed unlikely enough, yet it struck the knight that the man had spoken true. Wondering if perchance there might be some advantage to be worked from this nugget of information, he had relayed it to his noble friend and awaited his counsel.

It was no secret that the Woodville kin most heartily detested the King's youngest brother, largely because of the immense trust reposed in him by Edward. As the King's lieutenant in the north the young Duke wielded enormous influence, influence which the power-hungry Woodvilles coveted for themselves. In their view, therefore, any lessening of confidence between the brothers could only be to their advantage. Thus they were ever ready to seize on the slightest chance to damage Gloucester in his royal brother's eyes although until now they had signally failed to make any headway. That was why Rivers had paid close attention when he was brought word of the disreputable old soldier who spoke of a friendship with the young Duke.

Yet whatever else he was Rivers was a cautious man and so, before committing himself to any action, he set about ascertaining if this character, one Will Yorke, spoke the truth about his association with Gloucester. At first his discreet enquiries at Court yielded nothing for none he spoke to recognised the man's name. He had all but abandoned the notion when George of Clarence arrived at Court, full of swagger and bristling with barely concealed resentment at Dickon's favoured position with the King. Though a state of frigid enmity usually existed between Clarence and Rivers, the pragmatic Earl realised that George's timely arrival presented an opportunity for one final probe.

Putting aside his usual contempt for the hot-headed Duke, he took pains to greet him warmly and even went so far as to invite him to join him in a cup of malmsey which he knew to be George's favourite wine. As cup followed cup, he lent a sympathetic ear to Clarence's increasingly drunken allegations of injustice suffered at the hands of his brothers. By the time several flagons had been drained, Rivers had obtained the information he desired. The man known as Will Yorke could be none other than Will Fielding, a Yorkist soldier Clarence had thought long dead. Far gone in his cups, the Duke had furnished Rivers with the fascinating intelligence that the fellow had saved both his life and Gloucester's when they were boys. He had never cared greatly for the hulking brute, he said, but his brother Dickon had been much attached to him and their lady mother had sought to reward him until she received the news – false as it now turned out – of the fellow's death.

Now Rivers had been able to see how he and his friend could use this information to their mutual benefit. They would have the sickly nephew put to death, making it look as though Gloucester's disreputable old associate had killed the boy. He would be accused of the murder but then allowed to

174

escape, aided by someone he trusted. It would be the task of this same person to advise Fielding to seek succour from the one influential friend he had, the noble Duke of Gloucester.

In due course the justices would be advised to search for the fugitive at Middleham. They would apprehend him there and Gloucester would incur the censure of his royal brother for harbouring a man guilty of such a filthy murder. Most likely the incident would be insufficient to sunder entirely the King's trust in his youngest brother but it would at the very least lead to a disagreement. And when the story was put about, as Rivers would make certain it was, Gloucester's good name would stand discredited and for the Earl that would be sweet indeed. As for the knight himself, his reward would be the lush manor he would inherit on the death of his nephew.

To make all this happen, however, Rivers told Blanche that the knight needed a willing accomplice, one clever enough to win the ruffian's trust and skilful enough to engineer the boy's death so that suspicion fell in the right place.

"I am to be that person," Blanche had stated, "and my prize will be marriage to this knight."

The Dowager Duchess had nodded contentedly.

"I told you she would not cavil," she told her son. "She has been well schooled, she understands that in life one must grasp whatever opportunities appear."

"But can you do it, sweet girl?" Rivers had asked Blanche, and I could easily imagine him searching her violet eyes with his own intense green gaze.

"When the time comes, will you have the stomach to end the lad's life? And more to the point, mayhap, will you have the stomach to win the odious body servant's trust by whatever means possible?"

Blanche understood what he implied. She had always kept herself pure, she told me, because while she could bring little else to a future husband she could at least bring her virginity. Now that gift was to be taken from her but since it would be taken in pursuit of her most cherished dream, as the

Dowager Duchess had predicted, she would not cavil.

Having assured Rivers that she would gladly do all that was necessary to execute the plan, and sworn a solemn oath to reveal it to no one, Blanche was finally told the identity of her future husband. His name meant nothing to her but her excitement grew as the Earl described in rich detail the wonderful manor of Plaincourt and Sir Stephen's connection with the inordinately wealthy Lambert family, of whom Blanche had indeed heard. Behind her excitement, however, she claimed to feel a tremor of anxiety for she now knew that there could be no going back. Should she develop a conscious and refuse to carry out her allotted role her life would be extinguished as swiftly and effortlessly as a candle, for though the Earl had always trusted her, in a matter as grave as this he could afford to take no chances. Only when her own hands were tainted with the boy's blood would he and Plaincourt know they could truly depend on her silence.

The rest occurred much as Fielding had originally described to my lord of Gloucester and I. Blanche had arrived at Plaincourt and immediately set about winning Will's trust. She took to visiting Geoffrey's chamber, bringing him sweetmeats and sitting by his bed for hours at a time, telling him nonsensical stories and singing to him the comical songs of her childhood. Small wonder the affection-starved child lost his heart to her, and small wonder Will Fielding did also.

She confessed that she had unexpectedly enjoyed spending time with Will and Geoffrey but otherwise her life at Plaincourt Manor had been far grimmer than she had anticipated. While Sir Stephen had treated her with sufficient civility there was no warmth in his manner, yet even this coolness was preferable to the open hostility she received from the manor servants.

"The clods mistrusted me from the first," she admitted. "That wretched girl Cuckoo is wont to cross herself every time she sets eyes upon me and the others are little better. When I first set up my remedies in the still room they looked askance and grumbled loudly about unnatural practices. For all that my healing skills are valued by some of the greatest in the land, not a one of those superstitious dolts would suffer me to physic them when they fell sick. And when Flood cut his hand on his great gutting knife the ingrate dared to spit at me when I ventured to bind the wound.

"I know not why but they have always found fault with my presence here. He would not dare it now but before my betrothal to Stephen was made public, that tedious fool Rolf ranted that there was no rightful place for an unwed girl such as me about the manor. He refused to listen when I said I was skilled in healing and had come simply to help in the care of the young master. I was snarled at whenever I ventured into the kitchen, why even the washerwoman looked at me as if I was dirt beneath her lumpen great feet. Fanciful as it sounds, oft-times it struck me that they could look into my heart and see the true reason I was at Plaincourt.

"With such hatred all about me, I took to spending more and more time with Geoffrey and Will and soon I knew that both loved me right well. Alas for me, I found that I had not after all been sufficiently well schooled by the Woodvilles for I returned Geoffrey's affection in full measure. At first sight he was an unpromising scrap but the better I grew to know him, the easier I found it to love him. He was often fractious but with good cause, for he suffered greatly with a disease of the lungs which I believe was also responsible for his crippled state. He could not walk, nor stand unassisted, but he had such a capacity for joy which amply rewarded all the care Will and I lavished on him.

"As for Will, aye, his ruined face was repulsive to look upon but I liked him for the love he showed Geoffrey. The sad truth is that I could have been happy at Plaincourt had circumstances been different."

She stopped abruptly, startled into silence by a sound that seemed to issue from just outside the still room. Placing a warning finger to my lips, I flung open the door and glanced about the passageway. The only creature to be seen was a fat pigeon which had stunned itself by colliding with the closed door as it flew in from the courtyard. Now it stood stock still, alive yet seemingly unable to move. I had seen this before and knew the bird's movement would be restored soon enough if it was allowed some respite. I also knew that if Jem Flood were to happen upon it in this state it would likely end up in a pie. I have no great affection for pigeons but Flood I liked even less so I picked the creature up and brought it inside the still room that it might recover in safety.

With the door closed firmly once more, Blanche continued with her confession. When she had been at Plaincourt some seven months Stephen came to her and said it was time she fulfilled her promise to end the boy's life. Since she had been so successful in winning Fielding's trust, he said, they could progress with the next stage of their plan. She was to use her special talents to ensure Geoffrey was dead before Christmas and in return their marriage would take place in the new year. To strengthen her resolve he went with her to St. Oswald's church and swore before the altar his intention to make her Lady of Plaincourt.

As she reached this part of her tale Blanche began to weep once more. It was only now, she insisted through her tears, that she had fully comprehended the awful reality of what she had agreed to do. She acknowledged that her conscience might not have troubled her overmuch had she not learned to care so much for the boy but since she had, she now found it impossible to contemplate making away with him.

Yet, she demanded, what choice did she truly have? She considered running away but could think of no place that would keep her safe from discovery by the powerful Woodvilles whose tentacles reached everywhere. Another possibility that occurred to her was to confide all in Fielding but even as she thought of it she knew it was hopeless. He would be bound to despise her for having agreed to murder Geoffrey and in any case he was not in a position to guarantee her safety from Plaincourt or Rivers.

For nearly a week, Blanche said, she had anguished over

178

what course of action to take and then fate obligingly gave her an answer. Though generally poor, Geoffrey's health had been stable enough since her arrival at the manor but suddenly his lung disease took a turn for the worse and he began to suffer most hideously. As she tended him she became convinced that his poor body would soon not be able to withstand much more and then he would die a natural death after all, thereby sparing her the dreadful crime she was sworn to commit. Yet Geoffrey's will to live proved stronger than she had imagined and so he clung on, enduring the agonising pain that wracked his feeble body and rendered sleep impossible.

Watching the young lad's dreadful suffering, Blanche was suddenly struck by the realisation that it would in truth be a kindness to release him from such misery, or so she claimed.

"I could not bear to see him in such horrible pain," she told me, "so I started dosing his evening ale with poppy juice. This gave him several hours of blessed sleep and also furnished me with the chance to bind Fielding ever closer by giving him my body."

"How could you?" I interrupted, shuddering slightly as I pictured Fielding's terrible countenance in my mind.

"Keep your disgust in check, peacock!" she blazed at me. "It was not so very bad. Granted his face is ruined yet there is kindness in his eyes and his physique is well made.

"I was reluctant, I admit, yet he was gentle with me that first time and though it hurt it was no worse than I have heard it is for any maid. Thereafter our couplings were tolerable and even once or twice, I blush to say it, my body knew some pleasure. When he chewed the herbs I gave him to sweeten his breath and cleansed his hard body of sweat, he made an acceptable lover. Believe me or not as you will, Francis," she finished, "but it was no great hardship for me to lie with Will Fielding."

Though I found what she had just said unfathomable, I murmured a few conciliatory words that she might finish her confession with all speed.

Every night that she lay with Fielding she continued to

put poppy juice into Geoffrey's bedtime ale, increasing the dose every time so that his waking hours became gradually fewer. On the fifteenth or sixteenth night she mixed in a measure large enough to put him in a sleep from which she knew he would never awaken. For the first time she added some also to Fielding's ale, giving him just enough to make him insensible. Judging the precise dose was something of an art, she informed me, showing a degree of pride in her skills that I found unbearable coming so soon after her confession that she had used them to murder an innocent.

Unaware of my revulsion, Blanche progressed with her story. When sufficient time had elapsed she had returned to the chamber and discovered Will slumped on his pallet at the foot of Geoffrey's bed. In accordance with Plaincourt's orders she had seized the heavy ale pitcher and struck Fielding on his head as hard as she could manage. Then, with great difficulty she had managed to topple his inert form onto the floor.

"The next part was the hardest," she sobbed. "I knelt at Geoffrey's bedside and checked that he was no longer breathing. When I saw that he had truly gone I knew I should feel overwhelmed by the wickedness of my deed yet I did not. It was beyond me to be sorry that he was dead; instead I rejoiced that his long suffering was over. If I mourned for anything it was for the part I had played in the affair for it is a hard thing to kill someone you love whatever the circumstances.

"I laid a kiss on his pale brow as I had done so many times before and said a quick prayer for his soul. Then, again following Stephen's instructions I plucked a small feather from Geoffrey's pillow and inserted it between his lips so that the merest tip was visible. The pillow I arranged at his side to look as if it had slipped from his face."

This time I did not trouble to disguise my repugnance.

"You speak of love yet you slew the boy all the same!" I threw angrily at her. "I pray God spares me from such fond affection."

At these words she raised her violet eyes to me and gave me a look of the deepest reproach.

"You cannot understand, Francis," she moaned. "Geoffrey was in constant agony. Please, I implore you to believe me, I only did what I did to spare him further suffering. Yes, I came to Plaincourt intent on killing him but once I knew and loved him it was beyond me to do such a thing save for his own sake. I'll swear it before God if you'll let me."

I wanted to believe her and indeed part of me did. Yet I could not forget what Jacquetta of Bedford had said of Blanche by her own account. I recalled the words with blinding clarity.

"I told you she would not cavil," the old lady had said. "She has been well schooled, she knows in life one must grasp whatever opportunities appear."

Had snuffing out Geoffrey's life been an act of mercy, as she claimed, or had she in fact been grasping an opportunity too tempting to resist? It was not for me to decide; my job was to bring Blanche before my lord of Gloucester and let him be the judge and for that I was wholly thankful.

Aware that her confession was as yet incomplete, I urged Blanche to tell me now of Fielding's release from imprisonment.

"Stephen had given me the key to Will's cell and arranged to have a suitable horse saddled and waiting close by. I waited for darkness to fall and then made haste to free him. The poor fool did not question how I had been able to arrange these matters, so glad was he to see me. This was well, for had he but considered a moment he might have realised I could never remove a horse from the stables without anyone knowing of it.

"When I bid him be gone with all speed he dithered helplessly about where to go, leaving me no choice but to whisper Middleham to him. I had hoped to spare him this part of Stephen's trap and would have done so if he had been able to think of another possible refuge. Alas, his wits were so dulled by the shock of all that had befallen him that he gave me no option but to follow the plan.

"I knew Stephen would send word to the justices that a known murderer was being harboured by the Duke of Gloucester, delaying just long enough to allow Will to arrive safely at the castle. It saddened me to be sending him to his fate but what else could I do?"

I realised with some amazement that once again Blanche was seeking to excuse her despicable actions.

"What else could you do? You could have admitted your part in the affair and told him to ride for his life," I expostulated. "He is entirely innocent of Geoffrey's murder yet you are happy to see him hang for it. Have you no remorse?"

I saw her temper flare then.

"Who are you to judge me?" she spat back at me. "You who have only ever known comfort and high living! Who knows what acts you might have found yourself committing if life had not been so kind?

"I told you I felt sad sending Will into a trap but no, I feel no remorse! After all, I gave him his freedom. He should have ridden to the coast and taken ship somewhere far away but the clod had not the sense to think of that, leaving it to me to tell him where he must go. Must I be blamed for his lack of wit?"

With a lurching heart I understood at last that Blanche's perception of right and wrong was fatally twisted. Perhaps this crooked morality had always been in her nature yet I tended to believe otherwise. I was certain that some small root of goodness was embedded in her soul though it had failed to flourish in the poor soil of her Woodville upbringing. Sharing my master's low opinion of the Queen's kin, I could imagine all too readily the corrupting influence the old Dowager Duchess and her children would have brought to bear on the mind of a pretty and ambitious young girl.

Having grown to know and understand Blanche a little, my view was that in some ways she was as much to be pitied as poor Geoffrey yet I knew this was an opinion few would share. In any event, this was not the time to be dwelling on such questions. My priority now had to be to get her to Middleham without delay so that she might tell my lord of Gloucester her tale and bear witness against Plaincourt and Rivers. I would have a chance then to speak on her behalf, using what I knew of her circumstances to argue for leniency.

While I had been pondering these thoughts Blanche had subsided from her outburst and had taken the pigeon, now recovered and somewhat distressed, to the window. After releasing the bird she stood gazing out into the courtyard, twisting a sprig of dried lavender this way and that betwixt her fingers.

"After Fielding had fled, what did you then?" I asked her.

"There was naught left to be done save return to my chamber and wait for events to unfold," she answered.

I thought of telling her that she had been observed by Cuckoo as she stole back through the darkness but decided not to interrupt her flow.

"I knew the hue and cry would be raised on the morrow and I prayed, truly I prayed, that Will would find the wit to change his course and ride instead for the coast. I'll not deny that I also prayed most fervently the coming year would find me Lady of Plaincourt."

"Were you then already afeared that your less than devoted betrothed would renege on his promise?"

"Mayhap a small matter," she replied. "Were it not for my lord Rivers, I suspected Stephen would not hesitate to have me killed, so little eager is he for us to wed. And as you yourself have reason to know, having suffered at the hands of the bearded Tench brothers, he has loyal henchmen happy to obey his orders, however brutal. Yet at that time I remained confident that I was protected by the affection the Earl feels for me.

"Indeed, even now I am sure that my lord Rivers would be much loath to see me dead. But I also know that he is a great man with many pressing affairs to attend to and though he cares for my well-being, I fear it will not remain uppermost in his mind for long. Francis, once he has gone from Plaincourt I know it will be as you say, my life will stand in deepest peril."

Chapter 13
Time to Leave

The dinner hour was upon us by the time Blanche had finished her story. Knowing that her absence would be remarked on if she stayed away from the hall, I told her she must dine as usual even though, with Plaincourt and Rivers away from the manor, she would have to face the common folk alone. At this she quailed and asked why would she be alone, would I not be with her, to which I replied vaguely that some other business demanded my attention. From her face I saw that she found this intelligence displeasing so I hastened to assure her that it would be the last meal she took at the manor.

"You and I will quit Plaincourt this day," I told her, "but we must take care not to be seen leaving together lest we arouse suspicion. At dinner, let it be known that the minstrel has lost his appetite. All will imagine I am too craven to show my face in the hall without Lord Rivers to protect me. When the meal is done, keep to your chamber until dark. Then don all the warm clothing you have and make your way to the ruined hovel known as Old Lynet's cottage. Do you know where I mean?"

She nodded her assent.

"I will meet you there," I continued, "and then we will ride for Middleham."

"Thank you, Francis," she whispered, standing on her tiptoes to place a timid kiss on my cheek. "You are good to me, far better than I deserve."

Once more my senses were assaulted by her nauseating rose perfume and I struggled to control the impulse to push her away. Cease this coquetry, I wanted to scream at her, your powers of seduction will avail you naught with me. Can you not see that I am immune to your charms? Instead, knowing such incivility was pointless, I smiled blandly and chivvied her from the room.

After she had gone I sat awhile in the still room, leaving

what I judged enough time for her to reach the hall and take her place at the dais. Then I rose and went in search of Matthew.

To find him, of course, I would be obliged to enter the kitchen which was now unfriendly territory since I had managed to anger both Jem Flood and Cuckoo. Luck was with me, however, as neither were to be seen when I stepped warily into the room and I concluded that they must be occupied carrying dishes to the hall. Matthew was there, alone, but he at once informed me that Flood would be back presently and would likely give me a battering if he discovered me loitering within his domain.

In normal circumstances the likes of Jem Flood would not concern me. He was tough, I was tougher, that should have been an end to it. But these were not normal circumstances. I was recovering from a brutal attack and would be unable to bring my usual force and vigour to a fight for a good few days. Thus good sense recommended I should make myself scarce without delay but I still had urgent need of speech with Matthew.

"When they return you must find an excuse to slip away," I told him peremptorily. "Join me at the fishpond as soon as you can."

I turned and left before he could make an answer but I knew he would obey. I had unearthed plenty of corruption at Plaincourt Manor but I had also found a humble youth possessed of unexpected intelligence and rare humanity.

I had not been waiting long when Matthew arrived, rubbing his hands briskly against the raw chill of the day. I had chosen the fishpond as the location for our interview since I knew it to be well away from prying eyes, particularly when most of the manor folk would be at their dinner.

Without greeting the lad or waiting for him to speak I launched into an account of Blanche's confession and my intention to carry her at once to Middleham, there to lay her tale before the Duke of Gloucester. Sharp as ever, Matthew deduced at once that she was not my real quarry.

"Thee dost need Mistress Blanche to stand against master and his mighty friend," he commented.

"Correct," I said shortly. "Now I am in need of your assistance. I hope you recall your promise to give it to me."

The boy said nothing but nodded his acquiescence, whereupon I explained to him my plan. I told him that I intended to leave the manor immediately but it was essential I created the impression that I was simply venturing out for a ride. There must be no indication that I was leaving for good and therefore I could not be seen to leave with my possessions. Matthew, I said, must go in secret to my chamber and retrieve my things, most especially my lute.

"I have arranged to meet Mistress Blanche at Lynet's hovel," I explained to the lad. "Bring my things to me there and then get back here as quick as you can. I want no suspicion falling on you when we are found to be gone."

There was excitement in his eyes as he readily agreed to all I asked. From the very first, his presence at Plaincourt as a willing accomplice to my investigation had rendered my task more pleasant. Thinking of this, I recalled my earlier private resolution to improve his lot somehow.

"You have my gratitude, Matthew," I told him, "and when this sorry business is settled you will have more than that. I vow I will find a way to reward you. Now you'd best be about your business."

He smiled and slipped away without another word.

I knew the next part of my plan should be easy enough to effect. There was no call for anyone to suspect I was about to flee the manor, especially as I would be riding out without my lute and saddlebag. Yet even if the thought should occur to the groom who made ready my hired rouncey, he would probably surmise that I was quitting through fear of sustaining another beating. My only difficulty would be if Lord Rivers had left instructions that I should not leave the manor unattended for my own protection.

With this thought in mind, I was moderately anxious as I hailed the stable lad and asked him to bring me my horse. He was alone, his comrades taking their dinner in the hall just as I had hoped.

"Thee beant leaving us, master?" the fellow enquired. "I didst have a hankering to hear thee sing afore thee goes."

I flapped my arms about me to indicate the absence of my lute.

"No, no," I reassured him, "I have been asked by your master to bide here at Plaincourt over Yuletide and then I am to ride with Lord Rivers to London. He means to find a place for me at Court."

I allowed a note of pride to creep into my voice and the lad's eyes widened at my good fortune.

"For now," I continued, "I simply wish for a refreshing ride to shake the cobwebs from my head."

By now the rouncey was in the courtyard and it whickered softly as it recognised me. Again I noticed how much healthier it looked than when I had first encountered it at the tavern.

"For your trouble," I said, tossing a handful of coins at the fellow. When I had thought to reward the stable lads before, I had stopped myself with the knowledge that such largesse would look strange coming from a down-at-heel minstrel. Now I reckoned that from one gleefully anticipating a lucrative new post at Court it would seem entirely appropriate.

As the lad bent to retrieve the coins from the ground I scrambled onto the rouncey's back and cantered past the gatehouse, across the bridge and on into Plaincourt village. Few souls were about as I rode through the main thoroughfare and those that were there paid me no attention. Once beyond the limits of the village I checked the rouncey and turned its head in the direction of Lynet's ruined cottage.

As I approached the hovel I looked carefully about me, checking that I was not observed, before following a densely vegetated track that led around the back of the property. What had once been a neatly tended garden was now a depressing wilderness. Dismounting, I tethered the horse to an overgrown apple tree and settled myself in readiness for a long wait in the most sheltered spot I could find, all the while cursing the ill-luck that had brought me on this mission in the midst of winter. A short nap would have suited me very well but I knew the chill air would make that impossible, though I would stay warm enough enfolded in the rabbity depths of my cloak.

With naught to do but wait and shiver, I allowed my thoughts to stray to the complexities of familial ties since it struck me that family was the common thread binding the lives of those that dwelt at Plaincourt. An orphan almost from birth, I knew nothing of normal family relationships. I had heard of the bond said to exist between siblings but could conceive of no stronger bond than the one that existed between Dickon and I, though it was formed of love, trust and fidelity rather than blood.

At Plaincourt, blood ties seemed to count for nothing. While I could not know if there had been true affection between Stephen and his brother William the fact that Stephen had plotted to bring about the death of William's only child made it seem unlikely. Perhaps it was naïve of me but I imagined that a man who had loved his brother would feel at least a diluted measure of that love for that brother's offspring.

Thoughts of siblings brought me to Matthew and Cuckoo, half-brother and sister by dint of their bastard Plaincourt blood. They lived and worked side by side yet I observed no particular closeness between them. Matthew was mildly protective towards her, I could tell, but no more than had she been any other village girl.

Perhaps this was because Cuckoo was not an especially loveable person. Yet why should this be? She was unfairly despised by her adoptive father but at least she had a mother who cared for her whereas Matthew had no one. Raised on charity, he had known no mother's love, nor any other kind come to that, yet he had grown into a fine young man, cheerful, compassionate and unexpectedly agile of mind. So far as I could discern, Cuckoo was possessed of none of those admirable qualities.

I was unclear as to where these musings were taking me but I pursued them all the same, thinking again of Matthew and Cuckoo's fine half-brother, their master Stephen Plaincourt. Though their relationship with him would never be recognised, it existed nonetheless. Could I see aught of Matthew in Stephen's character? No, try as I might I could not envisage the good-natured cook's boy plotting to end his nephew's life. I knew Plaincourt had felt no compunction when it came to disposing of Geoffrey. Did that tell me that blood ties meant nothing to him, or simply that money and status meant more?

Status brought me to Blanche who craved it so badly she had committed murder in pursuit of it. Had her father not died, had her mother not consigned her to the care of strangers, had some suitable knight been prepared to overlook her lack of dowry, might she then have become a different person? I wanted so much to believe the answer to those questions was yes but if so, it suggested that our natures were decided by the circumstances of our upbringing. Yet surely Matthew's goodness in the face of a miserable childhood suggested otherwise.

Thus my thoughts ran on, spinning round and round in my head but reaching no resolution until my temples ached most abominably. It was with no little relief then, that just after darkness had fallen my ears detected the lightest of footsteps stepping through the undergrowth and I knew they could belong to none other than Blanche.

I was fully glad to see her, not only because my long period of inactivity had tested my patience to the limit but also because, as I was only now able to acknowledge to myself, I had not been entirely certain that she would come. During her confession I had recognised the sincerity of her desperation, her fear that Plaincourt meant to be rid of her just as soon as he was able, and I believed she understood that in leaving with me she had her best chance of survival. Yet during the long hours between dinner and our rendezvous she might have had time to reflect that the possible danger she faced by remaining at Plaincourt was outweighed by the reward if her fears proved groundless. Fortunately for my mission, this gamble had not occurred to her or if it had, she had decided not to take the risk.

When she stepped into the clearing behind Lynet's cottage I gave an involuntary gasp at the fairy-like figure she cut. Tiny, swathed in a dark hooded cloak and holding a small bundle in one hand and a lantern in the other, she put me in mind of a forest sprite from the stories Fat Nell used to tell when Dickon and I were small. I would hang on her knee, enraptured as she spoke of the Wee Folk who crept through the woodlands at dead of night, working mischief against humans wherever they could. I could never get enough of these stories and always begged for more but she paid me no heed until Dickon, who I knew was far less enamoured with the tales than I, would add his voice to the clamour and then she would comply.

Covering my surprise with a cough, I took her bundle without a word and secured it to the rouncey's saddle. She grabbed at my wrist then, compelling me to look at her face.

"I was followed," she hissed, her eyes flicking nervously around the clearing.

Before I could answer, heavy breathing and breaking bracken confirmed her words.

"Here thee be, master," Matthew announced cheerfully as he broke into the overrun garden. "Mistress," he added, nodding politely at Blanche who was still hanging on to my arm.

"What is he doing here?" she snapped at me. "The boy's an imbecile."

By the light of Matthew's lantern I could see that he was untouched by Blanche's harsh words but all the same I was not prepared to let them pass.

"He's far from that," I said shortly, gratefully retrieving my precious lute and other belongings from the youth.

When I had stowed them carefully I lifted Blanche onto the saddle and then turned to Matthew, instructing him to return to the manor with all speed.

"And remember my promise," I added as he made to go, "I will see you are rewarded, you have my word as to that."

At once, and to my horror, I heard the sound of many booted feet crashing through the vegetation. At the same time the darkness was sundered by spikes of bright, flickering light that bobbed eerily up and down as they moved inexorably towards Lynet's cottage.

As I stared, transfixed by the light, Matthew shoved me abruptly.

"Best get gone, master," he urged. "Thee's got company an' it looks like company thee doosnt want."

I saw that he was right. A rabble of men, numbering more than a dozen by the look of them, were heading towards us, coming from the wasteland that lay behind the ruined cottage. Without further delay I leapt onto the rouncey's back and with a curt command to Blanche to hold tight, kicked the animal into action.

We made it as far as the main track and then found our progress impeded by John and Walt Tench, the extravagantly bearded brutes who had delivered my beating. It was my intention to ride them down but the cursed rouncey checked itself, startled by the unexpected obstruction created by the men. As we slowed one of them caught hold of a fragment of Blanche's cloak and tugged on it, pulling her from the horse. She shrieked in pain as she toppled to the ground, leaving me little else to do but to jump down and defend her.

Still I thought all was not quite lost. If I could overcome the bearded ruffians and get Blanche back on the horse before the mob at our back arrived, we might yet make our escape. Easing my rondel dagger from its place of concealment in my boot, I planted myself in front of Blanche's supine figure and waited for the Tench boys to advance. Instead, to my chagrin, one caught hold of the horse while the other lunged at Matthew who had just made it from the clearing and put him in an armlock, holding a knife a hair's breadth from his throat. Reluctantly, I slid the dagger back into its hiding place, grateful at least that the ruffians had not appeared to notice it.

"Thee's going nowhere, pretty boy," the bigger of the two said mockingly to me. "Not wi'out a few words from a friend of thine."

Laughing insolently, they gestured for me to lead the way back to the clearing behind Lynet's house. A piteous yelp from Blanche told me that she was being manhandled behind me while a mild reproach from Matthew to his captor reassured me that he was also being brought along. Then all thoughts vanished as I cleared the narrow path and discovered the rabble awaiting us in the wreckage of Lynet's garden.

"Well now, Master Cranley," I heard a familiar voice say, "didst thee think to leave wi'out saying a farewell?"

With the eerie lights resolved into a blazing pool of torchlight, I saw Jem Flood standing at the head of a cluster of Plaincourt servants and villagers. Several of them I recognised, among them grooms, messengers and, I noted, even the kennelman whose fortuitous arrival yesterday had put a stop to the thrashing I'd been taking. He saw me looking at him and answered my enquiring gaze with a slight, apologetic shrug.

Then I was seized by rough hands and a knee in the back propelled me face down onto the ground. The bearded Tench brothers were back in action, eager to be laying about me once again. At least it means they have let go of Matthew, I thought, and the rouncey also. That information might prove useful if I could somehow contrive to overpower the assembled company, assist the injured woman onto the horse and arrange for the kitchen boy to go unmolested back to the manor. Snorting sardonically at the sheer impossibility of the situation, I braced myself for further blows.

When they failed to materialise I squinted up at Flood and saw that he had raised a hand to halt the onslaught.

"Thee mussen mind Walt and John," he declared. "When

they didst give thee a belting afore it were at master's order. He favours them for they be big strong lads what he can be sure dost allus do his bidding, no matter what. Yet for all that, they be true Plaincourt men and true Plaincourt men dost stick together, unlike that sneaking Matthew I see here."

As he named his kitchen boy he threw the lad a disapproving glare which would have quelled a lesser youth but Matthew, I noticed with approval, appeared unabashed.

"As for now," Flood continued, "there beant no reason for them to lay hands on thee. We dost have no quarrel with thee, Master Cranley. Thee's free to get on thy hoss and ride away. 'Tis the trollop we've come for."

Blanche cursed loudly and endeavoured to scramble to her feet but found she could not, for some bone had cracked when she had been pulled from the horse. No sooner did she make to stand than her legs crumpled and she collapsed back onto the grass, panting with pain and exertion.

"Thass right, witch," Flood spat at her, "stay in't dirt where thee dost belong."

The villagers murmured their approval and Blanche shrank into herself, too terrified to speak. With Walt and John no longer restraining me, I seized the opportunity to regain my feet.

"This is madness," I said angrily, striding towards Flood. "This woman is many things but she's no witch, I promise you. Now let me be about my business. I am taking her to the Duke of Gloucester to answer for her part in the murder of Geoffrey Plaincourt. If you attempt to prevent me you shall answer to him, also."

As I invoked the Duke's name, the kennelman and one or two others looked anxious but Flood's hide was too thick to let him be easily cowed and he carried the majority with him.

"Thee'll not be taking the witch anywhere, minstrel, for the lads an' me dost mean to punish her," he answered. "So thee best not think thee can turn us from our purpose with thy fancy words.

"Ever since she didst come to Plaincourt, full of how she

194

were raised by th'old hag Jacquetta, we've known her for a witch. The evil bitch that stood trial for witchcraft, thass who reared our fine Mistress Blanche! Then up she dost come to Plaincourt wi' her chests of filthy potions and her black heart intent on slaying Master Geoffrey.

"We didst suspect what she were about soon as she didst arrive but we're nowt if not fair. Proof was what we didst need. Well now we have it. We know she didst slay poor Master Geoffrey wi' her black arts."

Mention of black arts brought terrified murmurings from the crowd and a flurry of movement as several individuals made the sign of the cross. Again I had cause to realise that though they had been too cowardly or inert to attempt to help him themselves, in their own way the villagers had cared for Geoffrey and had been concerned for his welfare. I understood their anger yet I could not allow them to thwart my scheme to take Blanche back to Middleham, and not just because Dickon would need her if he was to bring Rivers to justice. Though Blanche was a confessed murderess my feelings for her were prodigiously confused and I found myself more than half-inclined to accept her protestation that she had only killed the boy to give him a merciful release.

"Listen to me," I said hurriedly, hoping to reason with Flood who seemed to be the villagers' leader. "Listen, I understand why you think her a witch but you are wrong."

"It's thee that's wrong," Flood interjected, "and thee dost know it. The girl Cuckoo didst overhear the witch telling you all. 'Tis how we didst know to seek you here. Cuckoo didst hear the witch say as how she put a devil's potion into Geoffrey's ale to kill him."

So Cuckoo had been lurking in shadows again, eavesdropping as Blanche unburdened her soul to me. Yet I was certain that I had been thorough when I searched the passageway after the pigeon had disturbed us.

"The store room, the one adjoining my still room," Blanche moaned through clenched teeth. "The wretched little spy hid there. The walls are thick but there's a small iron grille connecting the rooms. Our words would have passed clearly through it. How could I have been so heedless? I knew well enough that the grille was there but believed it was safe to speak freely for the simpletons are so afeared of my physics, I thought none would ever dare venture so close."

Aye, afeared, I thought, but jealousy and fury can lend courage to the meekest individual. With no little dismay I was beginning to comprehend that by spurning Cuckoo's advances I had turned her into a dangerous adversary.

"You should not believe all that ignorant chit tells you," I flung at the cook. "Poppy juice is no devil's potion, it is a known physic which has been used by learned men in the East for centuries past."

Flood smirked triumphantly at these words.

"Well that dost prove it then," he stated, "for nowt Christian ever came out o' those Eastern parts. Enough now, minstrel, the boys an' me, we dost have work to do. Plaincourt folk are God-fearing, and knowst what must be done with witches. They must be purged from the earth with fire."

"Jesu save me!" Blanche shrieked, scrabbling desperately to raise herself off the ground.

Swiftly and viciously, before I could intervene, Flood swung his booted foot into her face and she crumpled like a broken flower. Still enraged, he crouched beside her and yanked fiercely on her hair which had tumbled free from her headdress.

"Mention the Lord's name agin, thee sinful doxy, and I'll remove thy blasphemous tongue and feed it right back to thee!" he bellowed at her.

Lest he should strike again I hastily moved myself in front of Blanche's inert form and searched my mind for ways to save her. Casting about me, I noticed the shadows from the torches leaping against the crumbling back wall of Lynet's hovel.

"Lynet!" I shouted in relief. "Lynet was accused of witchcraft but her life was spared. If her, why not Blanche?

She will be punished for her crime, I give you my word on that, but it must be done properly, according to the law."

I noticed that more of the villagers were beginning to look uneasy but a few, including Flood and the Tench brothers, remained resolute.

"Lynet were one of us," Flood intoned, echoing the words Matthew had said to me just a few days before. "She were one of us and she were mad with grief. More'n that, no one didst blame her for wishing to harm Sir Thomas. Even so, we didst thrash her for her wicked intention and send her away, for Plaincourt folk wilst have no truck with witchery."

I tried to speak again but the obstinate man interrupted me.

"Thee mawt as well save thy breath," he remarked casually. "We dost know full well not to harken to owt thee dost say, for Cuckoo's told us of the love spell the witch didst put on thee. From thy own lips, she heardst tell that thee's so consumed with passion for her thee cain't lie with no other."

At first I could not comprehend the man's meaning and then enlightenment reached me. When I had refused Cuckoo's advances I had softened the rejection by telling her that I was in love with another to whom I had sworn to be faithful. In her feverish jealousy, the foolish girl had taken Blanche to be the object of my affections when the truth was that if I had been thinking of any woman at the time, it had been my lovely, sweet-natured Margaret.

"Why do you suddenly attend so closely to that miserable child's whispered half-truths?" I roared at Flood. "How is it that yesterday you could barely bring yourself to look at her yet today her every twisted word is holy gospel to you? She has gulled you for her own devices, you fool! Use your sense, man, and stop this madness at once!"

My efforts were to no avail. Pushing past me, Flood took hold of Blanche's arms and began yanking her into the cottage. She had been lying mercifully senseless for sometime but was awakened now as her body was jarred and jolted across the uneven ground.

"Help me, Francis, I beg you!" she called to me, her voice distorted by the cruel kick Flood had delivered to her face.

I sprang after Flood and was heartened that the crowd separated to allow me through, yet as I was nearly upon him I was grabbed from behind by Walt and John. Maddened by anger, I threw them both off but they recovered swiftly and came back at me. Drawing my dagger, I lunged at the one called Walt and he immediately dodged to my right. Holding him at bay, I span round and saw John sidling up behind me. I made a feint at Walt in an attempt to hold him off but the sight of his brother coming at me had renewed his courage. He ventured a low blow to my belly which I deflected with a deep bite from my dagger into his upper arm. As he recoiled from the wound I turned to deal with his brother.

Alas, I was too late. Perhaps my thrashing the day before had convinced Matthew that I was no match for the Tench brothers, for he had weighed in to assist me. As I parried with Walt, he had leapt onto John's back to prevent him from aiding his brother. They grappled thus for a few heartbeats and then the vicious dog spun about at such great speed that Matthew was startled into loosening his grip. His arms came free and he fell backwards, his head thudding onto the ground. Not yet content with his work, Tench lurched abruptly towards the cottage, his meaty arms clenching Matthew's long legs tight about his middle. The kitchen boy's head and shoulders were dragged along the ground but as the brute reached the hovel he gave a might heave which lifted them clear of the ground and then he smashed them with ferocious force into the wall. There was a sickening sound as the lad made contact with the cottage and then he was still, his head lolling at an unnatural angle.

Many of the villagers cried out in horror, aghast to see one of their own lying broken, all signs of life extinguished.

"Thee's slain Matthew!" the kennelman exclaimed in a voice ripe with dismay. "That were badly done, John. He were allus a good lad, thee shouldst not've done that."

All save Flood and Walt Tench nodded their agreement.

Mumbling, they threw down their torches and melted away into the darkness. Just before he disappeared from view the kennelman called out to Flood once more.

"Leave it be now, Jem," he exhorted. "Let minstrel take the witch and deal wi' her as he wishes."

Then he was gone and I was left alone with a corpse, a badly injured woman and three wild men intent on murder.

"If thee'd left when I didst say thee should," Flood snarled at me, "the daft lad'd not be dead. I'm sorry this didst happen but if he'd stayed true to the folk as raised him no harm would've come to him."

Having neatly salved his conscience by blaming Matthew for his own fate, the self-righteous villain began laying sticks of shattered furniture and bits of brush into a heap inside the ruins of Lynet's cottage. I realised that he was building a pyre and so did Blanche who, though falling in and out of consciousness, read the man's intentions all too clearly.

"Don't let me burn, Francis" she entreated before slipping once more into oblivion.

"Keep him busy, lads," the cook ordered, "while I see t' witch."

As he continued to build his pyre on the floor of the hovel, the blood-crazed Tenches renewed their attack. Though I'd stuck him in the arm Walt seemed ready enough to have another go at me and as for his devil brother, the very air around him seemed charged and noxious with murderous intent. They were formidable foes, there was no doubt, but I fancied scarce a match for a man schooled in fighting by the House of York. It was time to finish this.

Before the Tenches could advance on me I sprang at them, grasping a thick wedge of coarse beard in each of my fists. Without pause I wrenched down hard, knocking their bovine heads together with an almighty crack. Swiftly I released my hold on their beards and they stumbled backwards a few paces, whereupon I plucked from the ground one of the extinguished torches dropped by the villagers, swinging it hot end first into Walt's face. He gave a satisfying shriek and fell to the ground, his hands clutching madly at his head.

John saw his brother's distress and flew at me, roaring his fury. The roar stuttered, stalled and transformed into a cry of febrile horror as the dead boy's foot snaked out and tripped him, sending him crashing onto the earth. Then Matthew sprang from the ground and stamped heavily on Tench's hands.

"I doosnt kill so easy!" he yelled as he ground his erstwhile attacker's fingers into the dirt, taking special care to break them so that the brute's great fists would be rendered useless.

Unsure what was happening, Walt lumbered recklessly at me, guttural sounds of pain and wrath spewing from his mouth. I suffered him to pass close to me, then reached down and deftly sliced his left hamstring with my dagger. He groaned, staggered and hit the ground like a felled oak. His brother heard the fall and took to his heels, fleeing the scene with loud appeals to God to save him from the hell demon which had returned from death to hound him. Taking his cue, Matthew set off in pursuit, cackling with unholy glee as he ran.

Knowing what I did of his peculiar talent, I had suspected and indeed hoped that my young friend had been feigning death for his own purpose but the absolute certainty of it brought me an excess of joy. This I was able to savour for a scant few seconds before a scream of unearthly anguish punctuated the darkness, reminding me that Blanche's life remained in direst peril. As if to reinforce this point the night was at once lit up by menacing tongues of flickering orange flame. Clammy with fear I raced to the hovel, frantic to rescue her from a fiery end.

At the threshold of the hovel I stood a moment, urgently peering through the rapidly spreading flames in an attempt to locate Blanche. I could not see her at first, my efforts hampered by the heat of the blaze which seemed to scorch my eyes, making it difficult to focus. Yet I persevered and with relief finally located a recumbent figure near the far wall of the cottage. Retrieving her would be no easy task as I would have to dodge my way through the fire but in truth I did not hesitate.

"Blanche!" I shouted as loudly as I could. "Hold on Blanche, I'm coming!"

That was when I heard a soft footstep behind me but before I had time to turn a heavy blow to the head propelled me, insensible, into the burning cottage.

Chapter 14
A Grim Awakening

The resurrected kitchen boy was kneeling by my side when I regained my senses. We were a short space from the house which was by now an inferno, the like of which no mortal creature could survive. Wrenching my gaze from the conflagration to Matthew, I saw that he was urging me to stand as soon as I felt able, for the heat from the fire was making our present location uncomfortable.

"What happened?" I managed to croak before the ache in my head persuaded me to remain silent a moment longer.

"I knowst not," the lad answered. "I didst find thee a-laying here when I didst return from making sport wi' that bastard John Tench. But he were that frit already to be chased by a corpse, there weren't no fun to be had in fritting him some more. I didst soon give up the chase and return to thee."

Something here made no sense to me.

"But I was struck and the last thing I recall is pitching forward into the cottage!"

By the orange glow of the fire I saw Matthew shrug his shoulders in a gesture of vague incomprehension. His impassive manner irritated me but I did not doubt that he was telling me the truth. The lad had been my friend from the moment I arrived at Plaincourt and had risked much on my behalf.

"So if you didn't rescue me from the house," I elucidated, "then who did?

"Master, I knowst not," the lad repeated patiently, "but whoever it were, they didst thee a reet good turn, else thee'd've bin roasted like a hog on't spit."

I shuddered at the thought, and then remembered with a rush of sick dismay that Blanche had been inside the house when I was struck. I clutched at Matthew's hand and gestured feebly at the blazing ruin. The youth read my meaning and shook his head sadly.

"Fire were too far along when I didst return. Weren't no

chance o' getting in to bring her out. But master, I reckon as she must've bin dead afore the flames took hold, for there's bin no screams since I've bin with thee."

Too choked with bitterness at my inability to save Blanche, I didn't at first comprehend his meaning but understanding finally penetrated my misery.

"So she did not suffer the agonies of fire, at least," I said, glad to have some solace to cling to. "Then Flood must have finished her before he lit the blaze."

"I reckon so," Matthew agreed. "Seems as old Jem didst show her some mercy at the last."

Suddenly it seemed I must believe that Plaincourt was redolent with mercy. The cook had been merciful in killing Blanche before burning her, to spare her an agonising end. She in turn had been merciful in giving Geoffrey a painless death in order to end the suffering caused by his sickness. The latter notion I was almost ready to accept but the former, no, that I could never believe. I had seen the blood lust and hatred in Flood's eyes when he had accused Blanche of witchcraft. The man was violent and deranged and his particular brand of madness was fuelled by fear of the black arts. He would have shown her no mercy for he longed to see her suffer the torments of a fiery death. Therefore, if she had indeed been dead before the flames took hold, as Matthew suggested, Flood must have killed her accidentally in a struggle, or perhaps she had found a way to end her own life.

Either way she was dead and the abject failure of my mission tasted thick and sour in my mouth. I must return to Middleham and tell Dickon of all that had passed and he would know Rivers for a blacker villain than he had ever imagined. But what would that avail without Blanche to stand witness against him? Fielding would remain a wanted man and Stephen Plaincourt would be free to enjoy the estate he had inherited through murder and deceit. And Blanche would still be dead. I marvelled at the power that fact possessed to distress me. This was a woman I had barely known three days and certainly not loved nor even much liked. Yet her death left me feeling empty and bereft.

A drawn out groan from Walt Tench reminded me that the lumbering ox was lying hamstrung nearby. He would never again be able to pummel a man senseless and neither would his brother unless by some miraculous chance he regained the use of his broken fingers. With bitter mirth I realised that the fools had just helped burn the only person at Plaincourt capable of helping them.

Thinking of the Tench brothers brought to mind once again their ally, the cook Jem Flood. Everything pointed to him being the person who had knocked me senseless. He had seen that I was about to enter the house to rescue Blanche and had attacked me in order to prevent it but had then removed me from the burning cottage so that my blood should not be on his hands. Though it pained me to admit it I could not escape the conclusion that Flood had saved my life. Yet as I mused on all this a vagrant notion nudged my consciousness and refused to be ignored. If, as Matthew supposed, Flood had already slain Blanche, why should he seek to prevent me from entering the cottage since I would be rescuing nothing but a corpse. It was possible that he truly believed the evil in her could only be cleansed by fire and for this it made no difference if she was dead or alive. Yes, it was possible but I knew it more likely that Blanche had still been alive and that Matthew had sought to spare me the knowledge of her agony by saying he had heard no screams.

My strength was returning and I knew that soon I must stand and turn my thoughts towards home. I lingered a while longer, though, drowning in a fog of desolation until the unbearable stench of charred flesh, destruction and failure prodded me into action.

Climbing unsteadily to my feet, I asked Matthew to go in search of the rouncey. He located the petrified animal close to where we had first encountered the odious Tench brothers. The smell of burning had unnerved the poor beast and, lacking the skill to settle it, Matthew returned for my counsel. I knew the wisest course was to leave that ill-omened place of blood and fire at once so I put a temporary seal on my wretchedness and followed Matthew to the horse.

"Thee dost ride for home now, doosn't thee?" he asked fretfully as we walked and I concurred with a brief nod.

"But what of I, master?" he enquired. "Where shouldst I go now?"

The plaintive question brought me up short. I saw at once that by embroiling him in my affairs I had inadvertently rendered the lad homeless, for he could hardly return to Plaincourt now he had publicly taken my side against the villagers. The thought occurred to me that since arriving at the manor I had always taken his help for granted and had never questioned why he had been so ready to assist me. Now was the time to find out.

"What made you so willing to aid me in this matter, and fight alongside me against the people who brought you up?" I asked him abruptly.

"I doosn't rightly know," he answered lightly. "P'raps I dost know as I'll better prefer a life away from Plaincourt. I didst allus know I weren't never one o' them really, on account of my ma being a foreigner from Mablethorpe an' all. Only Dulcy didst ever show me kindness and she'll not live much longer."

He had not answered my question properly but I let it pass.

"Yet in a way you do belong here for you have family, or at least a sister. I mean Cuckoo, of course. What of her, will you not miss her?"

"Aye, some," Matthew admitted, "but she were wrong to make trouble for thee and to rouse Jem Flood and all t'others to burn Mistress Blanche. I doosn't say as I liked the mistress and I didst wish her to pay for what she didst to Master Geoffrey, but thee was seeing to it and that were good enough for me. Daft Cuckoo didst just make a mess o' things."

She certainly did, I thought angrily. The foolish girl had a great deal to answer for. Despite the grimness of her life it bothered me that she would likely never be brought to account for her actions. As for Matthew, I had promised to help him before and now I had the opportunity to do more than I had ever envisaged.

"You shall come home with me to Middleham," I told him. "When I tell my lord of Gloucester of the valuable service you have rendered me, he will gladly find a suitable post for you in his household."

The lad's face fell at these words.

"I thanks thee kindly, master," he replied, "but I weren't never that keen on kitchen work."

"But of course not the kitchen!" I exclaimed. "There are many more fitting ways in which a bright lad like you can serve my master. I promise you Matthew, he will see your worth just as I did and find you a role to suit your talents. You could go far in service to the Duke."

A stubborn gleam stole into the youth's eyes then.

"Master, I'll gladly come wi' thee to Middleham," he said, "but only if thee dost let me come as thy servant."

I sighed, much exasperated that the boy could not recognise the advantage being offered him.

"I have no need of a servant," I told him testily.

"Not looked at thy hose of late, has thee Master?" the impudent wretch shot back at me. "I reckon as thee dost need a servant and I reckon as that servant should be me."

"I see. And are you practised in caring for raiment?"

"Nay master, that I beant. In truth I know nowt about owt right now but I dost learn fast, thee may be sure of that. I'll soon give thee cause to bless the day thee took me on."

I could tell that he was set on becoming my personal servant but I truly felt I had no need of one since at Middleham all my needs were seen to by those that served the Duke and Duchess. In any case I was reluctant to squander my stipend on such an unnecessary luxury.

"You must not allow the fact of my friendship with the Duke to gull you into believing I am a man of wealth," I warned him. "I live well but at my noble master's expense. I would be hard pressed to find the wherewithal to pay you a decent wage."

At this Matthew chuckled as if I had just told him the drollest jest.

"As to that, I didst never get no payment from Sir Stephen so I'd not notice its lack if I didst serve thee."

By now we had been standing beside the horse for some minutes. I was restless and eager to put distance between myself and this place of misfortune. Matthew must have sensed my mood for his manner swiftly changed from jocund to earnest.

"Master, I dost wish to work for thee and will count my bed and board payment enough. Mebbe if thee dost ever have the odd copper to spare thee couldst toss it my way. I dost ask no more'n that."

Worn down by his persistence and anxious to be on my way, I gruffly agreed that he could come with me to Middleham as my personal servant. Behind my irascibility, however, I felt warmed by the knowledge that the boy had wanted me to be his master. Doubtless in time I would grow accustomed to keeping my own servant and if he should prove to possess musical ability I might even be able to train him in minstrelsy. I said naught of this to him, of course, but bid him sit behind me on the horse so that we may at last leave Plaincourt.

Riding in near total darkness is ever a tricky business. It was made more difficult still by the rouncey's displeasure at having to carry two well-made men, one of whom sat astride it with all the grace and agility of a sack of oats. After an hour or so of stumbling progress which greatly jarred my aching head, I decided that neither the beast nor I could endure much more and was thus heartily glad when the ghostly outline of a church appeared on the horizon. I prayed the entrance would not be barred and the prayer was answered, for it took but a small effort to force open the door. Inside was cold enough but at least the roof and walls provided shelter from the freezing wind. Silently begging forgiveness for the impiety, I watered the rouncey from the font and then tethered it to the reredos before huddling with Matthew beneath my cloak.

We stole from the church before dawn had broken and rode in haste to the tavern where I had left the palfrey, arriving in time for a dinner of questionable pottage and sour ale. I was relieved to discover the palfrey alive and apparently in good health. Wisely, the oily tavern keeper had heeded my instructions to tend it carefully. By way of reward I struck a bargain with him to buy the rouncey, realising wryly that within the space of twelve hours I had for the first time hired a servant and bought a horse. Dickon would say I was halfway to becoming a man of substance. Yet the rouncey was necessary to carry Matthew to Middleham and the lad's joy in learning the horse was for him marginally lessened the sting of parting with my coin.

Chapter 15
Fat Nell's Gift

As we approached Middleham, cold, sore and bone-weary after a gruelling three days on horseback, I could not fail to notice that an unnatural quiet hung about the castle. Alert with misgivings, I was much relieved when the burly guard at the gatehouse hailed us with a cheery Yuletide greeting before admitting us to the inner courtyard. All was well save that I had foolishly forgotten today was Christmas Day. That answered for the absence of bustle, since most of the castle's populace including the Duke and Duchess would be at Mass in the chapel at this hour.

Since the climactic events of my last day at Plaincourt all thoughts of Yuletide had been driven from my mind but I now recalled how Dickon had tasked me with attending to the festivities before Will Fielding's arrival had necessitated my employment elsewhere. I found it mildly galling that in my absence he would have assigned the role of lord of misrule to another of his retainers, for I knew that I would have excelled at all the disguisings and revelry. Now young Jack Conyers was perchance enjoying the responsibility, or Thomas Tunstall who was ever a merry fellow. Whomever he had chosen, loyalty to my noble friend obliged me to wish their endeavours on his behalf a success. In any case, I welcomed the thought of all the frivolities to come as they might serve to lift my sombre mood.

All the way from Plaincourt I had been anxious to reach Middleham as quickly as possible so that I might inform Dickon of all that had passed and discover if he had yet received a visit from the King's justices. Now I would have to delay a while longer for my friend took his devotions seriously and would not thank me for interrupting him during the Mass of the Divine Word, however pressing the reason. Curbing my impatience with difficulty, I saw that I would have to wait until the feast which would be held in the great hall soon after Mass had finished. Yet even then it could be some time before Dickon was free to speak with me for he would be fully occupied in exchanging Yuletide pleasantries with his retainers as befitted the King's lieutenant in the north.

Accepting the inevitable delay with ill-grace, I surrendered our horses to the care of a stable boy and led Matthew to the northwest tower and thence to my chamber, pausing only to cajole a loitering servant into bringing us hot water for washing and bread and ale that we might break our fast.

"Do not become too accustomed to such luxuries," I cautioned Matthew, "for soon enough it will be you fetching and carrying for me. I spare you these duties today simply because you are new here and would doubtless lose yourself searching for the kitchen."

I was jesting, of course, since I knew that like me the lad was far too travel weary to do aught but wash, eat a mouthful of bread and snatch a few moments of sleep. Nevertheless I expected him to make some sort of reply but when he made none I understood that he was in shock, awed by the scale and grandeur of Middleham. My apartment did little to lessen his astonishment since it was large, well-appointed and richly furnished. In truth, nothing I had told him about my personal circumstances could have prepared him for the grandness of my lodgings.

In the centre of the chamber stood my massive bed draped with elegant blue hangings embroidered all over with white roses, the emblem of the House of York, and Dickon's personal device of the white boar. In the corner of each hanging the outline of a small, one-eared fox had recently been added, the gift of the Duchess who knew it for the Cranley device. As a bastard I had no automatic right to use the device but the Duchess argued that since my father had acknowledged me as his son he would assuredly have granted me the right had he lived. When appealed to for his opinion Dickon had concurred, though whether from true conviction or a desire to please his cherished wife I could not say.

Now Matthew gazed in wonderment at this bed which I confess I had long since learned to take for granted, and then back at me.

"That's where thee dost sleep?" he asked incredulously. "Just thee, and nay other? And thee's truly a minstrel as thee didst say, and not a lord?"

I laughed at his confusion and agreed that this was so. When his perplexity continued unabated I realised it was necessary to explain to him the special nature of my relationship with my lord of Gloucester.

"Matthew, I have the rare privilege to be on very close terms with the Duke. In fact you could say that I am his brother in all but fact," I told him proudly.

"We were raised together from infancy and the friendship that was formed then has survived and strengthened. Since my lord of Gloucester is the most good and generous of men it pleases him to treat me kindly and spare me no comfort, as you see. Yet you must understand, Matthew, that though I am fortunate to stand high in my noble friend's affections, to the world at large I am a nobody, nothing but the bastard son of an unimportant adherent of the House of York. All that I have, I have because Richard, Duke of Gloucester calls me friend. Remember, that is the only reason for all this," I finished, gesturing at my snugly appointed apartment.

Flushed with excitement, Matthew nodded his head eagerly.

"Aye, master, I'll be sure I dost remember that. But master, I'm that glad to be thy servant!" he exclaimed happily.

We were interrupted at that moment by the arrival of our water and victuals. Having washed and then eaten sparingly of the soft white bread, not caring to spoil my appetite for the forthcoming Yuletide feast, I kicked off my boots and threw myself appreciatively onto the yielding softness of my bed. I was on the verge of closing my eyes when I recalled that I had not told Matthew where he was to sleep, so I pointed to the low truckle beneath my bed which was brought out whenever young Frank Lovell visited Middleham. The castle boasted chambers enough for him to have one all to himself but he and I had been on amiable terms for many years and though his rank placed him far above my humble status, it pleased him to pass his nights on the truckle at the foot of my bed so he might recall events from our shared past. Now Matthew arranged himself on Lovell's truckle and with no further speech between us we drifted into sleep.

We were snatched from our slumbers a scant few minutes later by a loud hammering at the door of my chamber. I was fuzzy-headed and still cursing the interruption when Matthew leapt to his feet and threw the door open, revealing the servant who had brought us the water and food. The diligent busybody had taken it upon himself to inform the Duke of my return the instant he had emerged from the chapel and now Dickon was demanding an immediate audience with me.

Bidding Matthew to stay where he was, I pulled on my boots, ran my fingers through my hair in a largely fruitless attempt to straighten it and then made haste to my lord of Gloucester's privy chamber. When I entered I saw that Anne was with Dickon and they both greeted me warmly, gently mocking my kneeling obeisance and directing me to be seated on the stool placed before them. When she caught sight of my battered face the gracious Duchess was much alarmed, so much so that I considered it well my other injuries were hidden from view. Dickon guessed at them, I was sure, for he frowned when I eased myself over-carefully onto the stool but refrained from commenting.

At a signal from the Duke a page poured me a cup of wine and then softly made his way from the chamber.

"So then, tell us everything," the Duchess urged me without further ado.

"Gladly, my lady, " I began, "but first if you will forgive me I would know if the King's justices have been here already, demanding you give up to them a man they believe to be a murderer. If they have delayed their coming thus far they will not do so much longer so we must hold ourselves in readiness. I fear they have been primed to come by those that wish you ill, it is a part of the diabolical plot that I uncovered at Plaincourt Manor."

Dickon smiled grimly at these words.

"My friend, the justices were here the very day you left."

He shook his head and stared glumly into the fireplace.

"Had you delayed your departure by a few hours poor Will would have been discovered and likely hanged by now."

I had always known that the justices would likely reach Middleham before my return from Plaincourt but all the same I found myself disheartened by the rapidity of their arrival. I suppose that against the odds I had hoped they would allow their own Yuletide celebrations to delay them from pursuing their duties so assiduously. Now the knowledge that they had wasted no time in riding for Middleham drove home to me the seriousness of the charge against Fielding and the perilous predicament he was in. Moreover, the sombreness of Dickon's tone was alarming me. Had things gone awry during the justices' visit to the castle?

The kind Duchess saw my anxious face and took pity.

"Look not so forlorn, Francis," she instructed me, "Dickon teases you. It is true that the justices were here but my clever lord bested them without uttering a falsehood."

She looked admiringly at her husband as he took up the story.

"With an outward show of apology and humility the knaves nevertheless had the impudence to tell me they had been given cause to believe I was harbouring a vicious fugitive, a fellow by the name of Will Yorke. Mercifully I was able to swear a solemn oath that no one of that name was being given succour within my castle.

"I gave them leave to make a search if they doubted my word but being for the most part decent, stout-hearted northerners they accepted what I said with good grace. All but one cunning fellow who probed further, demanding to know if I had knowledge of the whereabouts of this Will Yorke.

"This question did give me pause, for reasons you will readily comprehend, so I answered carefully that I had never known any man by that name. It is no less than the truth since my troubled friend's true name is Will Fielding, not Will Yorke, yet even so I regretted the necessity to dissemble with those honest men.

"At any rate they left satisfied that their quarry was not be found at Middleham and that at least was no lie. Now, Francis, I trust you are ready to tell me of your discoveries at Plaincourt Manor, for I fear I have annoyed the entire household by ordering the feast put back an hour that we might have this discourse."

Thus commanded, I gave a report of all the events that had unfolded at that blighted place, speaking succinctly as the Duke preferred but taking care to leave out no salient detail. The Duchess gave little murmurs of horror and sympathy at various stages of the story but Dickon made no comment and maintained his silence a long while after I had concluded my account. When finally he spoke his first words expressed his profound dismay at discovering the depth of immorality inherent in Rivers' character.

"Jesu, Francis!" he exclaimed softly. "Of course I have always distrusted him, as I distrust all his kin, but I never conceived of him being as black as this. His complicity in the murder of that pitiful boy is a thing that repels my soul. Anne, Francis, you will both say I am wrong yet I cannot shift the feeling that I bear a measure of blame for the lad's death since we know that Rivers' purpose in aiding his monstrous friend was to lessen my brother's regard for me."

The Duchess cried out at this and implored Dickon not to say such a detestable thing nor even think it. I held my peace; I knew that in time his thoughts would clear and he would see that he bore no responsibility in the matter but for now he was hurting and no words of mine would help. Perhaps my silence reminded Dickon that I might be suffering guilt pangs of my own for he shook off his brooding and clasped an arm about my shoulders.

"I must thank you, my friend, for your valiant efforts to save the life of that foolish woman. Witch or no, I cannot deny it would have been better had she lived for then she might have stood witness against Rivers and Plaincourt but Frank, I entreat you to feel no culpability for her death. I know you did all that you could to free her and put your own life in jeopardy in the process.

"Now we must make shift without her as best we can. On the morrow I will write to the King and appraise him of all you have uncovered. It may be that he will not heed me but I must try all the same. It is perilous for him to repose such deep trust in Rivers now that the full measure of his poisonous character has been revealed. Truly, if I cannot shake my brother's faith in his brother-in-law I do not doubt that one day we will all have cause to regret it.

"As for Stephen Plaincourt himself, he must pay for his unnatural crime against his brother's son with his own worthless life. I will ask the King to ensure he is brought swiftly to justice. And Will's name must be cleared. I cannot suffer poor Will to pay for the actions of those evil creatures."

His flow of discourse was broken by a discreet tap at the door followed by the entrance of the chamberlain, come to inform the Duke and Duchess that the kitchen could delay the feast no longer. Dickon exchanged a fond smile with his wife and then took her hand and helped her to her feet.

"So then," he said firmly, "let us put these cares away for the nonce and surrender ourselves to goose and frumenty. Francis, summon this new servant of yours. I am agog to see him and fancy he will greatly relish the mummeries that Tom Tunstall has been devising."

***

My noble friend was right, Matthew did indeed relish the mummings, as he did the mystery plays, the carolling, the hot lambswool beer with apples bobbing on the surface and most particularly the swan roasted with butter and saffron. Every part of Christmas at Middleham was a new delight to him and it gladdened me to see his eager enjoyment of it all.

For my own part, fatigue had caught up with me early on in the feast and near propelled me face first into my venison. As soon as was polite I murmured an excuse and slipped away to my chamber, catching sight as I exited the great hall of Matthew coaxing a buxom laundry wench towards the kissing bough.

The following morn I watched as my lord of Gloucester wrote a letter in his own hand to the King, appraising him of the Plaincourt Manor affair. When he had sealed it he summoned James Metcalfe, his fastest and most reliable messenger, and instructed him to make haste to Westminster where he was to deliver the letter into none but the King's own hand.

This matter dealt with, the Duke and Duchess sat together in front of the enormous Yule log that burned brightly in the hearth of the great hall, awaiting with good humour the next piece of foolishness ordered by Tom Tunstall, our northern lord of misrule. Though I was mildly interested to see what diversion he had concocted, I soon absented myself as I had another more pressing matter requiring my attention.

On a visit to York in November I had purchased a generous length of crimson flannel, intending it as a Twelfth Night gift for my old nurse. Now I fetched it from my chamber for I had decided to give it to the old dame a few days early in order to curry favour with her. Fat Nell was possessed of a famously uncertain temper. I was relying on the flannel to sweeten it since I needed some questions answered and only she could provide them.

I found her as I had suspected, guzzling ale in the cosy den she had made for herself in a corner of the nursery. She greeted me warmly enough, especially when her acquisitive eye spied the bundle under my arm, and thanked me kindly for the flannel when I had unrolled it from its protective sacking and presented it to her. Thus far all had gone well but nevertheless I was feeling edgy and strangely reluctant to begin my questioning. Stalling for time, I asked her if she had yet broken her fast and without waiting for a reply, hot-footed it downstairs to the bakehouse from where I cadged two pastry-wrapped umbles.

When I returned to the nursery Fat Nell accepted a pastry from me and then brusquely demanded that I stop playing the fool and tell her my business. As sharp of brain as she was of tongue, she had been set alert by the oddness of my manner and was primed for trouble. Even so, I took her unawares with my first question.

"What was my mother's name?" I asked her.

Her fat-drowned eyes widened but as ever she was ready with a cutting riposte.

"What nonsense is this? You great jackanapes, why in the Blessed Virgin's name would you ask me that? That nasty trull abandoned you when you were no more'n a few weeks old and that's all you need know of her. "

"This I know, since you have kindly mentioned it to me many times before," I told her, biting out each word clear and crisp so that she would understand I was not to be browbeaten by her this day.

"And yet I find I am curious and do wish to know, so be a good nurse and answer me. You are the only living soul of my acquaintance that ever met her. I would know my mother's name and I would know it now."

Though she heaved her colossal chest in evident disapproval, the fat old dame knew she must give me an answer for she could tell I would not leave off asking until she did.

"Very well, lord high and mighty," she said mockingly. "Since you command it I will tell you though it baffles me why you need to know so sudden when you never thought to ask her name before today.

"In truth I never knew her given name but your father called her Fayette. I once heard someone ask him why he called her that, making it plain it was not her real name. He answered that he did so on account of her being as tiny and perfect as a fairy or some such outlandish nonsense."

It was the name I had been both anticipating and fearing and it led me to ask a second question.

"Did you ever hear word of her again? I mean, after she abandoned me, did you ever hear word of her again and if so, did you hear tell that she had borne another child?"

"I did not," Fat Nell replied quickly, much too quickly. "I never heard of the worthless baggage again and never wanted to neither. Any mother that runs off without her babe and leaves him like to die is not deserving of the name. Now be off with you, Francis. Leave me in peace. You were ever a bothersome brat and I see manhood has not changed you for the better."

"You're lying," I hissed at her, causing her chins to wobble alarmingly.

"I know that you are lying. I have always found you an easy book to read. Your eyes turn meaner than ever and you fold your fingers and hide your thumbs inside them. You did it when I was a child, whenever you said you liked me as well as George and Dickon, and when you told George he was as handsome as the King.

"So you see, dearest nurse, I am certain you are lying when you protest that you know nothing more about my mother. Well then, here is something else for you to know. I will not leave your side, I will be your shadow, badgering you day and night until you tell me what you know, you mean-spirited, mendacious old sow."

It was harshest I had ever spoken to Fat Nell and she crumbled in the face of my anger. Between sobs and insults, she told me what I wanted to know.

"You think yourself so fine and clever, just because the old Duke had the goodness to raise you with his own sons. Yet you are naught but a bastard and not even a noble one, for all your fancy clothes and talk. Well, you are wrong about one thing. I never heard word of your filthy mother again after she cleared out but this I may as well tell you since you are so eager to know it.

"Your mother near died when you were born, so hard were her travails. Slight as she was, her belly was huge and when her time came she laboured well into the second day before you were brought forth. Aye, and then her troubles were not yet over for minutes later another babe appeared.

"Your foolish father was overjoyed that she had given him twins but I and all right-minded folk understood what it meant, that she had lain with another man besides him. Some tried to tell him of it but he would not listen, saying such things were naught but superstitious rubbish. He knew his Fayette was true to him, he insisted, the poor misguided soul.

"Who knows, mayhap after all it was a kindness that he thought so for it meant the last days of his life were filled with happiness. It was soon enough that some dirty Lancastrian dog slipped a knife between his ribs and he breathed his last. That was when your precious mother showed the full measure of her love for you! She had two babes, remember, but when she stole your father's fortune and ran away she took but one of them with her. Ha, how do you like that, boy? How do you like knowing that she cared for you so little she left you unprotected and like to die yet your twin sister she carried with her?"

I had listened closely to Fat Nell's ale-fuelled ranting, refusing to allow any of it to touch me until the very last when she identified the twin I had never known existed as a girl. Then I left her, found wine and drank myself into oblivion.

Inevitably it was my old adversary Smithkin who discovered me, lying vomit-streaked and insensible on the floor of a latrine in the southwest tower. He sent word to the Duke who arranged for Matthew and another strong lad to carry me to my chamber. There I slept the day through, waking only when an anxious-faced Matthew roused me with the news that my lord of Gloucester was asking for me.

Within Dickon's intimate circle of friends it was well known that he had little time for drunkards. Abstemious in his own habits, he deplored his brother George's pronounced partiality for expensive wines, blaming it for the gradual disintegration of Clarence's character. George was one concern but now, on recent visits to Court he had been pained to witness the King taking too many cups of wine. In fact Dickon had told me privately that his royal brother seemed to be over-indulging all his appetites and as a result his handsome face was filling out and taking on a florid complexion.

For these reasons I fully expected the Duke to chastise me when I came before him but his temper seemed concerned rather than vexed.

"What ails you, Frank?" he asked without preamble when I had shuffled sheepishly into the privy chamber. Anne was not present, unsurprisingly since my lord would wish to spare her the unsavoury details of my recent intoxication.

"Forgive me, Sire," I said humbly. "Nothing ails me save that I took too much Yuletide cheer and misjudged my capacity for it. It will not happen again, I swear it."

At this dissembling Dickon gave an exaggerated sigh.

"Don't 'Sire' me, Francis," he snapped, "for when you do I am forced to wonder to whom you speak before I collect that it is me.

"And don't lie to me, either. I understand you well enough to know that you would not have made such an inelegant display of yourself without some disturbing matter weighing on your mind. So pray spare me your falsehoods and tell me at once what ails you!"

I felt a warm flush of shame suffuse my cheeks as my dearest friend and master accused me of lying. From our earliest days we had always been open with one another and in all my life the only subject I had concealed from him was my love for Margaret. I held our friendship too dear to risk harming it with another concealment.

"Very well, my lord," I said in a contrite voice, "I must confess that I find myself sorely troubled by the awful fate the woman Blanche met at Plaincourt Manor. It grieves me more than I can say that I was unable to save her from the flames."

"I guessed as much," the Duke replied swiftly. "Now pray listen Francis, I understand right well your feeling of horror that the woman died in such a way, and that you were there yet could not help her. But you know that you tried and surely that is some consolation? She was after all a self-confessed murderess who might well have died later at the order of the King.

"Yes," he overrode me as I attempted to interject, "I would indeed have begged mercy for her and if Ned had been of a mind to listen he might have been persuaded to spare her life. And what then? You know as well as I that she would never have been allowed her freedom. Without question she would have been confined for life to a nunnery. Yet from what you tell me of this woman I believe she would have thought of that as another kind of death, would she not?"

I was obliged to agree that in this he had the right of it.

"When Blanche was but a small child she already knew that she was not fitted for the religious life," I admitted. "As a woman grown it would have been slow torture for her."

"Well then, and yet she must have known that this was the best she could hope for, long years of unrelenting piety and penitence," Dickon continued carefully. "Do you not see that perhaps death was kinder after all?"

Although I knew the Duke meant well, that as my friend he sought to help me in my grief, I could no longer disguise the depth of my emotions.

"Forgive me, my friend," he said gently, "I had not seen before how much this business has hurt you. Tell me true, Frank, though you knew her but a day or two, did you lose your heart to this damaged woman? Did you love her?"

I laughed then, a bitter laugh that I snapped off abruptly before it could develop into an unmanly sob.

"No, my lord, you have my word I did not lose my heart to her. But had I had the chance to know her better I may well have grown to love her a little, though not in the way you think. She was my sister, Dickon! Blanche St Honorine du

223

Flers was my twin sister."

I had rarely seen Dickon as astounded as he was at that moment.

"But that cannot be!" he exclaimed. "You were alone when your mother left you to the care of my father, there was no other babe! We have both heard the story many dozens of times. Had there been another child we would have heard of it."

"You are right, my lord," I agreed, "there was no other babe left behind. My damnable mother, for reasons of her own, chose to leave me behind but she took my twin sister when she fled.

"I knew nothing of this until very recently. In fact it was at Plaincourt Manor that I was first given reason to suspect I might have an unknown sibling. It started when I sat with Blanche in the hall there and noticed the ring she wore. At the time I remarked it only because the big, ungainly ornament looked so incongruous on her small hand. Regarding it more closely I was dumbfounded to see that the ring bore a highly unusual crest, that of a one-eared fox.

"Dickon, you have heard as often as I the story of the night my mother absconded with the meagre Cranley fortune. Among the items she took was my father's ring which carried the family's device, a one-eared fox. Seeing such a ring on Blanche's finger I at once entertained the suspicion that she might be in some vague way connected with my mother, although I was also well aware that she might simply have bought it, or indeed stolen it or been given it by a lover.

"Later, when Blanche told me the story of her tavern upbringing I began to speculate that the lovely, mysterious woman called Fayette was my mother though I assumed that Claud, the rough, kindly tavern-keeper, was Blanche's true father. Thus I thought that she might be my half-sister! The idea that I had possibly found an unknown sibling was enough to send my senses spinning, especially as I was already convinced she was complicit in the murder I had come to investigate.

"When she told me of Rivers' involvement in Geoffrey Plaincourt's murder I saw it as fortuitous that my duty to bring Blanche before you to speak against the Earl coincided with my own desire to rescue her from that ill-omened place. I cannot deny that her terrible death left me distraught yet I was able to cling on to the hope that I had been entirely mistaken, that she had not been my half-sister after all.

"These hopes were crushed yesterday when I visited Fat Nell and she confirmed something I only half recalled hearing once many years ago, when she was exchanging gossip with another goodwife. It was the time that I had fallen from my horse - do your remember Dickon? - and taken such a sickness of the head that I was obliged to lie abed while you, George and the others went a-hunting.

"I was wallowing in self-pity, paying little heed to the chatter of the women, until I heard Nell make a shushing sound. 'Little pitchers have big ears,' she said, or some such banality, and at once she had all my attention though I was careful to feign otherwise. That was when I thought I heard the other gossip mention the name Fayette, a name I recall for it was one I had never heard before that day. Nell shushed the woman again, exclaiming angrily that she never wished to have that most unnatural mother's name spoken in her presence again.

"I had all but forgot this trifling incident until Blanche told me her mother had been called Fayette and then the memory stirred. Fat Nell's confirmation that Fayette was my mother's name was bad enough for it seemed all the proof I needed that Blanche was my half-sister. But her grudging revelation that my mother had borne twins was more than I could bear, since it meant that Blanche was my twin sister. I had a sister, Dickon, and I allowed her to die!"

I gazed into the fire, ashamed that there were tears streaming down my face. My tactful friend effected not to notice them as he busied himself pouring us both a cup of wine. Then he spoke.

"In three days' time it will be the twelfth anniversary of

the death of my lord father and my poor brother Edmund. On that day I will pray for their souls as I always do. I would count it a favour, Francis, if you would join me, and afterwards we will pray also for the soul of your sister."

I dipped my head in assent, still too full of emotion to say more.

"And tomorrow," Dickon continued, "is the Feast of the Holy Innocents. It strikes me that would be a fitting time for us all to pray for young Geoffrey Plaincourt.

"Now Francis," he said as he held aloft his cup, "let us drink to happier times."

Chapter 16
Three Promises

It was into the month of January before James Metcalfe returned to Middleham with a letter for Dickon from the King. He wrote that he was happy to accept his beloved brother's word that Will Yorke, or rather Fielding, was innocent of the Plaincourt boy's murder but he could not believe that his wife's brother was in any way involved in the sordid affair. The blame, he stated, must rest fully with the dead waiting woman who had clearly concocted the ludicrous story in order to blacken Rivers' name for some malicious intent of her own. Furthermore, he rejected the notion that so honourable a knight as Stephen Plaincourt might have instigated the coldblooded murder of his nephew, and genially advised his youngest brother to dismiss the matter from his mind at once. He himself was more than half-inclined, he declared, to believe that witchcraft had indeed been involved and thus it was as well that the woman had burned.

Though he had been expecting it, all the same Dickon was sorely disappointed by the King's reluctance to believe ill of Rivers. His spirits were raised, however, by the full pardon that came with the letter for Fielding. Yet even this good news was not without barbs, for in his letter Edward suggested that Fielding would likely find the climate of Flanders more suited to his health for the time being. From this we both read the King's subtle warning that Plaincourt or Rivers meant to slay Fielding if he remained in England.

At the Duke's command Matthew and I made haste to York where we retrieved a grateful Will from his hiding place at the Pennicott's house. Both dreading and longing for a glimpse of Margaret in equal measure, I had taken more than usual care with my appearance but in the event she did not show herself and our business was conducted with Master Pennicott alone. I thanked him fulsomely for the great favour he had done my master and assured him it would not be forgotten, for loyalty lay at the root of my lord of Gloucester's character. The good merchant swore it had been his pleasure to perform this small service for the Duke but it was plain he felt no small relief to see the back of his clandestine guest.

In the private chamber of a tavern close by the Minster I handed to Will a weighty purse of gold which Dickon had entrusted to me for him, together with a letter of introduction to his sister Margaret, the Duchess of Burgundy. I told him it was my lord's will that he should take service with Margaret for she was ever in need of doughty, trustworthy fellows like him. What we made sure not to tell him was Dickon's opinion that working for his sister gave Will his best chance of staying out of his enemies' vengeful reach.

I greatly feared Fielding's reaction when the time came to tell him how his lady love had duped him, setting out to win his trust so that she might gain access to Geoffrey, kill him and leave Will to take the blame. To save his feelings I softened the story by saying that Blanche had been threatened with her own death if she disobeyed Plaincourt's instructions. Even so, it surprised me when the bluff old soldier took the news far better than I had anticipated; he was hurt and angry, yes, but declared he had always known it was too good to be true that one as exquisite as Blanche should feel love for him.

Giving him tidings of her death proved more difficult, particularly as I had yet to find a way to speak of it without experiencing the urge to destroy something. I was therefore thankful when Matthew, sensing my continuing unease over the matter, stepped in and told Fielding that Blanche had died during a scuffle with Plaincourt's bully boys. I found myself admiring his adroit intervention and the sensitivity he showed in sparing Will the full knowledge of Blanche's death.

Fielding wept a few salty tears after he heard the news but he recovered himself quickly enough. From this I guessed that during his concealment he had resigned himself to her loss one way or another. Our duties thus fulfilled, all that remained was for me to bid him take the horse we had brought him from Middleham and ride from York without delay.

"Get to the coast and find a ship to take you to Flanders," I told him. "There is enough gold in that purse both to pay for your passage and buy the captain's silence. And Will, as soon as you are able, be sure to send word to my lord of Gloucester of your arrival for he will not rest easy until you do."

With that I left him, trusting that the soldierly instincts that had kept him alive for twice as many years as I had lived would guide him to safety.

Back at Middleham I spent some days showing Matthew about the country, riding out with him over the moors to help him become better acquainted with his new home. At other times, when he was not busy attending to his new duties I sat a while with him, attempting to teach him his letters. I do not pretend he found them easy but he applied himself diligently and that was all I asked. I know not why but it had occurred to me that a lettered servant might prove more useful than an unlettered one and in any case the occupation eased my mind.

As for Dickon, though the vital business of strengthening ties with the local gentry left him little time for aught else, yet he rarely allowed more than a day to pass without seeking me out for a few moments of quiet conversation. Often at these times we discussed matters of little import but now and then he would touch on Blanche and her death, probing gently to discover if my hurts were healing. It was on one of these occasions that he revealed to me the extent of his own anger that Rivers and Plaincourt had escaped punishment for their part in Geoffrey's murder. He could never bring himself to criticise the King, his loyal code absolutely forbade it, so instead he laid the blame at the Queen's feet, claiming she had hoodwinked his brother into seeing only good in Rivers and all his kin.

Thus the weeks passed until it was February and the Duke was obliged to journey to London to attend Parliament. He would be gone several weeks but fervently hoped to return in time for Anne's lying-in. I gave him an assurance that I would see she came to no harm in his absence and would endeavour to keep her in good spirits. He thanked me seriously and said he would be relying on me, then begged me to spare her my more ribald jests which she rarely understood but which made her blush when she did.

Soon after he had left I rode again with Matthew to York, this time at the special request of the Duchess. She and her ladies had been working on a heavy damask bed cover, a gift for Master Pennicott to mark her gratitude for the service he had rendered her husband. Now that it was finished she desired me to deliver it to the merchant with her message of thanks. So once again I found myself facing the prospect of an encounter with Margaret, the woman I knew I still loved.

When we arrived at the Pennicott's door we discovered a household in turmoil. Since we were come from the Duchess of Gloucester the man of business who greeted us was obliged to admit us but he informed us tersely that we could not have arrived at a worse time. The house was newly in mourning, he said, the poor master having succumbed to illness in the night.

It seemed that Master Pennicott had shown the first signs of sickness after dining at a fellow merchant's house three days gone. From his symptoms of heavy vomiting and loose bowels, the hastily summoned physician decided tainted meat was to blame. Enquiries revealed that other guests who had taken the meat had experienced similar symptoms but all had been younger than Master Pennicott, their stronger bodies better able to withstand the rigours of the sickness.

"Not so our poor, frail old master," Pennicott's man lamented. "All that puking and shitting taxed him more'n he could bear and now he's gone, God save him. And now what's to become of us I don't know, with the mistress no more'n a girl and poor master having no childer. "

Aghast, I asked at once after Margaret and was informed that the mistress was bearing up but was seeing no one until her husband had been laid to rest. Realising that the fraught man had pressing concerns and urgently desired to be rid of us, we beat a hasty retreat from that place of grief. We took the bed cover with us, estimating that it would not be tactful to leave it under the present circumstances.

My head reeling with this new development, I gave Matthew a few coins and directed him to find some dinner at the tavern we had frequented with Will a few weeks earlier. Then I rode directly to the Minster and knelt before the altar in the Lady Chapel. There I remained some long moments as I struggled to compose my thoughts and then, when I was calm, I proceeded to swear three solemn promises with the Blessed Virgin as my witness.

Firstly, I vowed to enquire at all the religious houses in Caen until I located the one my mother had entered when Blanche and I were eight. If I succeeded in finding it, and if she lived yet, mayhap I could persuade her to explain her decision to keep Blanche but abandon me when we were babes.

Secondly, now that my beloved Margaret was so suddenly and unexpectedly a widow, I vowed I would do everything within my power to make her my wife. Only since losing her had I come to understand how much she meant to me and I was not about to squander this unlooked for second chance at happiness. Though I knew my foolish reluctance to wed her had left her both wounded and angered, I prayed that in time she would find forgiveness for me. With luck, perhaps then she would rediscover the love I knew she had once felt for me.

And thirdly, with granite in my heart I vowed I would not rest until I had found the means to make Sir Stephen Plaincourt and Anthony, Earl Rivers suffer for the murder of young Geoffrey. This I would do, however long it might take, for the sake of my friend Dickon whose sense of morality was outraged by the crime, for the boy himself whose short life had been filled with pain and misery, but perhaps most of all for my dead sister who to my mind at least, had been another victim of the Plaincourt Manor affair.

Acknowledgements

I am very grateful to a number of people for their interest in this project. Richard Fitzgeorge-Parker, Vicky Gwilliam, Bea Keen, Anita Lee and Eva Offord took the time to read the manuscript and share their thoughts with me. Their feedback was immensely helpful and encouraging although it hardly needs to be said that any flaws are entirely my own responsibility.

I'd like to thank the lovely Laura Hirst at Pen & Sword for being consistently positive and helpful and my copy editor Debbie Ambrose for her diligence.

Finally, two people lived this story every step of the way with me – my husband Alastair and daughter Amy. To them I can only reiterate what they already know, that I couldn't have done it without their love and support.